Diagnosis: IMPOSSIBLE

BOOKS BY EDWARD D. HOCH

The Shattered Raven
The Judges of Hades
The Transvection Machine
The Spy and the Thief
City of Brass
Dear Dead Days (editor)
The Fellowship of the Hand
The Frankenstein Factory
Best Detective Stories of the Year 1976-81 (editor)
The Thefts of Nick Velvet
The Monkey's Clue & The Stolen Sapphire (juvenile)
All But Impossible! (editor)
The Year's Best Mystery and Suspense Stories 1982-95 (editor)
The Quests of Simon Ark
Leopold's Way
Great British Detectives (coeditor)
Women Write Mysteries (coeditor)
Murder Most Sacred (coeditor)
The Spy Who Read Latin and Other Stories
The Night My Friend
The People of the Peacock
*Diagnosis: Impossible, The Problems of Dr. Sam Hawthorne
Twelve American Detective Stories (editor)
*The Ripper of Storyville and Other Ben Snow Tales
*The Velvet Touch

*These three books are available from Crippen & Landru, Publishers.

Diagnosis: IMPOSSIBLE

The Problems of Dr. Sam Hawthorn

EDWARD D. HOCH

Crippen & Landru Publishers
Norfolk, Virginia
2000

ISBN: 0-7394-1896-3

Printed in the United States of America

Crippen & Landru, Publishers
P. O. Box 9315
Norfolk, Virginia 23505-9315
USA

FOR MARV AND CAROL LACHMAN

CONTENTS

INTRODUCTION

Sometimes it's not easy to remember the origins of a series character, but in the case of Dr. Sam Hawthorne I remember the circumstances quite well. It was in January of 1974 and I'd just gotten a new wall calendar to hang by my typewriter. The page for each month showed a different watercolor painting of country life in the past, and the January illustration was of a covered bridge in winter.

I stared at that illustration all through January, and pretty soon I got to wondering what would happen if a horse and carriage went in one side of the bridge and never came out the other side. Some pondering over the next day or two produced a solution and a plot to go with it. All I needed was a detective.

Since the story had to be set in the past, I needed a new sort of sleuth, a new series character. I decided on a country doctor named simply Dr. Sam, probably with memories of the recently notorious Dr. Sam Shepherd still in mind. My Dr. Sam was young, just a year out of medical school, and his prized possession was a 1921 Pierce-Arrow Runabout that his folks had given him as a graduation gift. The story went off to *Ellery Queen's Mystery Magazine* as virtually all of mine do to this day. Frederic Dannay, who was half of "Ellery Queen" and who edited the magazine, liked it immediately but suggested a couple of changes.

First, my Dr. Sam would need a last name to avoid confusion with Lillian de la Torre's Dr. Sam Johnson series, something which had never occurred to me. Fred suggested two or three names and I immediately chose Hawthorne. What better name for a New England sleuth? His second suggestion was a bit more unsettling to me. He wanted old Dr. Sam, in narrating the story, to speak more in a country dialect, dropping his final letters and such. Although I'd had some of the other characters doing this, especially Sheriff Lens, I'd avoided it with Dr. Sam. Finally I agreed, and most of these changes were made by Fred Dannay himself. Gradually over the next several stories the use of this country dialect decreased, and finally Fred told me he thought the stories worked just as well without it.

From the beginning I'd planned the Dr. Sam series as one frequently involving locked rooms and other impossible crimes. Fred Dannay thought the same way, and when I submitted the second story in the series he suggested that all of them involve some sort of impossible crime. I was only too happy to oblige. There are all sorts of crime stories, but in the sub-species of the detective story there is nothing more intriguing, or more challenging, than a good locked room or impossible crime.

The stories collected here are the first twelve of Sam Hawthorne's fifty-two cases to date. They were originally published in *Ellery Queen's Mystery Magazine* between December 1974 and July 1978. I set the first story in March of 1922 and they continued chronologically, except for one instance which may have been caused by a typographical error. The setting is the vaguely located town of Northmont which is most likely in eastern Connecticut though it's been known to wander a bit. We do learn in a later story that the neighboring town is Shinn Corners, setting for Ellery Queen's novel *The Glass Village*.

In those days each story opened with old Dr. Sam welcoming a drinking companion for another narrative of his early years in Northmont, and most ended with a hint of the next case. Again, this was Fred Dannay's idea and it worked well for a long time. Finally, in an attempt to speed up the stories a bit, I greatly shortened the opening and eliminated the closing preview entirely. These days I only write about two Dr. Sam stories each year and there seems little point in coming up with the next idea six months before I'd be writing it.

Although just about all of my numerous series sleuths have tackled impossible crimes at one time or another, I think the best of my work in this sub-sub-genre is in the Dr. Sam series. Looking over these first twelve, I note that "The Problem of the Covered Bridge" has been the most reprinted story in the series. And locked room expert Robert Adey has cited "The Problem of the Voting Booth" as "one of the most satisfying of the Hawthorne stories." They seem to be good stories to include in this first collection of Dr. Sam's cases.

I hope you enjoy reading these stories of a past era as much as I enjoyed writing them.

Edward D. Hoch
Rochester, New York
November, 1995

THE PROBLEM OF
THE COVERED BRIDGE

"You're always hearin' that things were better in the good ol' days. Well, I don't know about that. Certainly medical treatment wasn't better. I speak from experience, because I started as a country doctor up in New England way back in 1922. That seems a lifetime ago now, don't it? Heck, it *is* a lifetime ago!

"I'll tell you one thing that was better, though—the mysteries. The real honest-to-goodness mysteries that happened to ordinary folks like you an' me. I've read lots of mystery stories in my time, but there's never been anything to compare with some of the things I experienced personally.

"Take, for instance, the first winter I was up there. A man drove his horse and buggy through the snow into a covered bridge, and never came out t'other end. All three vanished off the face of the earth, as if they'd never existed!

"You want to hear about it? Heck, it won't take too long to tell. Pull up your chair while I get us—ah—a small libation."

I'd started my practice in Northmont on January 22, 1922 (the old man began). I'll always remember the date, 'cause it was the very day Pope Benedict XV died. Now I'm not a Catholic myself, but in that part of New England a lot of people are. The death of the Pope was bigger news that day than the openin' of Dr. Sam Hawthorne's office. Nevertheless, I hired a pudgy woman named April for a nurse, bought some second-hand furniture, and settled in.

Only a year out of medical school, I was pretty new at the game. But I made friends easily, 'specially with the farm families out along the creek. I'd driven into town in my 1921 Pierce-Arrow Runabout, a blazin' yellow extravagance that set my folks back nearly $7,000 when they gave it to me as a graduation gift. It took me only one day to realize that families in rural New England didn't drive Pierce-Arrow Runabouts. Fact is, they'd never even seen one before.

The problem of the car was solved quickly enough for the winter months when I found out that people in this area lucky enough to own automobiles cared for them during the cold weather by drainin' the gas tanks and puttin' the cars up on blocks till spring arrived. It was back to the horse an' buggy for the trips through the snow, an' I figured that was okay by me. In a way it made me one of them.

·When the snow got too deep they got out the sleighs. This winter, though, was provin' unusually mild. The cold weather had froze over the ice on Snake Creek for skatin', but there was surprisin' little snow on the ground and the roads were clear.

On this Tuesday mornin' in the first week of March I'd driven my horse an' buggy up the North Road to the farm of Jacob an' Sara Bringlow. It had snowed a couple of inches overnight, but nothin' to speak of, and I was anxious to make my weekly call on Sara. She'd been ailin' since I first came to town and my Tuesday visits to the farm were already somethin' of a routine.

This day, as usual, the place seemed full o' people. Besides Jacob and his wife, there were the three children—Hank, the handsome 25-year old son who helped his pa work the farm, and Susan an' Sally, the 16-year-old twin daughters. Hank's intended, Millie O'Brian, was there too, as she often was those days. Millie was a year younger than Hank, an' they sure were in love. The wedding was already scheduled for May, and it would be a big affair. Even the rumblings 'bout Millie marryin' into a non-Catholic family had pretty much died down as the big day grew nearer.

" 'Lo, Dr. Sam," Sally greeted me as I entered the kitchen.

I welcomed the warmth of the stove after the long cold drive. "Hello, Sally. How's your ma today?"

"She's up in bed, but she seems pretty good."

"Fine. We'll have her on her feet in no time."

Jacob Bringlow and his son entered through the shed door, stampin' the snow from their boots. "Good day, Dr. Sam," Jacob said. He was a large man, full of thunder like an Old Testament prophet. Beside him, his son Hank seemed small and slim and a bit underfed.

"Good day to you," I said. "A cold mornin'!"

" 'Tis that. Sally, git Dr. Sam a cup o' coffee—can't you see the man's freezin'?"

I nodded to Hank. "Out cuttin' firewood?"

"There's always some to cut."

Hank Bringlow was a likeable young chap about my own age. It seemed to me he was out of place on his pa's farm, and I was happy that the wedding would soon take him away from there. The only books an' magazines in the house belonged to Hank, and his manner was more that of a funlovin' scholar than a hard-workin' farmer. I knew he and Millie planned to move into town after their marriage, and I 'spected it would be a good thing for both of 'em. Millie always seemed to be workin' in the kitchen when I made my calls. Maybe she was tryin' to convince the family she could make Hank a good wife. By the town's standards she was a pretty girl, though I'd known prettier ones at college.

She carefully took the coffee cup from young Sally, an' brought it to me as I found a place to sit. "Just move those magazines, Dr. Sam," she said.

"Two issues of *Hearst's International*?" It wasn't a magazine frequently found in farmhouses.

"February and March. Hank was readin' the new, two-part Sherlock Holmes story."

"They're great fun," I admitted. "I read them a lot in medical school."

Her smile glowed at me. "Mebbe you'll be a writer like Dr. Conan Doyle," she said.

"I doubt that." The coffee was good, warming me after the cold drive. "I really should see Mrs. Bringlow an' finish this later."

"You'll find her in good spirits."

Sara Bringlow's room was at the top of the stairs. The first time I went in, back in January, I found a weak, pale woman in her fifties with a thickened. skin and dulled senses, who might have been very close to death. Now the scene was different. Even the room seemed more cheerful, an' certainly Sara Bringlow was more vividly alive than I'd ever seen her. Sittin' up in bed, with a bright pink shawl thrown over her shoulders, she welcomed me with a smile. "See, I'm almost all better! Do you think I can git up this week?"

Her illness today would probably be classed as a form of thyroid condition called myxedema, but we didn't use such fancy words back then. I'd treated her, an' she was better, an' that was all I cared about. "Tell you what, Sara, you stay in bed till Friday an' then you can get up if you feel like it." I winked at her 'cause I knew she liked me to. "If truth be known, I'll bet you been sneakin' out of that bed already!"

"Now how would you know that, Doctor?"

"When Sally met me at the door I asked how you were and she said you were up in bed but seemed pretty good. Well now, where else would you be? The only reason for her sayin' it like that was if you'd been up and about sometime recently."

"Land sakes, you should be a detective, Dr. Sam!"

"I have enough to do bein' a doctor." I took her pulse and blood pressure as I talked. "I see we had some more snow this mornin'."

"Yes indeed! The children will have to shovel off the ice before they go skatin' again."

"The wedding's gettin' mighty close now, isn't it?" I suspected the forthcomin' nuptials were playin' a big part in her recovery.

"Yep, just two months away. It'll be a happy day in my life. I s'pose it'll be hard on Jacob, losin' Hank's help around the farm, but he'll manage. I told him the boy's twenty-five now—got to lead his own life."

"Millie seems like a fine girl."

"Best there is! Catholic, of course, but we don't hold that agin' her. 'Course her folks would rather she married Walt Rumsey on the next farm, now that he owns it an' all, but Walt's over thirty—too old for a girl like Millie. I 'spect she knowed that too, when she broke off with him."

There was a gentle knock on the door and Susan, the other twin, came in. "Momma, Hank's gettin' ready to go. He wants to know about that applesauce for Millie's ma."

"Land sakes, I near forgot! Tell him to take a jar off the shelf in the cellar."

After she'd gone I said, "Your daughters are lovely girls."

"They are, aren't they? Tall like their father. Can you tell them apart?"

I nodded. "They're at an age where they want to be individuals. Sally's wearin' her hair a mite different now."

"When they were younger, Hank was always puttin' them up to foolin' us, changin' places and such." Then, as she saw me close my bag, her eyes grew serious for a minute. "Dr. Sam, I *am* better, aren't I?"

"Much better. The thickenin' of your skin is goin' away, and you're much more alert."

I left some more of the pills she'd been takin' and went back downstairs. Hank Bringlow was bundled into a fur-collared coat, ready for the trip to Millie's house. It was about two miles down the windin' road, past the Rumsey farm and across the covered bridge.

Hank picked up the quart jar of applesauce and said, "Dr. Sam, why don't you ride along with us? Millie's pa hurt his foot last week. He'd never call a doctor for it, but since you're so close maybe you should take a look."

Millie seemed surprised by his request, but I had no objection. "Glad to. I'll follow you in my buggy."

Outside, Hank said, "Millie, you ride with Dr. Sam so he doesn't get lost."

She snorted at that. "The road doesn't go anywhere else, Hank!"

But she climbed into my buggy an' I took the reins. "I hear tell you've got yourself a fancy yellow car, Dr. Sam."

"It's up on blocks till spring. This buggy is good enough for me." Mine was almost the same as Hank's—a four-wheeled carriage with a single seat for two people, pulled by one horse. The fabric top helped keep out the sun and rain, but not the cold. And ridin' in a buggy during a New England winter could be mighty cold!

The road ahead was windin', with woods on both sides. Though it was nearly noon, the tracks of Hank's horse an' buggy were the only ones ahead of us in the fresh snow. Not many people came up that way in the winter. Before we'd gone far, Hank speeded up and disappeared from sight round a bend in the road.

"Hank seems so unlike his pa," I said, making conversation.

"That's because Jacob is his stepfather," Millie explained. "Sara's first husband—Hank's real father—died of typhoid when he was a baby. She remarried and then the twins were born."

"That explains the gap."

"Gap?"

"Nine years between Hank and his sisters. Farm families usually have their children closer together."

Hank's buggy was still far enough ahead to be out of sight, but now the Rumsey farm came into view. We had to pause a minute as Walt Rumsey blocked the road with a herd of cows returnin' to the barn. He waved and said, "Hank just passed."

"I know," Millie called back. "He goes so fast we can't keep up with him."

When the cows were gone I speeded up, still following the track of Hank's buggy in the snow. As we rounded the next corner I thought we'd see him, 'cause the road was now straight and the woods on both sides had ended. But there was only the covered bridge ahead, and the empty road runnin' beyond it to the O'Brian farm.

"Where is he?" Millie asked, puzzled.

"He must be waitin' for us inside the bridge." From our angle we couldn't yet see through it all the way.

"Prob'ly," she agreed with a chuckle. "He always says that covered bridges are kissin' bridges, but that's not true at all."

"Where I come from—" I began, and then paused. The interior of the bridge could be seen now, and no horse an' buggy were waitin' inside. "Well, he certainly went in. You can see the tracks in the snow."

"But—" Millie was half standing now in her seat. "Something's there on the floor of the bridge. What is it?"

We rode up to the bridge entrance and I stopped the horse. There were no windows cut into the sides of this covered bridge, but the light from the ends and from between the boards was enough to see by. I got down from the buggy. "It's his jar of applesauce," I said. "It smashed when it fell from the buggy."

But Millie wasn't lookin' at the applesauce. She was starin' straight ahead at the unmarked snow beyond the other end of the fifty-foot bridge. "Dr. Sam!"

"What is it?"

"There are no tracks goin' off the bridge! He came into it, but he didn't leave it! Dr. Sam, *where is he?*"

S he was right, by gum! The tracks of Hank's horse an' buggy led into the bridge. Fact is, the damp imprint of the meltin' snow could be seen for several feet before it gradually faded away.

But there was no horse, no buggy, no Hank Bringlow.

Only the broken jar of applesauce he'd been carrying.

But if he hadn't disturbed the snow at the far end of the bridge, he must be—he *had* to be—still here! My eyes went up to the patterned wooden trusses that held the bridge together. There was nothing—nothing but the crossbeams and the roof itself. The bridge was in remarkably good shape, protected from weathering by its roof. Even the sides were sturdy and unbroken. Nothin' bigger than a squirrel could've fit between the boards.

"It's some sort of trick," I said to Millie. "He's got to be here!"

"But *where?*"

I walked to the other end of the bridge and examined the unmarked snow. I peered around the corner o' the bridge at the frozen surface of Snake Creek. The skaters had not yet shoveled off the snow, and it was as unmarked as the rest. Even if the horse an' buggy had passed somehow through the wooden floor or the sides o' the bridge, there was no place they could've gone without leavin' a mark. Hank had driven his buggy into the bridge with Millie an' me less than a minute behind him, dropped his quart jar o' applesauce, and vanished.

"We've got to get help." I said. Instinct told me I shouldn't disturb the snow beyond the bridge by goin' forward to Millie's house. "Wait here an' I'll run back to Rumsey's farm."

I found Walt Rumsey in the barn with his cows, forkin' hay out of the loft. " 'Lo, Doc," he called down to me. "What's up?"

"Hank Bringlow seems to have disappeared. Darnedest thing I ever saw. You got a telephone here?"

"Sure have, Doc." He hopped down to the ground. "Come on in the house."

As I followed him through the snow I asked, "Did Hank seem odd in any way when he went past you?"

"Odd? No. He was bundled up against the cold, but I knew it was him. I kept my cows to the side o' the road till he passed."

"Did he say anything?"

"No, just waved."

"Then you didn't actually see his face or hear his voice?"

Walt Rumsey turned to me. "Wae-el, no. But hell, I've known Hank mosta my life! It was him, all right."

An' I s'pose it had to be. No substitution o' drivers could've been made anywhere along the road, and even if a substitution had been made, how did the substitute disappear?

I took the phone that Walt Rumsey offered, cranked it up, and asked for the Bringlow farm. One of the twins answered. "This is Dr. Sam. We seem to have lost your brother. He didn't come back there, did he?"

"No. Isn't he with you?"

"Not right now. Your pa around?"

"He's out in the field somewhere. You want Momma?"

"No. She should stay in bed." No need to bother her yet. I hung up an' called the O'Brian farm with the same results. Millie's brother Larry answered the phone. He'd seen nothin' of Hank, but he promised to start out on foot toward the bridge at once, searchin' for buggy tracks or footprints.

"Any luck?" Rumsey asked when I'd finished.

"Not yet. You didn't happen to watch him after he passed, did you?"

Rumsey shook his head. "I was busy with the cows."

I went back outside and headed for the bridge, with Rumsey taggin' along. Millie was standin' by my horse an' buggy, lookin' concerned. "Did you find him?" she asked.

I shook my head. "Your brother's on his way over."

While Rumsey and I went over every inch of the covered bridge, Millie simply stood at the far end, watchin' for her brother. I guess she needed him to cling to just then. Larry O'Brian was young, handsome, an' likeable—a close friend of both Hank Bringlow an' Walt Rumsey. My nurse April told me that when Walt inherited the farm, after his folks' death, both Larry and Hank helped him with the first season's planting. She'd also told me that despite their friendship Larry was against Hank marryin' his sister. P'raps, like some brothers, he viewed no man as worthy of the honor.

When Larry arrived he had nothing new to tell us. "No tracks between here an' the farm," he confirmed.

I had a thought. "Wait a minute! If there aren't any tracks, how in heck did you get over here this mornin', Millie?"

"I was with Hank at his place last night. When the snow started, the family insisted I stay over. We only got a couple of inches, though." She seemed to sense an unasked question, and she added, "I slept with the twins in their big bed."

Larry looked at me. "What d'you think?"

I stared down at the smashed quart of applesauce which everyone had carefully avoided. "I think we better call Sheriff Lens."

S heriff Lens was a fat man who moved slowly and thought slowly (Doctor Sam continued). He'd prob'ly never been confronted with any crime bigger than buggy stealin'—certainly nothin' like the disappearance from the covered bridge. He grunted and rasped as he listened to the story, then threw up his hands in dismay. "It couldn'ta happened the way you say. The whole thing's impossible, an' the impossible jest don't make sense. I think you're all foolin' me—maybe havin' an April Fool joke three weeks early."

It was about then that the strain finally got to Millie. She collapsed in tears, and Larry and I took her home. Their pa, Vincent O'Brian, met us at the door. "What is this?" he asked Larry. "What's happened to her?"

"Hank's disappeared."

"Disappeared? You mean run off with another woman?"

"No, nothin' like that."

While Larry helped Millie to her room, I followed Vincent into the kitchen. He wasn't the hulkin' ox of a man that Jacob Bringlow was, but he still had the muscles of a lifetime spent in the field. "Hank wanted me to come along," I explained. "Said you'd hurt your foot."

"It's nothin'. Twisted my ankle choppin' wood."

"Can I see it?"

"No need." But he pulled up his pants leg reluctantly and I stooped to examine it. Swellin' and bruisin' were pronounced, but the worst was over.

"Not too bad," I agreed. "But you should be soakin' it." Glancing around to be sure we weren't overheard, I lowered my voice and added, "Your first thought was that Hank Bringlow had run off with another woman. Who did you have in mind?"

He looked uneasy. "Nobody special."

"This may be serious, Mr. O'Brian."

He thought about it and finally said, "I won't pretend I'm happy about my daughter marryin' a non-Catholic. Larry feels the same way. Besides, Hank fools around with the girls in town."

"For instance?"

"For instance Gert Page at the bank. Wouldn't be surprised he run off with her."

I saw Millie comin' back downstairs and I raised my voice a bit. "You soak that ankle now, in good hot water."

"Has there been any word?" Millie asked. She'd recovered her composure, though her face still lacked color.

"No word, but I'm sure he'll turn up. Was he in the habit of playin' tricks?"

"Sometimes he'd fool people with Susan an' Sally. Is that what you mean?"

"Don't know what I mean," I admitted. "But he seemed anxious for you to ride with me. Maybe there was a reason."

I stayed for lunch, and when no word came I headed back to town alone. The Sheriff and some others were still at the covered bridge when I rode through it, but I didn't stop. I could see they'd gotten nowhere toward solvin' the mystery, and I was anxious to get to the bank before it closed.

G ert Page was a hard-eyed blonde girl of the sort who'd never be happy in a small New England town. She answered my questions 'bout Hank Bringlow with a sullen distrust she might have felt towards all men.

"Do you know where he is, Gert?"

"How would I know where he is?"

"Were you plannin' to run off with him before his marriage?"

"Ha! Me run off with him? Listen, if Millie O'Brian wants him that bad, she can have him!" The bank was closin' and she went back to countin' the cash in her drawer. "B'sides, I hear tell men get tired of married life after a bit. I just might see him in town again. But I sure won't run off with him and be tied to one man!"

I saw Roberts, the bank's manager, watchin' us and I wondered why they kept a girl like Gert on the payroll. I 'spected she was most unpopular with the bank's lady customers.

As I left the bank I saw Sheriff Lens enterin' the general store across the street. I followed and caught him at the pickle barrel. "Anything new, Sheriff?"

"I give it up, Doc. Wherever he is, he ain't out by the bridge."

The general store, which was right next to my office, was a cozy place with great wheels of cheese, buckets o' flour, an jars o' taffy kisses. The owner's name was Max, and his big collie dog always slept on the floor near the potbellied stove. Max came around the counter to join us and said, "Everyone's talkin' about young Hank. What do you think happened?"

"No idea," I admitted.

"Couldn't an aeroplane have come over an' picked up the whole shebang?"

"I was right behind him in my buggy. There was no aeroplane." I glanced out the window and saw Gert Page leavin' the bank with the manager, Roberts. "I hear some gossip that Hank was friendly with Gert Page. Any truth to it?"

Max scratched the stubble on his chin and laughed. "Everybody in town is friendly with Gert, includin' ol' Roberts there. It don't mean nothin'."

"I guess not," I agreed. But if it hadn't meant anything to Hank Bringlow, had it meant somethin' to Millie's pa an' brother?

Sheriff Lens and I left the general store together. He promised to keep me informed and I went next door to my office. My nurse April was waitin' for all the details. "My God, you're famous, Dr. Sam! The telephone ain't stopped ringin'!"

"Hell of a thing to be famous for. I didn't see a thing out there."

"That's the point! Anyone else they wouldn't believe—but you're some-thin' special."

I sighed and kicked off my damp boots. "I'm just another country doctor, April."

She was a plump jolly woman in her thirties, and I'd never regretted hirin' her my first day in town. "They think you're smarter'n most, Dr. Sam."

"Well, I'm not."

"They think you can solve this mystery."

Who else had called me a detective that day? Sara Bringlow? "Why do they think that?"

"I guess because you're the first doctor in town ever drove a Pierce-Arrow car."

I swore at her but she was laughin' and I laughed too. There were some patients waitin' in the outer office and I went to tend to them. It was far from an ordinary day, but I still had my practice to see to. Towards evening, by the time I'd finished, the weather had turned warmer. The temperature hovered near 40 and a gentle rain began to fall.

"It'll git rid o' the snow," April said as I left for the day.

"Ayah, it'll do that."

"Mebbe it'll uncover a clue."

I nodded, but I didn't believe it. Hank Bringlow had gone far away, and the meltin' snow wasn't about to bring him back.

The telephone woke me at four the next mornin'. "This is Sheriff Lens, Doc," the voice greeted me. "Sorry to wake you, but I gotta bad job for you."

"What's that?"

"We found Hank Bringlow."

"Where?"

"On the Post Road, about ten miles south o' town. He's sittin' in his buggy like he jest stopped for a rest."

"Is he—?"

"Dead, Doc. That's what I need you for. Somebody shot him in the back o' the head."

I t took me near an hour (Doctor Sam went on) to reach the scene, drivin' the horse an' buggy fast as I could over the slushy country roads. Though the night was mild, the rain chilled me to the bone as I rode through the darkness on that terrible mission. I kept thinkin' about Millie O'Brian, and Hank's ma only just recoverin' from her lengthy illness. What would the news do to them?

Sheriff Lens had some lanterns out in the road, and I could see their eerie glow as I drove up. He helped me down from the buggy an' I walked over to the small circle of men standin' by the other rig. Two of them were deputies, another was a farmer from a nearby house. They hadn't disturbed the body— Hank still sat slumped in a corner o' the seat, his feet wedged against the front o' the buggy.

I drew a sharp breath when I saw the back of his head. "Shotgun," I said curtly.

"Can you tell if it happened here, Doc?"

"Doubtful." I turned to the farmer. "Did you find him?"

The man nodded and repeated a story he'd obviously told 'em already. "My wife heard the horse. We don't git nobody along this road in the middle o' the night, so I come out to look around. I found him like this."

In the flare of lantern light I noticed somethin'—a round mark on the horse's flank that was sensitive to my touch. "Look here, Sheriff."

"What is it?"

"A burn. The killer loaded Hank into the buggy an' then tied the reins. He singed the horse with a cigar or somethin' to make it run. Could've run miles before it stopped from exhaustion."

Lens motioned to his deputies. "Let's take him into town. We won't find nothin' else out here." He turned back to me. "At least he's not missin' any more."

"No, he's not missin'. But we still don't know what happened on that bridge. We only know it wasn't any joke."

The funeral was held two days later, on Friday mornin', with a bleak winter sun breakin' through the overcast to throw long March shadows across the tombstones of the little town cemetery. The Bringlows were all there, 'course, and Millie's folks, and people from town. Afterwards many of us went back to the Bringlow farm. It was a country custom, however sad the occasion, and many neighbors brought food for the family.

I was sittin' in the parlor, away from the others, when the bank manager, Roberts, came up to me.

"Has the Sheriff found any clues yet?" he asked.

"Nothin' I know of."

"It's a real baffler. Not just the *how,* but the *why.*"

"The *why?*"

He nodded. "When you're goin' to kill someone you just do it. You don't rig up some fantastic scheme for them to disappear first. What's the point?"

I thought about that, and I didn't have a ready answer. When Roberts drifted away I went over to Sara Bringlow and asked how she was feelin'. She looked at me with tired eyes and said, "My first day outta bed. To bury my son."

There was no point arguin' with a mother's grief. I saw Max bringin' in a bag of groceries from his store and I started over to help him. But my eye caught somethin' on the parlor table. It was the March issue of *Hearst's International.* I remembered Hank had been reading the Sherlock Holmes story in the February and March issues. I located the February one under a stack o' newspapers and turned to the Holmes story.

It was in two parts, and called "The Problem of Thor Bridge."

Bridge?

I found a quiet corner and sat down to read.

It took me only a half hour, and when I finished I sought out Walt Rumsey from the next farm. He was standin' with Larry O'Brian on the side porch, an' when he saw me comin' he said, "Larry's got some good bootleg stuff out in his buggy. Want a shot?"

"No, thanks, Walt. But you can do somethin' else for me. Do you have a good stout rope in your barn?"

He frowned in concentration. "I s'pose so."

"Could we ride over there now? I just read somethin' that gave me an idea about how Hank might've vanished from that bridge."

We got into his buggy an' drove the mile down the windin' road to his farm. The snow was melted by this time, and the cows were clustered around the water trough by the side of the barn. Walt took me inside, past empty stalls an' milk cans an' carriage wheels, to a big shed attached to the rear. Here, among assorted tools, he found a twelve-foot length of worn hemp.

"This do you?"

"Just the thing. Want to come to the bridge with me?"

The ice of the creek was still firm, though the road had turned to mud. I handed one end o' the rope to Rumsey and played out the other end till it reached the edge of the frozen creek. "What's this all about?" he asked.

"I read a story 'bout a gun that vanished off a bridge by bein' pulled into the water."

He looked puzzled. "But Hank's buggy couldn'ta gone into the crick. The ice was unbroken."

"All the same I think it tells me somethin'. Thanks for the use o' the rope."

He took me back to the Bringlow house, puzzled but unquestioning. The mourners were beginning to drift away, and I sought out Sheriff Lens. "I've got an idea about this mystery, Sheriff. But it's sort of crazy."

"In this case, even a crazy idea would be welcome."

Jacob Bringlow, tall and unbent from the ordeal of the funeral, came around the corner o' the house with one of the twins. "What is it, Sheriff?" he asked. "Still searchin' for clues?"

"We may have one," I said. "I got an idea."

He eyed me up an' down, p'raps blamin' me for what happened to his stepson. "You stick to your doctorin'," he said with a slur, and I knew he'd been samplin' Larry's bottle. "Go look at my wife. She don't seem right to me."

I went inside and found Sara pale and tired-looking. I ordered her up to bed and she went without argument. Max was leavin', and so was the O'Brian family. The banker had already gone. But when I went back on the porch, Jacob Bringlow was still waitin' for me. He was lookin' for trouble. Maybe it was a mixture of grief and bootleg whiskey.

"Sheriff says you know who killed Hank."

"I didn't say that. I just got an idea."

"Tell me. Tell us all!"

He spoke loudly, and Larry O'Brian paused with Millie to listen. Walt Rumsey came over too. In the distance, near the buggies, I saw Gert Page from the bank. I hadn't seen her at the funeral, but she'd come to pay some sort of last respects to Hank.

"We can talk about it inside," I replied, keepin' my voice down.

"You're bluffin'! You don't know a thing!"

I drew a deep breath. "All right, if you want it like this. Hank was reading a Sherlock Holmes story before he died. There's another one he prob'ly read years ago. In it Holmes calls Watson's attention to the curious incident of the dog in the night-time. I could echo his words."

"But there was no dog in the night-time," Sheriff Lens pointed out. "There's no dog in this whole danged case!"

"My mistake," I said. "Then let me direct your attention to the curious incident of the cows in the daytime."

It was then that Walt Rumsey broke from the group and ran towards his buggy. "Grab him, Sheriff!" I shouted. "He's your murderer!"

I had to tell it all to April, back at my office, because she hadn't been there and wouldn't believe it otherwise. "Come on, Dr. Sam! How did the cows tell you Walt was the killer?"

"He was bringin' them back to the barn, across the road, as we passed. But from where? Cows don't graze in the snow, and their waterin' trough is next to the barn, not across the road. The only possible reason for the cows crossin' the road in front of us was to obliterate the tracks of Hank's horse an' buggy.

"Except for those cows, the snow was unbroken by anything but the single buggy track—all the way from the Bringlow farm to the covered bridge. We know Hank left the farm. If he never reached the bridge, whatever happened to him had to happen at the point where those cows crossed the road."

"But the tracks to the bridge! You were only a minute behind him, Dr. Sam. That wasn't long enough for him to fake those tracks!"

I smiled, runnin' over the reasonin' as it first came to me. "Roberts the banker answered that one, along with Sherlock Holmes. Roberts asked *why*—why did the killer go to all that trouble? And the answer was that he didn't. It wasn't the killer but Hank Bringlow who went to all the trouble.

"We already knew he'd fooled people with his twin sisters, confusin' their identities. And we knew he'd recently read 'The Problem of Thor Bridge,' which has an impossible suicide of sorts takin' place on a bridge. It's not too far-fetched to imagine him arrangin' the ultimate joke—his own disappearance from that covered bridge."

"But *how*, Dr. Sam?" April wanted to know. "I read that Sherlock Holmes story too, an' there's nothin' in it like what happened here."

"True. But as soon as I realized the purpose o' those noonday cows, I knew somethin' had happened to those tracks at the barn. And only one thing could've happened—Hank's buggy turned off the road and went *into* the barn. The tracks from the road to the bridge were faked."

"How?" she repeated, not yet ready to believe a word of it.

"*When* is the more important question. Since there was no time to fake the tracks in the single minute before we came along, they had to have been done earlier. Hank and Walt Rumsey must've been in cahoots on the scheme. Walt went out that mornin', after the snow had stopped, with a couple o' old carriage wheels linked together by an axle. On his boots he'd fastened blocks o' wood a couple o' inches thick, with horseshoes nailed to the bottoms.

"He simply trotted along the road, through the snow, pushin' the pair o' wheels ahead of him. He went into the bridge far enough to leave traces o' snow, then reversed the blocks o' wood on his boots and pushed the wheels back again. The resultin' tracks looked like a four-footed animal pullin' a four-wheeled buggy."

"But—" April started to object.

"I know, I know! A man doesn't run like a horse. But with practice he could space the prints to look good enough. And I'll bet Hank an' Walt practiced plenty while they waited for the right mornin' when the snow was fresh but not too deep. If anyone had examined the tracks o' the horse carefully, they'd've discovered the truth. Careful as he was, Walt Rumsey's prints comin' back from the bridge woulda been a bit different, hittin' the snow from the opposite direction. But they figured I'd drive my buggy up to the bridge in his tracks, all but obliteratin' them, which is what I did. They couldn't really be examined then."

"You're forgetting the broken jar o' applesauce," April said. "Don't that prove Hank *was* on the bridge?"

"Nothing of the sort! Hank knew in advance his ma planned to send the applesauce to Mrs. O'Brian. He prob'ly suggested it, and he certainly reminded her of it. He simply gave Walt Rumsey a duplicate jar a day or two earlier, an' it was that jar Walt broke on the bridge. The jar Hank was carrying went with him into Walt's barn."

"What if it hadn't snowed that mornin'? What if someone else came along first to leave other tracks?"

I shrugged. "They would've phoned one another and postponed it, I s'pose. It was only meant as a joke. They'd have tried again some other day, with other witnesses. They didn't really need me an' Millie."

"Then how did it turn from a joke to murder?"

"Walt Rumsey had never given up lovin' Millie, or hatin' Hank for takin' her away from him. After the trick worked so well, he saw the perfect chance to kill Hank and win her back. Once I knew he was in on the trick, he had to be the killer—else why was he keepin' quiet 'bout his part in it?

"Hank had hidden his horse an' buggy in that big shed behind the Rumsey barn. When we all went back to town, an' Hank was ready to reappear an' have a good laugh on everyone, Walt Rumsey killed him. Then he waited till dark to dispose of the body on the Post Road. He drove the buggy part way, turned the horse loose to run, and walked home.

"This mornin' after the funeral I made an excuse of wantin' a piece of rope so I could see the inside of Rumsey's barn again. He had spare carriage wheels there, and the shed was big enough to hold a horse an' buggy. That was all the confirmation I needed."

April leaned back and smiled, convinced at last. "After this they'll probably give the you the Sheriff's job, Dr. Sam."

I shook my head. "I'm just a country doctor."

"A country doctor with a Pierce-Arrow car!" . . .

That's the way it happened, back in '22. I've often thought I should write it up now that I'm retired, but there's just never enough time. Sure, I've got other stories. Lots of 'em! Can I get you another—ah—small libation?"

THE PROBLEM OF
THE OLD GRISTMILL

"Now murders didn't come every day to our little town o' Northmont, and after the covered-bridge affair it was more than a year before I was faced with another mystery that seemed impossible to solve. By July of 1923, after eighteen months of medical practice in the area, I'd become an accepted member of the community. I knew most o' the men by their first names, and their wives an' children, too. They'd stopped kiddin' me about my yellow Pierce-Arrow Runabout—a med-school graduation gift from my folks—and sometimes the kids would even ask for rides in it."

Dr. Sam Hawthorne paused to take a sip from the small glass in his hand.

"The year had started violently, when a convict named Delos killed a guard while escaping from state prison on New Year's Day. Now, beneath a hot an' brooding July sun, the odor of death was still in the air. Word had come from Mexico of the assassination of Pancho Villa, shot sixteen times as he drove down from the hills in his car. And within weeks we were to learn of the death of President Harding on the west coast.

"But the death that concerned me was much closer to home. . . . Could I interest you in a—ah—small libation?"

"Land sakes, Dr. Sam! What you doin' out this neck o' the woods? Someone sick, or you lookin' for a good still?"

"Neither one," I told Minnie Dranger, pulling my car off the side of the road so I could chat with her. She was one of those buxom country women who seemed ageless, going on from year to year like the endless flowing of the mill stream. She always joked about bootleg whiskey out in the woods, but in truth we were only 150 miles from the Canadian border and everything we needed came in that way. "I'm on my way to Hawkins' gristmill to see Henry Cordwainer before he leaves."

"So'm I. Can I ride along?"

"Sure can, Minnie, if you don't mind bein' seen in my car."

She climbed into the seat beside me, depositing her bulky string bag on the floor by her feet. "Folks hereabouts name it a treat to ride with you, Dr. Sam."

"Glad to hear that."

I turned the yellow Runabout onto the mill road and we bumped along in silence for a few moments. Henry Cordwainer had become something of a local celebrity in the months he'd been living at Hawkins' gristmill, and it was a measure of his fame that two people as different as Minnie and me were coming to see him off.

Cordwainer was a full-bearded naturalist in the best New England tradition of Thoreau. He'd settled into old mill ten months earlier, arriving with the first chill of late September. They said he was writing a book about the seasons along Snake Creek, but during those first few months hardly anyone ever saw him. Even his food and supplies were delivered to the mill. But after a few months things changed. People began to see him, and to like him. He really was writin' a book, and he even let us read some of the early passages.

I took to stopping by the mill on spring evenings, sitting with him beneath the flowering dogwoods, joining him in an illegal beer and listenin' to his rambling reminiscences. Then he would bring out the journal and I'd read his beautifully phrased notes about autumn on Snake Creek.

"Who'd be interested in reading this sort of book?" I asked one night, when the beers had strengthened my courage.

He shrugged and scratched at his beard. "Who reads Thoreau?"

"Not very many people, at first."

"True enough."

I picked up one of the recent journals, but there was nothing in it but a handwritten copy of a newspaper clipping. "Take this, for instance." And I read:

Fifty Pounds Reward—Mysteriously Disappeared on the afternoon of the 20th ult., a Young Lady, 22 years of age, rather less than 5 feet in height, of sallow complexion, grey eyes, brown hair, and bearing evident marks of recent illness. She wore a black silk dress, a straw hat trimmed with white, and had with her a black travelling trunk. Information should be forwarded to Mr. C. F. Field (late Chief of the Metropolitan Police), Private Inquiry-office, 20, Devereux-court, Temple.

"That," Henry Cordwainer explained with a smile, "was a classified advertisement which had been circled in pencil on the front page of the London *Times* for August 6, 1873." When he saw my puzzlement he added, "I found the newspaper right upstairs, on the second floor of this very mill. There was a pile of old rags and magazines and papers, and this was one of 'em. I put it in my journal as a curiosity, because what would a fifty-year-old London newspaper be doing in an old New England mill? And especially with an item marked that way?"

"Many of the people hereabouts came from England. Hawkins, who used to operate the mill here, was English. He might have come over at about that time. Maybe he brought the newspaper from his last day in the mother country."

"Maybe," the bearded naturalist agreed. "But I can't help wondering about Mr. C. F. Field, late Chief of the Metropolitan Police. D'you think he ever found the young lady?"

That was the way one o' the conversations had gone. More often they dealt with the creek itself, with the various forms of wildlife Cordwainer found along its banks, and with the changing of the seasons. Though he avoided socializin' with the town residents, the naturalist was quick to lend a hand on community projects. During the winter when the creek froze over, he could be seen helping to saw ice for storage in the commercial icehouse that adjoined the mill. And on the first warm weekend of spring he joined the others for the annual cemetery cleanup.

Now, in late July, his journal was completed. It filled some three-dozen composition books such as students used, and bore the title *A Year on Snake Creek*, though in truth he'd been there only a bit over ten months. But now he was leaving, and Minnie Dranger and I had come to say our goodbyes.

I parked the Runabout next to Seth Hawkins' black Ford and we went inside. Cordwainer was busy packin' his books and journals inside a big wood-and-metal strongbox I'd seen before, all the while carrying on a running conversation with young Hawkins. "Hate to leave this place," he was saying. "You've all been mighty friendly to me here."

Young Seth Hawkins was a gangly farm lad just turned 20. His father had died five years ago and Seth had been too young to carry on the gristmill business himself. So the mill had closed down, though Seth's mother was reluctant to sell it. She still hoped Seth would take it over someday and build it back into the profitable business her husband had once had. Renting it to Cordwainer for a year had been a small source of income to the family, and now that he was leaving, the question of Seth's future was bein' raised again.

"We were mighty glad to have you here," Seth told Cordwainer. "Mebbe your book will make the old mill famous."

The naturalist gazed up at the stone walls and the roughhewn wood ceiling. "I'll have fond memories of the place," he admitted. "I loved it even when the grain dust made me sneeze." Then he saw Minnie and me. "Two more good friends! How are you, Dr. Sam? Minnie?"

"Land sakes, Henry Cordwainer, the old mill ain't goin' to be the same 'thout you!" She put down her bag and went to him, embracing him like a mother. "Why not stay another year?"

"I wish I could, Minnie. But I'm only on a sabbatical. I have to go back to teaching in September. Even Thoreau left his cabin, you know." He liked mentioning Thoreau, and at times I wondered just how good a journal he had written. I wished he'd let me read some of his later notes.

"I'll help you with those," I said, taking a pile of books from Seth Hawkins and loading them into the strongbox on top of the journals. I wasn't that much older than Seth, but there seemed a world of differernce between us. The death of his father had done nothing to thrust maturity onto his narrow shoulders.

"Is there anything else of yours upstairs?" Seth asked Cordwainer.

The naturalist hesitated. "I think that's everything, but you might check upstairs for me, Seth."

"That boy'll be lost without you," Minnie said when he was out of earshot. "Now that you're leavin', his mom wants him to start the mill up again."

Cordwainer shrugged. "Maybe it's good for him that I'm going. It'll force him to make a decision." He closed the lid of the strongbox. "Will you help me get this chest to the depot, Dr. Sam?"

"Where's it going?"

"I'm shipping it on to Boston. I'll pick it up there in a few days and then take the journals to my publisher."

I'd reached out to touch the familiar worn spots on the strongbox lid when we heard a muffled shout from above. "What's that lad into now?" Minnie asked, starting for the stairs as I followed.

We found him in the upper room of the gristmill, near a pile of rubbish Cordwainer had mentioned to me earlier. "Look at this!" he said.

In his rummagings he'd uncovered a human skull. Minnie Dranger gasped and stepped back, but I took the skull in my hand. "It's from some medical school or doctor's office," I assured them. "See how the lower jaw is wired onto the rest? They don't just *come* that way."

"What's it doin' up there?" Minnie wanted to know.

"Some kids probably stole it and left it here." I turned to Seth. "The place is your property. If you don't want this, I'll take it back to my office."

"Go ahead, take it! I don't want it."

"Every good doctor's office needs a skull."

We went back downstairs and I showed my acquisition to Cordwainer. He was just closin' the lid of his strongbox, and securing the hasp with a big padlock. "I'm ready whenever you are," he told me.

"Seth found this skull. I'm taking it for my office."

"That should scare the patients away," he said with a grin.

We carried the strongbox out to my car and stowed it in the side luggage well. I wondered how to fit both Minnie and Cordwainer into my two-seater, but Seth solved the problem by offering to take her in his car. "Will I see you agin before you go?" she asked.

Cordwainer smiled. "Sure, Minnie. I have to wind up some business in town and then come back out here. I probably won't leave till morning."

Seth's black Ford followed us into town, but turned off towards Minnie's farm when we reached the depot. I helped Cordwainer get the box inside and waited while it was weighed and tagged for railway-express shipment to Boston.

"That's forty-five pounds," the clerk said, accepting Cordwainer's money.

"There's some mighty valuable notes and journals in this box," the naturalist said. "Take good care of 'em."

"Don't worry," the clerk told him. "You can watch me put it on the train right now if you want."

We stood on the station platform while the strongbox was wheeled with a shipment of other parcels to a waiting freight car. "How soon will it reach Boston?" Cordwainer asked.

"Tomorrow mornin', I expect," the freight clerk answered.

That seemed to satisfy him and he turned towards the car. "Thanks for helpin' me, Dr. Sam."

"The least I could do. Can I give you a lift somewhere? How about some coffee?"

"No, no. I have to close out my account at the bank and pay a bill at the general store."

I dropped him at the bank and drove to my office. Not surprisingly, my nurse April was on the phone, making frantic excuses for my absence. When she hung up she said, "Dr. Sam, where've you been? There are patients waitin' to see you, and Aaron Spring just went an' fell of'n his tractor."

"Aaron? Badly hurt?"

"He mighta broke somethin'."

I started for the door again, picking up my bag on the way. "Explain to the patients, April. I'll be back soon as I can."

In the winter the women had babies, and in the summer men had accidents on the farm. It was an endless cycle that I'd discovered after only 18 months. But Aaron Spring was luckier than most. He had a dislocated right shoulder and a bump on his head, but no broken bones. I taped up the shoulder and told him to take things easy for a few days.

Then I went back to the office and sat through the usual assortment of afternoon patients. At least half of them seemed to have some illness that demanded the prescribing of alcohol, and this was always a problem. Generally I ended up silently cursin' the Volstead Act and writin' the prescription.

That evening, after my usual dinner alone, I decided on a drive to the next town. I knew some cockfights were being held in a barn there, and though I disapproved of the sport it always furnished a colorful evening. Some bootleggers would surely drive over from Boston, and I felt the need of a drink. Prescribin' it for others could give one a mighty big thirst of his own.

As I was drivin' along the dirt road to Calkins' Corners, I saw Sheriff Lens in his car ahead of me. "Evenin', Sheriff," I called out as I passed.

"Hi there, Doc. How's things?"

"Haven't lost a patient all day. You out patrollin'?"

Sheriff Lens grunted. "There's a light up at the mill. Somebody called me about it. Didn't that naturalist fella go back to Boston?"

"I think he's leaving in the mornin'. He's probably still up there."

"Guess I'll go check. The Hawkins family pay their taxes. They deserve to have their property protected."

I drove on into Calkins' Corners. There was a crowd at the barn for the cockfight, and I had to park in a field down the road. They were city people mainly, thrilled at the thought of doin' something illegal. There were college boys and their dates, drinkin' from silver hip flasks as they moved among the locals. There were darker, quieter men, too—the professional gamblers who traveled the cockfight circuit up from the south. And there were the bootleggers conducting their business out behind the barn.

As the bets were placed on the first match, I bought a quart of good Scotch and locked it away in the side luggage well of my car. It was a likely place for the police to search, but I knew Sheriff Lens wasn't going to stop me. I went inside the barn, staying near the edge of the crowd, and was surprised when I saw young Seth Hawkins there, too.

"Hello, Dr. Sam. What brings you to a cockfight?"

"I could ask you the same thing, Seth."

He shrugged. "Just somethin' to do."

A roar went up from the crowd as the two birds clashed. "Now that Cordwainer's leaving, are you going to reopen the gristmill?" I asked him.

Seth seemed pained by my question. "My father was one man and I'm another. Why does everyone expect me to follow in his path?"

"Everyone doesn't."

"My mother does, and she's the most important one." He glanced toward the cockpit but seemed uninterested in the battle. "Jeepers, I wish I had a drink!"

Perhaps he'd seen me buying the Scotch. In any event, it was not a request I could ignore. "Come on, I've got some in the car." My fingers felt some dampness in the luggage well, and for a moment I feared my bottle o' Scotch was leakin'. But the bottle was full and unopened. I poured us each a drink in two small metal cups I carried in my bag. "Tastes good."

He nodded in quick agreement. "The real stuff."

I put the bottle away. It would do neither of us any good to be picked up for drunken driving. "Are you staying for the rest of the fights?"

He took out his pocket watch. "No, I'd better head on back. Tomorra I'll have to start cleanin' out the mill."

"Sheriff Lens said there was a light up there. I told him it was Cordwainer's last night."

"I hate to see him go. First time I met him, when he rented the place, I didn't like him a'tol. Next time I saw him, helpin' with the ice in January, he seemed like a pretty good fella."

"You've spent a lot of time up there."

He nodded. "Two, three nights a week. I learned a lot from him, and not just about science neither. He knows about life."

I started out for home with Seth following behind me in his Ford. We passed a state police car on the road, and I wondered if it might be on the way to raid the cockfight. Probably not, I decided.

While we were still some distance from Northmont I spotted the reddish glow in the night sky. I waited till the Ford drew abreast and called out, "Looks like a fire."

Seth Hawkins nodded. "Somewhere up around the mill road."

We turned off our route and headed in the direction of the blaze. Before long I saw that it was on the mill road—the gristmill was in flames!

I drove as close as I could and then abandoned the car behind the horse-drawn town pumper. A hose line had already been run to the creek and the volunteers were pourin' water onto the blaze. The first person I saw was Aaron Spring, runnin' with the others despite his taped shoulder and bandaged head.

"You should be home in bed, Aaron," I shouted, running alongside of him.

"I'm the fire chief, Doc! We don't often git ourselves a blaze like this one."

It was true. The entire mill seemed about to be consumed, though I realized quickly enough that the stone walls of the lower floor would not burn. I saw Sheriff Lens and called out to him, "Anybody inside?"

"Hope not," he replied.

"How about Cordwainer?"

"Don't know. The fire had too good a start when I came up here to check on that light. I couldn't get inside to search for him."

Within another hour the volunteers had the blaze under control—meaning most everything that could burn had already done so. As they doused water on the last of the glowing embers, Sheriff Lens and I entered the lower floor through a door on the river side.

Using lanterns to guide us, we found Henry Cordwainer's body in the ruins. Though his skin and clothes and beard were charred, the body itself was not too badly burned. The stone walls of the lower floor had protected it. And there was no doubt as to the cause of death. The side of his skull had been crushed by repeated blows.

Cordwainer's body was sent to the county seat for an autopsy (the old doctor continued), and even by their primitive standards they were able to determine that the lungs were free of smoke. Cordwainer had been dead before the fire started, which didn't really surprise any of us.

"It's another case for you, Dr. Sam," the sheriff said. "Like that covered-bridge thing last year."

Aaron Spring, the fire chief, joined in. "Our own Sherlock Holmes! You even got the same initials—Sam Hawthorne and Sherlock Holmes."

I didn't take well to their jokin', because I'd liked Cordwainer. The man had been murdered, and most likely it was someone we all knew.

That first afternoon Cordwainer's brother and a fellow professor came down from Boston to claim the body. He'd been unmarried, and something of a loner, apparently. The brother, John Cordwainer, stared hard at the body and nodded. "It's Henry, all right. Burned, but I can tell. Haven't heard from him in months. I guess he was never very friendly."

"I knew him quite well," I told the brother. "He was a friend to all of us here."

"What about his notes, his journals?"

It was the first time I'd thought of them. "We shipped them to Boston by train. I helped him take the strongbox to the depot."

John Cordwainer gave a mirthless laugh. "That damn strongbox! I used to kid him about it. You'd think he was transporting Wells Fargo gold!"

"The key's probably one of these," Sheriff Lens said, producin' the ring we'd taken from the body. "I don't know about the claim check, though. It mighta got burned up."

"I'll go with you to get it," I volunteered. "We can get the claim-check number from the depot at this end."

For some reason Cordwainer's journal had become very important to me. I was remembering the skull on the second floor and the old newspapers the naturalist had found. Had he speculated in that journal of his about some forgotten crime he'd come across? I remembered how he'd never let me read his most recent entries—my browsin' was always confined to entries for the first few months or to the clippings and items he had inserted in the journal. What had he been writin' during those final months? Was it something important enough to cost his life?

We obtained a copy of the baggage claim check and went into Boston the following morning. It was two years since I'd seen the city, and driving past the Common on the way to the North Station I had a sudden longing for it again. Life in rural New England had its charms, but it had its lack, too. There was not a young lady in all of Northmont as pretty as the ones who now passed across my line of vision.

Cordwainer and I waited impatiently as the familiar strongbox was located and brought out. The first chill of something on my spine came when I saw the clerk carrying it under his arm without effort. Henry Cordwainer and I had struggled to get it to the depot.

"Feels empty," the clerk said, putting it on the counter.

The brother stared at me. "Empty?"

"That can't be," I said. I found the correct key, opened the lock, and threw back the lid.

The strongbox was empty.

The journals of Henry Cordwainer had vanished.

My nurse April was far more sympathetic than Sheriff Lens (the old man went on). She canceled all but the most urgent of my patients for that afternoon, then sat with me in the office after the last of them had gone. She may not have been as young or lovely as the Boston girls, but I was willin' to bet she was a better nurse than any of 'em.

"The strongbox was empty?"

I nodded. "Empty. Three dozen journal books and a couple of dozen of his regular books—all gone. Not a trace of them."

"Someone stole them!" she decided at once.

"Sure, but how?"

"The box was broken into."

"No. It was solid wood, with metal edges and metal bands going around it. The padlock hadn't been tampered with—I examined it closely. Hell, April, it's the sort of strongbox that banks use! The only thing I could find was a tiny hole that had been drilled through the wood at the bottom. And, I almost forgot, some grains of sawdust inside the box."

"Sawdust?"

I nodded again. "Our thief somehow got to the box while it was on the train or in Boston. He got by all the guards, tipped the box over, drilled an eighth-inch hole in the bottom—and through that tiny hole took out those thirty-six journals and the books. And all without being seen."

"Well, that's plain impossible, Dr. Sam."

"I know," I said gloomily.

But if April was in sympathy with my puzzlement, Sheriff Lens was not. He didn't want to hear about any missing journals. "Let the Boston police worry about that," he told me. "I've got a murder case on my hands."

"Don't you see the two are the same, Sheriff? The person who stole those journals killed Cordwainer to keep him from ever duplicating them."

Sheriff Lens shrugged. "The box was probably empty all the time."

"The box was *not* empty! I helped load it myself. I helped carry it to the depot. The bill of lading shows it weighed forty-five pounds. Empty—the way we found it—the box weighed only eleven pounds. That's thirty-four pounds of books and journals missing!"

"You say there was a hole drilled in the bottom. Maybe someone poured acid in it."

"Acid that destroyed everything but left the strongbox itself untouched?"

The sheriff waved his hand. "I don't know. Don't bother me about it. I'm close to makin' an arrest."

That news surprised me. "An arrest? Who?"

"You'll find out."

And I did find out, the following day. Old Minnie Dranger brought me the news. "Land sakes, Dr. Sam, the sheriff's gone an' arrested Seth Hawkins for the murder!"

"Seth?" I couldn't believe it. "But that's impossible!"

"Sheriff Lens says the boy was so feared of havin' to start operatin' the mill that he burned it down. Cordwainer caught him at it and got killed."

I went storming out of my office. "That's the damnedest fool thing I ever heard of!"

I found Sheriff Lens at the jail, just completing the arrest forms. "I think I've got a pretty good case," he said. " 'Course he hasn't confessed yet."

"Sheriff, listen to me! I was with Seth Hawkins at the time the mill caught on fire. We were twelve miles away, at a cockfight over in Calkins' Corners."

"Yep, he told me that."

"Don't you believe him? It's the truth!"

"Oh, I believe him all righty. An' I believe you, Dr. Sam. But that's just the sorta alibi a killer would think up now, ain't it? He bops Cordwainer on the head, kills him, and then sets a candle to burnin' on a pile of oily rags. The candle burns down slow, the rags catch fire, an' by that time he's twelve miles away."

"Did you find any evidence of that?"

"No, but I will. This time I beat you to the killer, Doc."

"I didn't know we were having a contest."

I went back to my office in low spirits and found Minnie Dranger still waiting. "What'd he say?"

"Not much," I admitted. "He thinks Seth's guilty."

"What do *you* think, Dr. Sam?"

"He's about as guilty as you are, Minnie. And I'm going to prove it."

I had made a purchase at a medical supply house in Boston. It was strictly experimental, and I knew full well I could lose my license if anything went wrong. Still, I felt it was worth the risk. Later that day I outlined my plan to April.

"I'll need your assistance at the jail," I said.

"It sounds risky, Dr. Sam."

"Everything's risky."

"Will Sheriff Lens agree to it?"

"Don't know," I admitted. But I intended to find out.

I found the sheriff in his office and came right to the point. "Suppose there was a chemical—a drug—that could tell you whether or not Seth Hawkins is guilty."

"Sure, Doc, if there was a chemical like that I'd be out of a job!"

"Listen—there is! It was written up a few weeks ago, in the July ninth issue of this new magazine, *Time*. It's called scopolamin, and it's a poisonous alkaloid anesthetic derived from deadly nightshade. It's like hypnosis, and a person injected with it is powerless to lie. They've tested it at San Quentin, and in Chicago and Texas."

"A sorta truth serum?" Sheriff Lens said with a chuckle. "You believe that hogwash?"

"I believe it enough to have bought a sample of scopolamin when I was in Boston. With your permission, and Seth's, I'd like to try it on him."

"That's crazy," the sheriff growled, losing his good humor.

"What have you got to lose? If he's guilty you'll have a confession."

"Yeah . . ."

The magazine article had been careful to say that such confessions could not be used in court because of the rule against self-incrimination, but I didn't feel I needed to tell Sheriff Lens that. I was utterly confident there'd be no confession for him to hear. "How about it? Willing to back up your arrest with a scientific test?"

He thought about it some more. Finally he said, "We'll see what the prisoner says."

Seth Hawkins trusted me, and he agreed at once. April arrived in her nurse's uniform to assist, and I opened my bag. I'd never used scopolamin before, but I'd read enough about the dosages to be sure I could administer it properly.

As soon as the drug had taken effect I started questionin' him. "Seth, do you know anything about the fire at the mill?"

"No."

"Did you start the fire or have someone else start it for you?"

"No."

"Did you kill Henry Cordwainer?"

"No."

"Did you ever hit him with anything or push him down?"

"No. He was my friend."

Sheriff Lens edged me aside and took over the questioning. "Now, listen here, Seth. You didn't want the mill to reopen, did you?"

He hesitated, then answered, "I couldn't keep it goin' like my dad did. I was afraid it would be a failure."

"So you burned it down."

"No!"

"Do you know who burned it?"

"No."

I took over again. "Seth, do you know who stole Cordwainer's journals from the strongbox?

"No."

"Do you know how it was done?"

"No."

Sheriff Lens held up his hand. "We're not gettin' anywhere, Doc. I told you I wasn't interested in the strongbox. And as for your truth serum—it don't prove a thing to me. Unless you want to inject everybody in the county till you find someone who admits to killin' him, the boy stays in jail."

I looked at April and saw her nod. The sheriff was right. I may have satisfied myself of Seth's innocence, but I hadn't satisfied the law. The fact that the sheriff had no real evidence against Seth didn't really matter. Cases like this one were tried by public opinion as much as by evidence.

"All right," I said. "Let him rest now. The effects of the drug will wear off soon."

As we walked back to my office April asked, "Did you really expect an old goof like Sheriff Lens to roll over an' sit up like a puppy jus' because you sprung some new drug on him?"

"I suppose not. But it was worth a try. At least I'm sure Seth is innocent."

"You knew that all along."

"Yes," I agreed.

"Then who's guilty? Do you think Cordwainer fell an' killed himself accidental, startin' the fire at the same time?"

I shook my head. "His skull was crushed by repeated blows. It wasn't from a fall. Besides, if the death and fire were somehow accidental, who stole his journals from the strongbox?"

"You always get back to the strongbox!"

I slumped in my office chair, feet on the desk. "I'm convinced that's the key to it, April. The strongbox with its bits of sawdust."

"You said the claim check wasn't found. Maybe the killer used it to get the real strongbox and replace it with a substitute."

"No, I'm sure the claim check simply burned in the fire. If the strongbox had been picked up and a substitute returned, it would have had a different claim number. Besides, I remember some worn spots on the lid. It was the same strongbox, all right. When I put it in my car—" I stopped short.

"What is it?" April asked.

"My car."

"What about it?"

I held up a hand. "Just let me think this through."

"Land sakes, Dr. Sam—"

My feet hit the floor and I headed for the street. "I have to check something at the newspaper office, April."

"What sorta somethin'?"

"An address."

An hour later I was back in the Sheriff's office. He looked at me through bleak, tired eyes and said, "What sorta tricks you up to now, Doc? More truth-serum monkeyshines?"

"No tricks. If you'll come with me, there's a chance I can break this case for you and hand you the real killer."

"Come where?"

"To Abernathy."

"Abernathy! That's over in the next county!"

"I know. I looked it up on the map, after I found the address I wanted. It's a long shot, but it's worth a try. You coming?"

"What for?"

"To make an arrest, if we're lucky."

"I can't arrest nobody in Abernathy!"

"Then we'll pick up some local deputies on our way. You must know the sheriff there."

"Well, sure, I know him. But—"

"Come on, then. There's no time to lose."

I took Sheriff Lens in my Runabout and we picked up a carload of local deputies on the outskirts of the town of Abernathy. It was larger than Northmont, with neat rows of houses lining shady streets. I found the street I wanted without difficulty.

"That white house there," I said, pointing it out from down the block.

"Looks like no one's to home," Sheriff Lens observed.

"It was a long shot at best, but let's make sure."

Then, suddenly, I saw the front door open. A clean-shaven man in a dark suit came down the front steps and glanced in our direction. I hated what I had to do, but there was no turnin' back. I crossed the street to intercept him.

"I believe we know each other," I said.

His eyes hesitated just a moment as he weighed his chances. "You're mistaken," he mumbled.

"I'm sorry, Delos," I said. "But we know it all."

His left hand moved fast, pulling me off balance, while his right hand snaked inside his jacket to emerge holdin' a snub-nosed revolver. I'd done it all wrong, I realized with a pang of fear. Now he would get away and I'd end up dead for my troubles. He was no friend. He was a cornered killer.

But then there was the crack of another weapon behind me, and Delos spun around, clutchin' his side. Sheriff Lens came runnin' up, kicking at the fallen gun, snapping the handcuffs on the wounded man. I'd never seen the sheriff move so fast.

"Get an ambulance," he shouted to the local deputy. "He's bleedin' bad." Then to me, "You satisfied?"

"I guess so."

"This is Delos, the escaped convict?"

I nodded. "But we knew him better as Henry Cordwainer."

"Cordwainer! He's dead!"

"I know. Delos killed him six months ago, and then took his place at the gristmill."

I had to go over it on the drive back to Northmont, and even after I told it Sheriff Lens still had his doubts. He only knew he'd shot and captured an escaped convict. It took a while for the rest of it to sink in.

"You see, Sheriff, the missing journals were the key to it after all. I saw Cordwainer putting them into that strongbox—I even helped him. I carried the box and watched while it was weighed an' shipped. Yet when it reached

Boston it was empty. Impossible? It seemed so at first, until I remembered feelin' some dampness in my car's side luggage well, where I'd had the strongbox during the drive to the depot. Dampness plus a small hole in the bottom of the box plus traces of sawdust inside—what did that add up to?"

"You got me," Sheriff Lens admitted.

"Melting ice, Sheriff."

"*Ice?*"

"Ice. I remembered seein' Cordwainer close the strongbox lid before I was called upstairs in the mill to look at an old skull. When I came back down he was closin' the lid again. He figured Seth would find that skull and call out to Minnie an' me. If Seth hadn't, Cordwainer would have gotten us out of the room on some other pretext. While we were out he quickly took the journals and books out of the strongbox and substituted a block of ice weighing about thirty-five pounds. The strongbox was locked, and I helped carry the ice to my car."

"I'll be damned!"

"Of course the tiny hole was to allow the water to escape, as it started to do in my car. The rest of it probably made a small stream in the railroad baggage car, but by the time the box reached Boston the water either evaporated or ran out the baggage-car door. In any event, the baggage handlers didn't pay any attention to it. And we found an empty strongbox waitin' for us."

"What about the sawdust?"

"That's the clue that clinched it for me. We know Cordwainer helped cut ice in the creek last winter for storage in the icehouse next to the mill. And ice stored like that is always packed in sawdust to preserve it. Cordwainer got a block of ice from the icehouse to substitute for the weight of his journals and books. The ice melted without a trace, but left some of the sawdust behind."

"All right, all right," Sheriff Lens agreed. "But why would Cordwainer steal his own journals? It don't make sense!"

"That's how I knew Cordwainer wasn't Cordwainer," I said. "The real Cordwainer would have no reason in the world to arrange such an elaborate disappearance, not when he'd be pickin' up the strongbox himself in Boston in a few days. The disappearance only made sense if he expected *someone else* to call for the strongbox and *if he knew he'd already be dead by then.* Since suicide was out of the question with a head wound like that, I had to consider the likelihood that the man we knew as Cordwainer was the killer."

"But why did the journals have to disappear? You skipped over that part."

"They had to disappear because part of them didn't exist! Thinkin' back over it, I remembered that Cordwainer would only allow me to read his journals of the first few months. What I saw of the later notes were only collections o' clippings from old newspapers and the like. In truth, there was no evidence that Cordwainer wrote a single thing after the first of this year.

"And what else did I know? The bearded naturalist had kept to himself before that, then suddenly, a few months later, had become friendly, even helping with the ice on the river. Seth Hawkins didn't like him when Cordwainer first rented the mill, but when he saw him again in January they became friends. Cordwainer's whole personality seemed to change after the first of the year. His personality changed, and his writin' stopped. Why? Because Henry Cordwainer became a different person."

I paused to let it sink in, then hurried on. "Then I remembered the prisoner Delos, who'd killed a guard while escapin' from the state prison on New Year's Day. It was a long shot, but it held together. Delos came to the mill the night of his escape, learned what the naturalist was up to, killed him, an' took his place. Luckily for Delos, they were about the same size, and he merely had to grow a beard to complete the disguise. Men with full beards tend to look alike.

"As you know, an escaped convict's greatest danger is always in the first six months or so when police are watchin' his home and family. When I decided it was Delos, I looked up his address and took you there. He'd gone back for a brief visit or stopover, as I hoped he would."

"Why didn't he just stay on at the mill?"

"Because the real Cordwainer had been on a sabbatical. If he didn't return to teaching in September, his friends would come looking for him and discover the truth."

We were nearing Northmont now, but Sheriff Lens still had questions. "All right. But what about the body in the fire? Even our poor excuse for a coroner could tell when a man's been dead over six months! Where was the body all that time, and how come it looked as if it had just been killed?"

"You should know the answer to that. Delos hid Cordwainer's body in the icehouse next door. The body was frozen, along with all that ice from the creek. I suppose that's why Delos had to pull out in July instead of waitin' till September. He kept track of the ice and must have seen they were getting close to uncovering the frozen body as they used up the blocks."

"Then the fire—"

I nodded. "To burn those empty journal books, of course. But the main reason for burnin' the mill was a truly unique one. Delos had to thaw out the body of the man he'd killed six months ago."

THE PROBLEM OF
THE LOBSTER SHACK

"**N**ow I want to tell you 'bout the lobster shack, which was just 'bout the most bafflin' of all the mysteries that confronted me during those early years. It would have been in the summer of '24 (Dr. Sam Hawthorne was saying), when Harry Houdini was still alive and popular. I was only a strugglin' young New England doctor at the time and still somewhat in awe of people like magicians and brain surgeons.

"Pour yourself another—ah—small libation and settle back while I tell you . . ."

The magician's name was Julian Chabert, but perhaps I'd better begin with the brain surgeon since he was my introduction to Chabert. Even in a little town like Northmont I'd heard plenty of stories about the fabulous Dr. Felix Dory. Back in 1924 there weren't that many brain surgeons 'round and his fame had spread from Boston like the ever-widening ripples in a pond.

I'd been practicin' medicine some two years in Northmont when the serious illness of a nearby farmer brought me into personal contact with Dr. Dory. When I determined that a brain operation was the only chance of savin' my patient's life, I telephoned the great man at his Boston hospital. He was willin' to see my patient, so I drove into the city myself, using the Pierce-Arrow Runabout as a makeshift ambulance. Dr. Dory operated that night and saved the farmer's life.

When I met him for the first time that day, I was startled by the quiet diffidence of the man. I'd expected someone brash and confident, with white hair flyin' in all directions, issuing orders to his nurses as he moved through the hospital corridors like some sort o' whirlwind. What I found instead was a pleasant man in his mid-forties who spoke softly and took credit for virtually nothin'.

I was young enough to be his son, but he took the time to explain the surgical procedure in great detail. When I praised his skill and suggested that he was a forerunner in the newest techniques of brain surgery, he merely scoffed. "Nonsense, Dr. Hawthorne! Is that what they call you back home? Dr. Hawthorne?"

"Mostly it's Dr. Sam," I admitted.

"Well, Dr. Sam, the art of making openings in the skull was known to the ancients, though I'll admit that surgery of human brains has progressed more slowly than other forms of surgery. We know that prehistoric man performed trephination, but we don't know why. And there's evidence of brain surgery in pre-Christian Peru."

Despite what he said, brain surgery was still a rare procedure in 1924. The few doctors who practiced it usually developed their own ingenious surgical tools, and Felix Dory was no exception. That first time we met he showed me a probe with a tiny light on it and a barbed steel wire that could be used as a bone saw. Today variations of both these tools are used in surgery, but back in '24 I could only stare at them and gape. To me the man was a magician.

I saw Dr. Dory two or three more times during the spring of that year, whenever some aspect of my profession brought me to Boston. Unlike the other country doctors I'd come to know, I was not content to sit out the years of my life in Northmont, unfamiliar with the progress being made in the world around me. The great teaching hospitals of Boston were a source of knowledge, and it was knowledge that could help my patients back home. So I came to get it.

It was in the late spring that Felix Dory first mentioned his daughter's impending marriage. "Linda is a fine lovely girl," he said with more than a fatherly pride. "She's just turned twenty, and I suppose I still think of her as a child. But she's a young woman and they're very much in love."

"They met at college?"

Dr. Dory nodded. "Tom Forsyth is graduating in June, then going on to law school. Naturally I wanted them to wait, but you know how young people are these days."

I certainly did, since I still considered myself one. "Is she your only child?"

He nodded sadly. "The house will be empty without her. Even away at college she often comes home weekends. But I suppose Edith and I will get used to it." He had a sudden thought. "The groom's family has a summer place up the coast, near Newburyport. The third weekend in June they're having an engagement party for Tom and Linda. Would you and your wife like to come?"

The invitation from this man I hardly knew so astounded me that I had no answer. All I could think to say was, "I'm not married."

"Well, your girl, then."

"I'm afraid it would have to be my nurse. But are you sure it'll be all right?"

"Certainly! I like you, Dr. Sam. And I want to convince my daughter that my colleagues aren't all bearded old fogies. Give me your address and I'll see that you receive an invitation."

M y colleagues.
The phrase repeated itself in my mind all the way back to Northmont that day. I was a colleague of the most famous brain surgeon on the east coast. He'd said so himself.

"How'd you like to go to an engagement party?" I asked April as I entered the office. She was a plump jolly woman in her thirties, and she'd been my nurse since the day I arrived in Northmont.

"Who's gettin' engaged?" she asked.

"The daughter of Dr. Felix Dory."

"Land sakes! And you're invited?"

"I will be. And I'm going to take you, April." I could see the idea pleased her. "Will you go?"

"Mebbe. I gotta get used to the idea."

But pleased as she was I don't think she really believed it till the engraved invitation arrived two weeks later. The party was to be an all-day affair, on a Saturday at the Forsyth home. There would be tennis and swimmin', with a special performance by the world-famous escape artist, Julian Chabert.

I had to admit they knew how to do it in style.

When the big day finally arrived on the third weekend in June, happily without any last-minute complications from injured farmers or their pregnant wives, April and I started out in the morning for the two-hour trip to Newburyport in my Runabout. I'd never seen her quite so dressed up with her hair close-cropped up the back and wearing a deep cloche hat that matched her pale pink summer dress.

"Do I look all right?" she asked, as we drove across the North Bridge and left the town behind us.

"Beautiful! You should dress like that in the office."

"Oh, it wouldn't be right for a nurse!" she answered, taking me seriously. Then, after we'd driven a ways in silence, she asked, "Who is this Julian Chabert?"

"I suppose you'd call him a poor man's Houdini. He performs the same sort of escape tricks. From what I hear he's just as skillful, but he lacks Houdini's showmanship." During the past few years Houdini's name had been often in the public press. When he wasn't escaping from a packin' box under water, he was makin' an elephant disappear from the stage of New York's Hippodrome, or exposin' the trickery of a fake medium.

"Will he do some tricks today?"

"I expect so. I wonder how the Forsyths got hold of him."

The road to Newburyport was narrow and rutted, with only the trail markings to guide us. We were still two years away from the present numbering system for highways, and lengthy journeys by car we're somethin' of an adventure.

When we finally reached the Forsyth home, it proved to be a sprawlin' white house set smack-dab in the middle of an estate that ran from the highway all the way to the edge of the ocean. I could see that the sight of it took April's breath away, and it very nearly did the same for me.

Happily, Dr. Dory and his wife were already in attendance. He welcomed me with a gracious handshake and I introduced April. "So glad you could both make it! This is my wife, Edith."

She was a pleasant woman with large diamond rings on her fingers. "I'm pleased to meet one of my husband's younger colleagues. Our daughter Linda says all doctors are old fogies."

"That's what your husband told me," I said. "Where is the happy couple?"

"In the back with our hosts." Dory led the way around the side of the big house, and we saw that a huge tent had been erected for the party. There must have been a hundred people present already, and many of them were sippin' champagne cocktails though it was barely noon. "We won't be raided," Dory assured me, as if readin' my mind. "The police chief is one of the guests."

Linda Dory and Tom Forsyth were close to each other, at the center of the crowd of wellwishers. I had to admit they were a handsome couple—she with a natural beauty that reflected and enhanced her mother's friendly good looks, and he with a wealth of charm that could work equally well on college girls and juries.

Forsyth's parents, the party's hosts, were a bit of a surprise. I'd been expectin' the poise and charm of Dr. and Mrs. Dory, and they weren't in evidence. In fact, Pete Forsyth looked downright uncomfortable in his open polo shirt and ice-cream white slacks. I wondered how he made his living and decided not to speculate. It was none of my business.

"Are you at the Boston hospital, too?" Mrs. Forsyth asked. She wore too much makeup and was tryin' too hard to be the mother of the groom. But again, it wasn't my business.

"No, I have a small country practice in Northmont. This is my nurse, April."

"I sure do admire your house," April said. "Nothin' like this back in Northmont!"

"Thank you," Mrs. Forsyth said, glancing around nervously for her husband. An orchestra had started playin' dance music at the other end of the tent.

Suddenly there was a stirring, a murmur of anticipation. I saw Dr. Dory tug nervously at a bandaged finger as he strained for a view. "Chabert is here!" Linda Dory announced.

The crowd before me parted, and there he was, sweepin' into our midst with black cape flowing in the best tradition of the stage magician. He *was* a showman, it seemed, and maybe he'd equal Houdini's success someday. Pete Forsyth held out his hand, but the escape artist didn't take it. Instead, he motioned to a short bald man at his side. "This is my business manager, Mark Ernst. Some of you met him last evening. Are we ready for the performance?"

Forsyth nodded. "We'll use the lobster shack down by the shore, as we discussed last night."

"Fine. You may choose a committee of guests to search the shack, to search me, and to tie and chain me in any way they please. I'll be left alone and the shack locked from the outside. You may guard it, all of you. I will walk out of the shack, free of my bonds, in five minutes, no more."

While he spoke, my eyes had settled on the future bridegroom's face. Tom Forsyth seemed unusually nervous, and I was tryin' to determine why.

"Dr. Sam."

The sound of my name interrupted my thinkin'. Felix Dory was speakin'. "Pete suggests you and me for the committee. How about it?"

"And our police chief," Forsyth added. "He should be an expert on locking people up."

"I'll get him," Mrs. Forsyth said. She was gone only a few moments and returned with an overweight, red-faced man. "Chief Banner, this is Dr. Felix Dory. And Mrs. Dory. You know, Linda's parents."

"Happy t' meet you," the Chief said, shakin' Dory's hand, then hoistin' his pants a little.

"And Dr. Sam Hawthorne, all the way from Northmont."

I took his hand and introduced April. "I don't want ye to think all this open drinkin' goes on here all the time," he confided to us. "But the Forsyths are somethin' special hereabouts. And a weddin' is a weddin'—right?"

"Right," I agreed. "Just when is the weddin'?"

"First Sat'aday in August. Big affair." He reached into his pocket. "Want a cigar?"

"No, thanks."

"We should go down to inspect the lobster shack," Dr. Dory suggested.

I followed along behind Dory and the Chief, and some of the other guests trailed us. The wide lawn sloped gradually down from the tent to the shoreline, perhaps a hundred yards away. It was a rocky shore, with only a narrow beach. At one point, where the land jutted into the sea, stood a small wooden structure. Even at a distance I could make out the details of its construction—one door and two windows at the side, a short pier connected with the door and running to the water, and a chimney which told me there was a fireplace inside.

The three boats tied up at the dock were hardly the craft of lobster fishermen, and it was obvious the place was no longer used for its original purpose. Even the old wooden lobster traps piled near the doorway were present only for scenic effects, as was a fishin' rod propped against one of the two windows.

"Pete gave me the key," Dr. Dory said as he unlocked the door. "He uses it as a boathouse—keeps his fishin' gear here."

The inside was not as cluttered as I'd expected. There were a number of fishin' rods and reels, one of the reels unwound on the floor, but otherwise the place was neat and reasonably clean.

"They do surf castin'," Chief Banner observed. "Expensive gear, too."

Felix Dory strode over to a wooden post in the center of the room. It was a support for the roof and ran from floor to ceiling. "This seems sturdy enough," he decided, after giving it a hard tug. "Suppose after they get the chains on him we bring him in here and tie him to this post? Then we'll lock the door from the outside. If he can get out of this shack in five minutes I'm willing to grant he's a magician."

"We better search the place first," Chief Banner said. "Make sure he hasn't got a friend hidin' here already."

A careful search revealed nothing. There was really no place anyone could hide in the lobster shack, except for a tall wooden cupboard against one wall. This proved to be empty, and the wall behind it was solid.

"What about the chimney?" Chief Banner suggested as we were about to leave. We checked it together and found the tiny opening plugged at the top by a bird's nest.

"They haven't used this fireplace in a long time," I said.

We went back outside to the crowd of spectators, who'd formed themselves into a semicircle around the lobster shack. At first I didn't see Julian Chabert, but then he broke through the crowd, stridin' down the grassy slope in bright green bathin' trunks. I heard a few gasps from the women guests when they saw his bare chest. Even Olympic swimmer Johnny Weissmuller still wore a top to his bathing suit.

But I wasn't surprised. I'd seen newspaper photos of Houdini, chained and wearin' only bathin' trunks, ready for one of his impossible escapes. In fact, they said he'd once escaped from a jail cell in New York's Tombs while completely naked.

While Chabert's business manager stood to one side with a faint smile on his lips, Pete Forsyth came forward. "All right, now we need a committee to chain him."

"How about the future bride and groom?" someone shouted. "They'll get to know what married life is like!"

Linda and Tom came forward amidst good-natured kidding and took up the lengths of chain. They wrapped them tightly around Chabert's arms and legs until he could barely hobble into the lobster shack. Padlocks were produced and examined, then snapped into place. It seemed impossible that the man could free himself without aid.

We guided him into the shack while the guests crowded around the open door to watch. Chief Banner had produced a stout length of rope which he wrapped around Chabert's shoulders, towering above the magician as he worked. He made a firm knot, tying the already chained man to the stout wooden post. I took another length of rope and secured him at the knees. His hands, already tightly chained in front of him, were further restrained by a final chain that locked him to the wooden post.

"There you are!" Pete Forsyth announced with somethin' like pride. "Tied and helpless, roped and chained, nearly nude so you can see he conceals no tools or keys."

"One last precaution," Dr. Dory suggested. "I'll take this hammer and nail the windows shut." He went around to the outside while Pete Forsyth prepared to lock and bolt the door.

"Any final words?" Forsyth asked.

Julian Chabert merely smiled at us, lookin' not the least uncomfortable. "I will be with you in five minutes. You might start timing me from right now."

Forsyth slammed the door, threw the bolt, and padlocked it. Around the side we heard Dr. Dory finish with his hammerin'. "I don't suppose that was really necessary," he said, comin' around to rejoin us. "There are people on all sides of the shack, so no one could get in there to free him without being seen."

"That's for sure," young Tom Forsyth agreed. I noticed he was holdin' Linda's hand tightly.

I'd almost forgotten April, but she reminded me with a tug at my sleeve. "Stay with me now, Dr. Sam! I don't know any o' these people!"

"Neither do I, April." Glancin' around at their eager, slightly drunk faces, I decided I'd never know them. I was a country doctor, and these were the people in an F. Scott Fitzgerald short story—people right out o' the pages of *The Smart Set* or *Vanity Fair*.

"Two minutes gone!" Pete Forsyth proclaimed.

April and I walked over to where Mark Ernst, Chabert's manager, was standin'. "This must be old stuff for you," I said.

The little bald man shrugged. "Every escape is a little bit different. He likes unusual settings, and it's tough finding ones that Harry Houdini hasn't already used."

"How does he do it?"

Mark Ernst merely smiled. "Magic, Doctor. Pure magic."

"Just one more minute!" Forsyth proclaimed. We could feel the tension in the guests as they waited for the locked door of the lobster shack to open.

"Thirty seconds!"

All conversation had stopped. I saw Felix Dory give his daughter's arm a little squeeze, saw Mrs. Forsyth refill her glass of champagne.

"Ten seconds!"

I watched a gull circle slowly overhead, perhaps wonderin' what all these foolish people were doing standin' outside a lobster shack on a hot June afternoon.

"The five minutes are up," Forsyth said, his voice flat, even harsh.

Everyone watched the door of the lobster shack.

Nothin' happened.

We waited a full minute.

Nothin' happened.

"I guess we did too good a job tyin' him up," Chief Banner remarked.

Mark Ernst edged forward to reassure Forsyth. "I've seen him do this trick a hundred times. Don't worry, he'll get out. It's just taking him longer than usual."

By the end of the second minute past the deadline, the guests were growin' obviously restless. Pete Forsyth walked to the door and called out, "Are you all right in there, Chabert?"

There was no answer.

Cursing softly, Mark Ernst stepped forward. "I told you not to worry!" he pleaded.

So we waited some more.

After five minutes had passed, Tom and Linda tried to peer in the side windows, but they were painted over in black on the inside. Nothin' could be seen.

After seven minutes Forsyth said, "I'm unlockin' the door."

I stepped forward and was at his side when the door swung open. The first thing I saw was the bloodstained huntin' knife on the floor near the window.

I pushed past Forsyth and entered the shack first. "Keep everyone else back!" I warned.

Julian Chabert was still tied and chained to the wooden post. But now his head sagged at the unmistakable angle of death.

Someone had entered the locked lobster shack, unseen by a hundred witnesses completely surrounding the shack, and cut Chabert's throat.

C hief Banner took charge immediately, and in these first moments of panic and confusion he seemed secretly pleased with himself. Maybe he was enjoyin' his temporary mastery of these wealthy people with their fancy home overlookin' the ocean.

"All right, now!" he bellowed. "Everybody quiet down! We got a murder here, an' I'm gettin' to the bottom o' it! Now I helped search that shack myself — me an' the two docs here—an' we know there wasn't a livin' creature hidin' there. We jus' searched it agin with the same result. Nobody's in there but the dead man. That means somebody killed him while we was all standin' around out here. Now who saw anythin'?"

Mrs. Forsyth was the first to reply. "Nobody entered that shack, Chief Banner. Nobody even went near it!"

"He must have killed himself," young Tom Forsyth said.

"With his hands tied and chained?" Chief Banner asked. "An' where'd he have the knife hidden—in his throat?"

Felix Dory stepped forward, the cool professional brain surgeon always in control. "There's no doubt he was murdered. If we find out why, maybe we'll find out who."

"None of us even knew him!" Pete Forsyth argued. He was taking the killing as a personal affront to his party. "He was just a hired performer." He turned on Chabert's manager. "And speaking of that, I'll expect a refund of my five hundred dollars!"

Through it all Mark Ernst's behavior had been the strangest. The bald little manager seemed alternately terrified and delighted, movin' with a sideways step that was almost a skip, yet at the same time wipin' away the tears from his eyes with a tremblin' hand. "What'll I do without him?" he moaned. "He's been my whole life!"

I glanced around at the millin', confused guests and saw that some order must be made out of this chaos. Already some of them were headin' across the great lawn towards their cars, anxious to avoid any involvement. Seein' what was happenin', Chief Banner ran up ahead of them and drew a revolver from under his coat.

"Now listen here you folks! I'm plantin' myself smack-dab in the center o' this lawn, an' if anyone tries t' run by me an' git away, they's gonna git a bullet in the leg! Understand?"

They understood. The exodus came to a sudden halt.

But Pete Forsyth came runnin' up, wavin' his arms. "Look here, Chief, you can't talk that way to my guests! My God, you're treating them like common criminals!"

I stepped quickly between the two men. "Let's go into the house," I suggested. "Mr. Forsyth, if you'll be good enough to furnish us with a guest list, Chief Banner can check off the names on it and then allow most of these people to leave. It's obvious they had nothin' to do with the crime."

My suggestion seemed agreeable to everyone, and we trooped into the big white house. Banner was crankin' up the telephone to summon his men, so I took advantage of the delay to pull Pete Forsyth aside for some questionin' of my own.

"How did you happen to hire Chabert for the entertainment?" I asked.

Forsyth nervously lit a cigar. "My God, how could this happen to me? The worst possible publicity!"

"How did you happen to hire him?" I repeated.

"He came to me. He showed up at my office one day last month with his manager. He'd heard my son was gettin' engaged and suggested I book his act. Well, I thought it would be a nice diversion."

"Did you or your wife know Chabert or Ernst before?"

He hesitated only a second. "No."

"But—?" I prompted.

"But Tom might have. I don't know."

Chief Banner stormed into the room, interruptin' us. "I'll do the questionin' here, Doc."

"Are your men on the way?"

He nodded. "We'll get to the bottom o' this. Don't you worry none, Mr. Forsyth."

I drifted out to the big living room, where I spotted Mark Ernst across the room and headed for him.

When he saw me he gestured towards the high ornate ceiling. "This is quite a joint, eh, Doc?"

"Could I talk to you privately? Before Chief Banner does?"

"Sure, Doc. What's on your mind? Got a little act you'd like me to manage?"

I led him past a knot of anxious, babbling guests, thinkin' that they were all gettin' drunker by the minute. Forsyth had made no effort to lock up the champagne, despite the imminent arrival of more police.

Once I had Ernst safely in the study, I closed the door and said, "You don't seem too broken up by the death of your star client."

"Sure I'm broken up! He was a good guy!"

"Was Julian Chabert his real name?"

"No. That was the name of some French magician from a hundred years ago. He found it in a book."

"What was his real name?"

"Sammy Gorman. He was from New York. Learned his stuff watching Houdini."

"How was he supposed to escape from that shack?"

"Those were his secrets. He didn't even tell me!"

"But you must have some idea."

The little man shifted nervously. "I can't tell you. Maybe I'll find another magician to take Chabert's place."

I tried a different approach. "Chabert must have been insured. Some of his underwater stunts were dangerous."

"Sure he was insured."

"Any wife or kids?"

"Him? You kidding? He didn't like girls."

"Then who was the beneficiary on his policy?"

"Well . . . I guess I was."

"A strong motive for murder, isn't it?"

"Hell, I didn't kill him."

"Someone did." I tried again. "How was the trick supposed to be done?"

"They won't pin this on me, will they?"

"Maybe."

"I was outside. Everyone saw me. I never even went in there!"

"But maybe there was somethin' in the way he did the trick, some way you could kill him by remote control."

"All right," he said. "I'll tell you what I know. He had a key to the locks hidden in his mouth, under his tongue. As long as his hands were chained in front of him, which he insisted on, he could spit the key out and catch it."

"What about the ropes?"

"He flexed his muscles while you were tying him up."

"And the locked door?"

"He had a couple of ways of working that. Do you have to know all his secrets?"

"I guess you've told me enough," I agreed. "Except who might have killed him—if *you* didn't."

"Honest, I don't know a thing about that!"

"Whose idea was it to come here?"

"His. He read about the engagement in the papers."

"Did he always approach rich people for jobs?"

"No, never before. But he thought Forsyth might be good for a bundle. Said he was a bootlegger, running the stuff in from boats offshore."

The revelation didn't surprise me. In fact, it explained a great many things. "All right," I said. "Stick around and tell your story to the Chief." I headed for the French doors overlooking the back lawn.

"Where you going?" Ernst asked.

"Back to the lobster shack."

Chief Banner's men were there now, carefully untying the body, examining the doors and windows and every inch of the shack. "Nothin' on the floor, nothin' outa place," Banner complained. "It's just like it was when we searched it earlier, Doc."

"Did you check the chimney again?"

"Sure did. And the windows that Dr. Dory nailed shut. There's nothin' to go on. The thing's impossible."

Felix Dory had joined us in the doorway. "I could have opened the window and thrown a knife at him."

Chief Banner snorted. "Sure you coulda! Except that you were hammerin' away while we was still inside talkin' to him. And a hundred witnesses swear the windows weren't opened, then or later. And the knife couldna been thrown an' leave a wound like that. It had to be drawn across his throat by a human hand."

"Then it must be suicide," Dory insisted. "Anything else is impossible!" He picked up the fishin' rod that was leanin' against the outside of the shack and kicked at one of the old lobster traps.

While they argued about it, I stood lookin' at the pile of old traps. Their wooden slats were broken and rotted. They hadn't been used in a long time. I thought about Chabert, lured into the shack like a lobster into its trap. The only difference was that the lobster stayed alive, Chabert hadn't.

I saw Edith Dory walkin' along the shore with a comforting arm about her daughter, and I went to meet them. "Don't worry," I said reassuringly. "I'm certain the police will straighten it out."

But Linda Dory was close to tears. "They think Tom did it!" she wailed.

"What's that? How could they?"

"Apparently Tom knew him," Mrs. Dory explained. "We don't know the details, but Chief Banner's men are questioning him now."

I left them and trotted back up to the house, anxious to see what was goin' on. Apparently Tom Forsyth had just been interrogated. He stood in the front hall, pale and shaken, talkin' softly to his father. When they saw me they both fell silent.

I motioned to some departin' guests. "Are the police checkin' them off all right?"

Pete Forsyth nodded. "Thanks to your suggestion."

"What's this about your son?"

Tom glanced away, embarrassed, and his father replied, "The damn fool is too honest for his own good. He had to go and tell 'em he knew Chabert."

"Where did you know him from, Tom?"

"New York. I spent last summer there."

I was beginnin' to see the light, and it wasn't a very pleasant light. "Chabert told his manager he thought you'd be good for a bundle of money, Mr. Forsyth. He knew you were a bootlegger. I think he came here with blackmail on his mind. Under the guise of payin' him for his performance, you'd really have been payin' for his silence."

Pete Forsyth grimaced. "You've seen Chief Banner. Do you think he cares if I'm a bootlegger?"

"Maybe Chabert wasn't blackmailin' you because of whiskey. Maybe he was blackmailin' you because of your son."

Forsyth glanced at Tom, then looked at me. "How much do you know?"

"Tom must have been a pretty close friend to tell Chabert his father was a bootlegger. And it was the announcement of Tom's engagement that brought Chabert here. His manager implied that Chabert was a homosexual—"

"All right," Tom Forsyth interrupted, his face contorted with agony. "It was a foolish, crazy thing that happened last summer and lasted exactly one night. I was sick with myself for months afterwards. I'd hoped with Linda I could get over even the memory of it!"

"And Chabert wanted money?"

Pete Forsyth nodded. "Fifty grand to keep his mouth shut."

"What did you tell him?"

"That I knew guys who'd put him at the bottom of the ocean in a concrete coffin."

"And that scared him off?"

"It seemed to. He didn't mention it again—just talked about today's performance."

"When did all this happen?"

"Last evening."

"Was anyone else present?"

"Not during this. Felix and Edith Dory joined us when we were talking about using the lobster shack for Chabert's escape."

"So only you and your son knew of the blackmail attempt." I turned to Tom. "Did you tell all this to the police?"

"Most of it. I didn't say my father threatened him."

"All right." I moved away as some of the departing guests headed in our direction.

One of them was April. "I'm all checked off the list. We goin' purty soon, Dr. Sam?"

"Yes, April, soon."

Chief Banner appeared in the doorway. "Okay, you, Doc. Down t' the lobster shack. You, too, Pete. By gum, I'm goin' to show ye how this trick was worked!"

"You mean you know who killed him?"

"I mean I know how he killed hisself."

We walked down and stood round the shack while Chief Banner leaned against the post inside, his arms crossed in front of him, in the manner of the dead man. "Look here, now. We know Chabert was—well, queer. Call it what ye want, he was sick. So he decided to kill hisself, but in a magical way. I guess he figured he'd go out with big headlines."

"He wouldn't kill himself," Mark Ernst insisted from the sidelines.

"Oh, no? Well, I'm gonna show you how he done it! You told me, Ernst, that he had a duplicate key hidden in his mouth. Well, he used that key to unlock his chains, then he reached up here for the knife he'd hidden earlier." His hands went above his head, barely reaching one of the ceiling beams. "He put the key back in his mouth where we found it, cut his throat, tossed the knife away, and while he was bleedin' to death he snapped shut the padlock on his hands agin!"

"It doesn't seem very likely," Pete Forsyth observed.

"Likely or not, it's the only way! There weren't nobody in here with him, and nobody entered or left. We was all watchin'. He killed hisself—it's the only way!"

The police began packin' up their equipment, and the Forsyths headed back to the house. I walked out onto the dock and stood for a time gazin' off into the choppy water. Presently Dr. Dory came and stood at my side.

"What do you think, Dr. Sam? Are you satisfied with the Chief's solution?"

"No," I answered simply. "It would take a superhuman effort to lock those chains again after cutting one's own throat. Besides, you saw how Chief Banner had to stretch to reach that beam, and Chabert was much shorter. He couldn't have done it."

"Why didn't you tell the Chief?"

I shrugged. "The truth wouldn't bring Chabert back. Besides, he was a blackmailer. Worse than a blackmailer, for what he did to Tom Forsyth."

"Yes."

I bent and picked up a pebble from the dock and sent it spinnin' out into the water. "I know you killed him, Felix." It was the first time I'd ever used his given name.

"Yes," he said again.

"And I know how. When he found he couldn't blackmail Pete Forsyth, Chabert must have tried you. You knew how much the weddin' meant to your daughter, and you had faith in Tom. So you killed Chabert to silence his filthy mouth. What tipped me off to your method was the fishin' line, of course.

"When we searched the shack earlier the reel was unwound on the floor. But later, when the police searched the place, the floor was bare—the Chief said so. Forsyth had given you the key to the shack. It was a simple thing for you to come down in the night, or early this morning, and set the stage for your impossible crime."

"This morning," he said in confirmation. "Just at sunrise."

"You arranged the fishin' line very carefully, so when it was pulled tight it rose to just the level of Chabert's throat. It was you who suggested tyin' him to the post, and you who suggested nailin' the windows shut. While you were nailin' the far window—*after* we'd closed the door and locked it—you used your body to shield what you were really doin'—reelin' in that fishin' line. It pulled taut, some five feet or so off the floor, and caught naturally in the soft flesh of his neck.

"Chabert was still chained and helpless. You reeled in the line fast and cut his throat with it, in much the same manner that a few London residents were killed by the danglin' cables of barrage balloons, during the World War. The window only had to be open a fraction of an inch to allow the fishin' line to pass through the openin'. You'd tied the huntin' knife loosely to the end of the line, and stained it with blood, probably chicken blood—"

"Human blood," Dr. Dory corrected, holding up his bandaged finger. "I took no chances."

"When the knife hit the window sill it came free of the line and fell to the floor. Chabert was dead, the shack was locked from the outside, and the illusion was complete. He couldn't have done it better himself."

Felix Dory smiled. "You're forgetting the human element. The fishing line might have done no more than give him a bad skin burn, and he might have screamed for help."

"The sound of your hammerin'—while you were reelin' in the line with your other hand—would have covered any yellin' unless it was lengthy. And you made sure it wasn't. This is guesswork, but I think a portion of the line was replaced with your own specialty—the barbed steel wire you use as a bone saw. You'd carry a length of it in your medical bag surely, ready for any emergency."

"You're a clever young man, Dr. Sam. You'll go far."

"I should have tumbled to it earlier. The fishin' rod was leanin' against the window outside the first time we searched the shack. And I saw you pickin' it up a while ago—disposin' of the evidence. Your steel wire came directly out the window, at the level of Chabert's throat, and onto the reel you wound with your left hand. A fake line runnin' to the top of the rod didn't move, so anyone watching your back while you hammered wouldn't realize the reel was even movin'."

"What are you going to do?" he asked finally.

I stared at the water for a long time. "It's not for me to do anything, Felix. It's for you."

"I see." He chewed his lower lip. "Give me till after the wedding. All right?"

"All right." He'd saved a good many lives in his day. Maybe he'd have a chance to save a few more.

"I drove back to Northmont with a slightly drunk April that evening (Dr. Sam concluded) and I never heard from Felix Dory again. The Chabert case was closed with a verdict of suicide. Three months later, some weeks after his daughter's marriage, Dory was killed when his car hit a tree on the Boston Post Road.

"But there were other things on my mind that summer. For one, it was the summer of the haunted bandstand. Now if you've got time for another— ah—small libation, I'll tell you about that one. You see, folks were gettin' ready for a big Fourth o' July celebration . . . ."

THE PROBLEM OF
THE HAUNTED BANDSTAND

"**W**ell now, I promised to tell you about the haunted bandstand, didn't I? You comfortable in that chair? Your glass filled? These aren't stories to listen to without—ah—a small libation. No, sir!

"This was still the summer of '24, shortly after I'd returned to Northmont from the wedding that involved me in the lobster shack affair. It was a healthy summer as summers go, and there wasn't too much call for my services. Nobody'd even missed us the day my nurse April and I were away, but that was prob'ly because folks were already gettin' ready for the big Fourth o' July celebration.

"You see, that's when it happened, with the bandstand and all. On the Fourth o' July . . ."

It came on a Friday that year (the old man went on), and it was a big treat for the folks 'round Northmont. 'Course there were no long weekends in those days. Most everyone worked at least a half day on Saturdays, but nobody ever worked very hard the day after the Fourth.

About a week before the celebration I happened to meet Doc Henry Church, the local druggist, near the park in the town square. Doc Church was always friendly to me, prob'ly 'cause I sent him most of his business. This was in the days before drug stores started sellin' everything from perfume to picnic grills. Doc Church sold drugs an' tobacco, an' he had a soda fountain—but that was all.

"Big doings here next week, Dr. Sam. You comin' to the band concert an' fireworks?"

"I wouldn't miss it, Henry. This is my third summer in Northmont, and the Fourth o' July is one of the highspots."

He was a smiling man of medium build, around 40, who lived in the town with his wife and two children. I liked Doc Church, even though he was forever kiddin' me about bein' a young available bachelor. "Thought a fella like you would have more important things to do on a summer's night than listen to me playin' the flute in the town band," he chided.

"That's a pretty important thing," I answered with a wink. "All the young girls will be there."

We'd strolled together into the park and now we reached the old bandstand. It was a tall wooden structure, well weathered and in need of repainting, with eight open sides and a roof that tapered to a point with a weathervane atop it. The floor was maybe four feet off the ground and was reached by seven steps that led up from the ground. There were railings along the steps, and railings enclosin' the other sides of the bandstand, prob'ly to keep overzealous trumpeters from topplin' backwards into the crowd. The space beneath the bandstand was completely enclosed with wooden latticework, guarding against wanderin' children.

"Sheriff Lens ever tell you about the ghost?" Doc Church asked.

"Here? By the bandstand?"

"Yes. Happened back around 1880, right after this bandstand was built."

"What happened?"

"Couple o' drifters—a colored man an' his gypsy wife—came to town. He was prob'ly a freed slave who'd been roaming the country since the Civil War, but nobody knowed for sure. One night he broke into the hardware store and they caught him. They said he had a knife a foot long and he near killed the sheriff. I guess the townsfolk weren't takin' any chances. They strung him up from the top o' the bandstand."

"Lynched him?" I was incredulous. "Lynchings didn't happen in New England."

"They was rare, but they happened. Indians in colonial days an' witches, too—in Salem. Anyway, his gypsy wife put a curse on the bandstand before they drove her out o' town, and they say he still comes back here at times, still wearin' a hood an' the rope 'round his neck."

"Sounds like an old wives' tale to me."

"I'll admit he hasn't been seen in recent years," Doc Church conceded.

"I'll bet not! People today are too smart for that nonsense."

"I s'pose you're right," he agreed as we headed back.

"Mayor Dwiggins return from Washington yet?"

"Just this mornin'. Came in to get his prescription refilled. He says Washington is hot an' full of flies. Hell of a place for the capital of our country, huh?"

"I guess it's not too pleasant in the summer. The British Foreign Office lists it as a subtropical climate. Did he have any luck with Secretary New?" Mayor Dwiggins, recently elected and brimming with campaign promises, had journeyed to Washington by train to ask Postmaster General Harry New to give Northmont its own post office.

"Never even saw him. New was out o' town somewhere—prob'ly fishin' —and the mayor had to meet with his assistant. He's hopeful, though.. But then Mayor Dwiggins is always hopeful."

We'd reached his drug store, and I could see Mrs. Church workin' behind the counter. "I gotta get back to my patients, Henry."

"Write lots of prescriptions, Dr. Sam!"

D uring the week of the Fourth my office was mildly busy, mostly with the usual summer complaints of farm injuries an' poison ivy. When there weren't any patients, April kept me hoppin', insistin' it was the perfect time for an office house-cleanin'.

"I'm not in the mood," I complained on Thursday as she was emptyin' my wooden file drawers for a thorough dusting. "Can't we do it some other time?"

She moved her stocky body around my desk. "In the winter there's flu and in the spring there's babies. This is the time for it."

"There's babies all year."

"Seems like more in the spring. Anyway, you been here two and a half years, Dr. Sam, an' this is the first good cleaning we've had! What will the patients think, with you wipin' cobwebs from the files?"

I had to laugh at that. "It's not quite that bad, April."

"You goin' to the band concert an' fireworks tomorrow night?"

"Sure. How about you?" I knew she didn't have a regular beau, and some-times I felt a little sorry for her. "Want to come with me?"

She didn't wait to be asked twice. "Sure do!"

"Maybe we can grab somethin' to eat at Dixie's first." Dixie's was a lunch counter, the only place in town with decent food. "Pick you up about seven."

Her eyes widened. "In your Runabout?" Ever since the wedding a few weeks earlier she'd been enchanted by my car, a yellow '21 Pierce-Arrow that had been a graduation gift from my parents.

Before I could answer, the outside bell signaled the arrival of a patient. "Are we expectin' anyone, April?"

"Calendar was clear for this afternoon. I'll go see who it is."

She returned in a moment with Tom Younglove in tow. Tom was a local real-estate man who'd been buying up some farms in the neighborhood. His ultimate purpose was a source of much gossip and not a little fear. "Dr. Sam," he said, breathin' hard, "I need your help."

"Better catch your breath first. I been tellin' you to lose some of that pouch around your middle."

"It's not me—it's Mayor Dwiggins. He won't see me."

"What can I do about that?"

"He canceled an appointment for today, says he's ill. Is he?"

"I couldn't rightly answer that without examinin' him, now could I? I've been prescribin' a medication for his heart trouble, but I haven't heard of any other complaint. He was just back from Washington the end o' last week. Maybe he picked up somethin' down there. Hear tell they got lots o' bugs in the summertime."

"It's not bugs that's keepin' him from seein' me!" Younglove exploded. "It's my land deals. He knows I need the town board's approval by Monday an' he's just draggin' his feet."

"What are these land deals?" I asked, as curious as the next one.

But Younglove clammed up then, switchin' back to the subject of Mayor Dwiggins's health. "Can't you call him to see if he's really sick?"

"If he was sick, I'd be hearin' from him. Can't you wait till tomorrow?"

"Tomorrow's the holiday."

"But he'll be at the band concert tomorrow night. Nothin' would keep him away from his first Fourth o' July celebration as mayor."

"You're right," Younglove admitted. "I'll see him there."

April stepped in then. "Now you get goin', Tom. The doctor's very busy today. I shouldn't of let you in without an appointment."

Younglove retreated somewhat sheepishly and she went back to cleanin' out the files. But the episode bothered me. "What do you think he's up to, April, buyin' that land? And why is Dwiggins pretendin' to be sick so he won't have to see him?"

"Politicians are all alike," she answered. "They stay clear o' the voters, except at election time."

I got to my feet. "Come on, I'll buy you a soda."

It was something of a ritual, on quiet days, for me to escort April to Doc Church's drug store for a chocolate soda. His place was just down the street, a long narrow store with a checkered tile floor and an embossed tin ceiling. The tobacco was in a glass showcase on the left, with the six-stool soda fountain on the right. Doc Church waved from the back as we entered.

"Remind me," April said. "Before we leave I have to get some witch hazel for mother."

I lowered myself onto one of the fragile-looking stools with their twisted wire legs. "Chocolate sodas as usual?" Doc Church asked us.

I shook my head. "Glass of lemon phosphate today, Henry."

"And a malted milk for me," April decided.

"Tom Younglove was just in my office," I told Doc Church. "Blowin' off steam 'bout the mayor bein' sick and not seein' him."

"Or at least sayin' he's sick," April corrected.

The glass of lemon phosphate slipped from Doc Church's hand and the contents spilled on the counter. "Damn! There goes the week's profits!" He poured another glassful and set it in front of me. "What's Younglove up to with all the land he's buyin?"

"Wish I knew," I replied. "Maybe we should be buyin', too."

On the way out I reminded April to get the witch hazel for her mother . . .

F riday evenin' was bright and balmy, with the daylight lastin' till well after eight. Our state was one of the few in the nation to go on daylight-savings time in those days. Most others had rejected it after the unpopular law of 1918 and '19. The farmers around Northmont still complained, but they went along with it.

So it was nearly nine o'clock before the band concert finally got under way, with husky ol' Roy Pinkerton leadin' his brightly uniformed musicians up to the bandstand. "I'm goin' to hate this night," Roy whispered to me as he passed by, and I could understand why. Mayor Dwiggins was scheduled to play an important part in the evening's program, and Roy was the man he'd defeated in the election.

Which I guess proved you could woo more votes with words than with music.

I waved to Doc Church as he went by with his flute, thinkin' how spruce he looked in his brass-buttoned uniform. 'Cept for him and Roy Pinkerton, I didn't know any of the fifteen musicians that well. None of them was a patient, and I knew for a fact that several had been recruited by Pinkerton from Shinn Corners after he failed to find enough local talent.

As the band struck up its opening selection, I glanced around for April. She'd wandered off somewhere in the crowd, and instead of her I spotted Tom Younglove, comin' at me with his usual distraught expression. "I still haven't seen Mayor Dwiggins."

"Cheer up. He'll be here soon."

The band was renderin' a slightly off-key version of *The Stars and Stripes Forever*, and off in the distance I could see the crew settin' up the launchers for the fireworks. Sheriff Lens and a couple of his men were busy keepin' kids away from the scene. Twilight had faded now, and the lights around the edge of town square were comin' on.

"Ever hear the story about that bandstand?" Younglove asked at my side. "How they hanged a man from it?"

"I heard. Is it true?"

"Sure. They say his ghost used to—"

A roar went up from the edge of the crowd, and we turned to see Mayor Dwiggins and his wife Vera threading their way through a sea of well-wishers. Always the politician, Dwiggins was pausing to shake everyone's hand. He wasn't a bad sort, really, despite lookin' like a Boston ward boss. He wanted badly to become a Congressman someday, but it was a long trip from Northmont to Washington, even though he'd just taken it last week.

His wife Vera was tall and graceful, just a bit superior to other town ladies. Oddly enough, they didn't resent her for it. When I saw I couldn't get through to His Honor, I settled for reachin' out to touch Vera's arm as she passed. "Hello, Dr. Sam," she said.

"Did you enjoy Washington?"

"Terrible place in the summer! I'm happy to be back home." Tom Younglove tried to speak to her at this point, but she merely said, "The music's lovely, isn't it?" and hurried on her way.

The first half of the concert ended with a crashing of cymbals, and the bandsmen stood up to take a break. Several of them drifted into the crowd for a cold beer, not feelin' obliged to remain on the bunting-draped bandstand during the mayor's speech. But Roy Pinkerton, always the good loser, came forward to introduce his rival.

"Ladies an' gentlemen!" he called through the megaphone. "While the band takes a much-deserved rest an' we get ready for the fireworks, it's my great pleasure to present the mayor of our town—the Honorable David Dwiggins!"

Somewhere behind me a balloon burst and a baby started to cry. But the sounds were quickly drowned out by a loud and sincere round of applause for the man we'd elected. Dwiggins and his wife went quickly up the bandstand steps. He shook hands with Roy Pinkerton while Vera waved to the crowd. Then she went back down the steps as he started to speak.

"It's a pleasure to join you on my first July Fourth as mayor. . . ." His voice was strong as he waved aside Pinkerton's megaphone, but his face seemed pale and I wondered if he really was sick. He wasn't the sort to come runnin' to the doctor with every little pain.

Doc Church passed by me with a beer. "He's good for an hour. The kids'll be asleep before the fireworks even start."

He was right, and I decided to do something about it. I pushed my way through to the edge of the crowd where kids were playin' in the darkness, and walked across the open space to the launchin' racks for the fireworks. I knew the person in charge, a farm youth named Chris, and I gave him the word. "Mayor says start the show."

He eyed me uncertainly. "Now? He's still talkin', ain't he?"

"Now."

He shrugged and struck a match on the seat of his pants. "Okay—here goes."

I was halfway to the bandstand when the first skyrocket burst above us. Mayor Dwiggins stopped in midsentence, then recovered long enough to say, "Looks like the big show is starting, folks, so I'll turn the program back to my good friend, Roy Pinkerton. How about a big hand for Roy and the band?"

While the spectators applauded dutifully, the rest of the band was driftin' back to the stand, takin' their seats and pickin' up their instruments. Most eyes were turned skyward at the starbursts of red and blue and white rockets, and the young folks were joinin' in with their own fireworks on the ground.

That was when it happened, so suddenly that for a moment we couldn't believe our eyes.

A figure in a black flowin' cloak pushed past the bandsmen on the steps and rushed at the mayor. The figure wore a hood over his head and a rope noose dangled from his neck. In his right hand was an upraised carvin' knife. Mayor Dwiggins turned towards him, more puzzled than alarmed. Then the knife plunged deep into Dwiggins' chest, and women in the crowd screamed.

The hooded figure whirled around, leaving the knife buried in his victim's chest. I saw Roy Pinkerton and the others lunge forward to grab the assassin, but in that instant there was a sudden blindin' flash and a puff of thick smoke. For maybe ten seconds we could see nothin'. Then as the smoke cleared I saw Pinkerton and the other musicians standing over the body.

The killer had vanished.

I rushed forward, pushin' past the musicians who still blocked the steps of the bandstand. There were screams and cries of panic from the crowd now, and general confusion. Above us the fireworks were still burstin' against the night sky.

"What in hell was it?" Pinkerton demanded. "A ghost?"

At his side Doc Church held a danglin' rope noose. "I grabbed the rope round his neck, but he just disappeared!"

I turned over Mayor Dwiggins's body and felt for a pulse, but I knew there wouldn't be one. The knife had gone straight to the heart. "He's vanished!" Pinkerton said in something like awe. "The man who stabbed him has disappeared."

I straightened up and shouted down to Sheriff Lens. "Get this crowd out of here, Sheriff. The celebration's over!"

"What happened?" he asked, fightin' his way to the bandstand.

"Mayor Dwiggins has been murdered. And his killer vanished right before our eyes—vanished in a puff of smoke!"

"**D**amnation!" Sheriff Lens exploded an hour later back in his office. "Killers don't disappear in puffs o' smoke! And lynchin' victims don't come back to life after forty years!"

"Of course not," I agreed. "I don't believe this business of a haunted bandstand any more than you do."

"Then what happened to the killer?"

"I'll know better in the mornin', after I've examined the bandstand by daylight."

April was standin' by the window, lookin' out at the street. Though it was nearly eleven, most of the crowd was still about, the adults talkin' in small quiet groups while the kids were still settin' off occasional strings of firecrackers. "I saw a magician in Boston once," she volunteered. "*He* vanished from the stage in a puff o' smoke."

I nodded. "Trap door."

Sheriff Lens snorted. "You think there's a trap door in that bandstand?"

"I'll know in the mornin'. There's not enough light for a thorough examination now."

"What the hell kind of a bandstand would have a trap door in its floor?"

"One that was used for a gallows," I told him.

Doc Church was waitin' for me outside. His brass-buttoned band uniform was scorched and he was still nervous from the night's events. "My God, Dr. Sam, do they know anything yet?"

"Nothin'," I admitted. "Suppose you tell me just what you saw."

"Only this—this man with the hood an' black cloak. Honest, Dr. Sam, I was close enough to touch him!" He brushed at his sooty band uniform.

"Think carefully, Henry. Is there any chance—any possibility at all—that the figure we all saw wasn't real? That it was merely projected by some sort of magic lantern?"

"You kiddin' me, Dr. Sam? He was as real as you or me! Hell, I grabbed at him just as he stabbed the mayor. I was hangin' onto this noose round his neck, an' when he disappeared I still had it. Besides, projected images can't stab people. You know that."

"If the image was projected, someone standin' close to the mayor could have wielded the real knife and set off that smoke bomb or whatever it was."

Doc Church looked frightened. "Hell, Dr. Sam, I wasn't *that* close to him." Roy Pinkerton was lots closer than me."

"I remember seeing him there," I agreed. I also remembered seeing the killer push past two bandsmen on the steps. Thinking about it, there could be no doubt he was flesh and blood.

"Couldn't he have dived over the railing during the confusion?"

I shook my head. "The stairs were blocked and there were people all around the sides. The flash and smoke together only blinded us for maybe ten seconds. If he was a real person, he couldn't have gone anywhere except up or down."

"I could help you investigate it, maybe," he volunteered. "I could take pictures o' the bandstand for you an' Sheriff Lens."

I'd forgotten Doc Church was one of Northmont's few amateur photographers. "I might be able to use you at that," I said.

As I left him and started down the street towards Dixie's Diner, April came runnin' up. "Wait for me," she called out. "Were you goin' to leave me with Sheriff Lens all night?"

"Hardly. Come to think of it, though, that might improve the ol' boy's disposition. No, I wanted to stop at Dixie's to see if anyone was still around there." You could get bootleg whiskey in your coffee cup at Dixie's, and I figured people might be needing it that night.

The first one we saw when we entered Dixie's was Tom Younglove, sittin' at a table up front. "This whole thing is terrible," he said. "I've got land options expirin' Monday morning. His death could ruin me!"

"It sure ruined him."

"I'm sorry if I seem heartless, but it's an important business matter."

"I guess the police will want to know just what that business of yours is all about."

He motioned April and me to join him at the table. "I suppose I have to talk about it sooner or later. I've been buyin' up farm land, as you know. I'm negotiatin' with one of the new automobile companies that wants to build a plant here."

April snorted. "A car factory here in Northmont! It's a wonder somebody didn't kill you!"

"Listen, the day is comin' when every American family will own a car. A Pierce-Arrow like yours, Dr. Sam, or a Stutz or Jordan or Packard. Plants are springin' up all over the country. It's a chance for Northmont to get its share of the coming prosperity."

"There are a lot of 'em around Detroit."

"Sure, but the Jordan's made in Cleveland. This company, which I can't name, wants two plants—one in New England for the east coast, an' the other near Denver for the west."

"This is why you needed to speak with Mayor Dwiggins?"

"Exactly. I needed the town's approval to put that farmland to industrial use."

"You might be right about the future of the automobile," I said, "but I doubt if Northmont's the place for a car factory."

Roy Pinkerton came through the door at that moment, his spotless band uniform giving him the appearance of a general in some operetta army. He stopped at our table and said, "Hell of a night! The young Brady boy jus' got burned by a firecracker, on top o' everythin' else."

I stood up immediately. "Where is he?"

"Over near the bandstand. They got him pretty well bandaged up, though."

"I'd better have a look anyhow." I was a doctor first and a detective second. My first responsibility was to the boy.

April came along, and we found young Brady propped against a tree in the square. I was surprised to see Vera Dwiggins just finishin' the job of bandagin' his hand. "Glad you're here, Dr. Sam," she said. "Better check over my work."

I examined the whimperin' boy's injured hand as gently as I could. She'd done a good job of first-aid treatment. "If April ever retires I'll take you on as a nurse," I said.

"Thank you."

"I thought you'd be home."

"I couldn't face that empty house. I'm staying the night with friends, but I can't quite face them yet either."

"You'll be all right," I reassured the boy. "Have your mom call me in the mornin'." April took him in tow and I turned back to Vera. "I'm right sorry about your husband. I only knew him as an occasional patient, but I liked him. I know what you must be going through."

"He always had a high regard for you, Dr. Sam."

I pulled at a piece of crepe-paper bunting nailed to the tree. "What was his opinion of Tom Younglove?"

"He didn't take him too seriously."

"Your husband claimed to be sick yesterday when Younglove tried to see him."

"He *was* sick. His stomach was upset. I wanted him to call you, but he wouldn't let me."

"I see. Well, how about Roy Pinkerton? Was there any bitterness after the election?"

"None that I know of."

I glanced up at the church clock. "We should both be gettin' some sleep. Thank you for helpin' with the boy's injury."

"It was nothing," she replied.

In the morning, just after sunrise, I went back to the park in the town square. It was deserted when I arrived. The crepe-paper bunting still hung from the trees and the bandstand, but there was somethin' forlorn about it now.

I went up to the bandstand and studied the floor where the hooded killer had stood just before he vanished. It was scorched a bit, and there were a few charred bits of black paper about. But no trap door. The planks of the floor were solid. I straightened up and glanced at the cupola above my head. The wooden beams supportin' it showed no evidence of a rope or wire.

And yet—our phantom must have gone somewhere.

"Got the case solved?" a voice behind me asked. It was Sheriff Lens lookin' as if he hadn't been near a bed all night.

"Just checking on this floor, Sheriff. There's no trap door."

"I coulda told you that."

"Then what happened to him?"

"You believe in ghosts?"

"I know—the man who was hanged from the roof forty-odd years ago. I've heard that story."

Sheriff Lens nodded sadly. "I'd sure like some other answer before all them Boston reporters start troopin' in here." He looked around in dismay. "Who in hell ever heard of a haunted bandstand?"

"The thing that bothers me," I said, "is not so much *how* it was done as *why*? Why murder in public with such long odds against escapin' when it could be done easier an' safer in private?"

Before Lens could answer, a black Ford pulled up on the street. Vera Dwiggins was behind the wheel, beckoning to us. I ran over, with the sheriff coming along behind. " 'Mornin', Mrs. Dwiggins. What's the trouble?"

"I told you I was staying with friends overnight. I just drove back to my house and discovered someone had broken in while I was away. The pane of glass in the side door is smashed."

"They take anything?" Sheriff Lens asked.

"Nothing seems to be missing, but—well, I'm afraid it might have been the killer and that he was looking for me."

"I'll go have a look-see," Lens said, mainly to calm her. "You comin', Dr. Sam?"

"Yes." I glanced back at the bandstand. "There's nothin' more to be found here."

It was obvious that someone had entered the dead mayor's house by the side door after breakin' the glass and reachin' through to pull the bolt. There were traces of ground-in glass on the floor, where the intruder had stepped in it. I bent to examine them and then went into the kitchen to look around. "You're sure nothin's missin'?" I asked Vera Dwiggins.

"Pretty certain, Dr. Sam."

I walked into the livin' room. It was a nice house, larger than most in Northmont, and this was my first visit to it. Dwiggins had never been sick enough to request a house call.

Sick enough.

"Could I see your bathroom?" I asked suddenly.

She looked surprised. "Of course. It's up here, right at the top of the stairs."

The first thing I saw when I entered it was a tiny sliver of glass on the tile floor near the claw-footed bathtub. "Were you in here this morning?" I asked her.

"No," she replied.

That sliver of glass told me the intruder had gone into the bathroom. And that fact told me who killed Mayor Dwiggins.

A little girl was sitting at the soda fountain of Doc Church's drug store when the sheriff and I entered a half hour later. "Kinda early in the mornin' for ice cream," Sheriff Lens teased her, rustlin' her hair as we walked by.

Doc Church was in the back of the store, standin' on a step ladder while he arranged bottles of liniment on a shelf. "You want to come down a minute, Doc?" I asked. "We gotta talk to you."

He glanced down at me and Sheriff Lens, and I could see in his eyes that he knew. "Lot o' work to do here," he mumbled.

"You better talk to us, Doc," I said.

"Dr. Sam's got some ideas about the killin'," Sheriff Lens said quietly.

Doc Church came down off his ladder. "You think I did it, don't you?" he asked. His hands were tremblin'.

I nodded. "I know you did it, Henry. More than that, I know *when* you killed him."

"When?" Sheriff Lens repeated, lookin' baffled. "The killin' was last night. Hell, everybody *saw* it!"

"You're wrong, Sheriff," I said, keepin' my eyes on Doc Church. "Mayor Dwiggins *died* last night, but in a very real sense Henry killed him over a week ago, when he gave him the wrong prescription for his heart trouble."

oc Church collapsed onto a chair and buried his head in his hands. "You know! But how could you?"

"The thing that was botherin' me right along, ever since last night's stabbin', was why the killer went to the trouble of imitatin' a ghost and committin' murder before hundreds of witnesses. It had to be dangerous, with so many things that could go wrong, so many chances of bein' captured. But when you realized that Dwiggins was already dyin' from your mistake, you had to kill him in public in such a way that there'd be no question as to the cause of death.

"You see, I knew he'd had his prescription refilled by you last week—you tol' me so—and when we were in your place Thursday, April and I were talkin' about Dwiggins bein' sick and not seein' Tom Younglove. The news upset you so much that you spilled my glass of lemon phosphate—remember? It upset you because you were already afraid you'd made a mistake and my words confirmed it in your mind.

"When someone broke into Dwiggins's house last night, but apparently took nothin', it gave me an idea. I went up to the bathroom and found a sliver of glass the intruder had tracked there. The bathroom was your goal, wasn't it—because you had to steal that bottle of pills from the medicine cabinet."

Doc Church lifted his head and I saw that he was sobbing. "It was a terrible mistake I made. He was talkin' about his Washington trip an' I wasn't payin' enough attention to my work. I used the wrong white powder to press into tablet form. When I saw him a few days later he seemed pale an' outa sorts. I came back here to check and found how I coulda made the mistake. I still hoped I was wrong in what I feared, but then Thursday you tol' me he was sick an' I knew the worst.

"I knew he was dyin', an' there was no way to save him. He'd been takin' the wrong medication for a week already. Even if I went to him an' admitted the truth, it would be too late to save him. And my life—my family's life—would be ruined forever. Who'd ever trust a prescription to the druggist who had poisoned the mayor?"

"But why the stabbin'?" Sheriff Lens asked.

I answered for him. "Doc Church had to kill him by a method so bizarre that no one would think about doing an autopsy. With several hundred witnesses, who could possibly question the cause of death? I hope someday an autopsy will be required for every violent death, but we haven't reached that yet in this state. Dwiggins's killing was accepted for what it looked like—a stabbin' in public. The poison eatin' away at his insides would go undiscovered."

"How did he disappear from the bandstand?"

"He didn't disappear—he simply became himself by shedding his disguise. Once we know the killer, the method almost explains itself. Doc Church knew the legend of the haunted bandstand—he told me about it himself—and he decided to put it to use. He played the flute in the band, and he knew the musicians would be given a break while Mayor Dwiggins spoke. I saw him in the crowd drinkin' a beer, but I didn't see him return to the bandstand.

"You'll remember the musicians were just resumin' their seating, with the fireworks goin' off and much confusion, when the killer struck. Nobody—not even Pinkerton—could have sworn if Doc Church was on the bandstand or not at that instant. But he was there when the smoke cleared a few moments later, holdin' tight to the noose he said he snatched from the killer's neck.

"What really happened was simple, and I was pretty certain of it when I remembered those charred bits of black paper I found on the bandstand this mornin'. During the break, Doc Church went over behind the trees, out of range of the street lights, and slipped a cloak of black crepe paper over his band uniform. He put a cloth hood, with eyeholes, over his head, an' a noose round his neck to complete the ghost illusion. Then he ran up on the bandstand and stabbed the mayor."

"And the flash o' light? The smoke?" Sheriff Lens asked.

"He'd covered the crepe paper with flash powder, prob'ly pasted on. He's an amateur photographer, remember, and he'd have some at home. When he set off the powder, it not only blinded us but also burned up the flimsy paper cloak. Doc stuffed the hood under his uniform jacket and held the noose in his hand, explainin' that he'd tried to grab the killer."

"How'd you know?" Doc Church asked, raising his head again.

"The bits of burned crepe paper and your scorched band uniform. The hood protected your face, but the flash of burnin' paper naturally scorched your uniform. We were supposed to think it got burned when you lunged for the killer, but you admitted Pinkerton was *closer than you*—yet his uniform was spotless!"

Sheriff Lens shook his head. "He was takin' an awful chance with a scheme like that. So many things coulda gone wrong!"

"His victim was dyin' already, Sheriff. It was a long chance, but it was his only chance."

"Come on, Doc," Lens said. "I'll have to take you in."

Near the front door the little girl still sat at the soda fountain.

"You'll have to go now," Doc Church told her. "I'm closin' up."

"When will you be back?" she asked.

He looked up at the shelves and answered, "Maybe not for a long time."

"So that's how it was, back in 1924, and I guess I'll never forget that Fourth o' July."

The old man paused, his eyes dreamy and far-off.

"Yes, there was one other thing that told me I was right that morning. Remember the broken pane, an' that sliver of glass the intruder tracked into the bathroom? Well, when we walked into the drug store and I saw Doc Church up on his ladder, I could see another bit of glass stickin' to the heel of his shoe.

"Here, let me refill your glass. Now, did I ever tell you about a train ride I once took, and about the impossible robbery that happened on the way?"

THE PROBLEM OF
THE LOCKED CABOOSE

"**C**aboose!" Dr. Sam Hawthorne exploded. "It's a wonderful word and we hardly hear it any more. It's a word that was important back when trains were important—more important than they are now, anyway. Let me fill your glass . . . another small—ah—libation . . . an' you settle back in your chair. I'll tell you about a train trip I took in the spring of 1925, and about the impossible theft—and impossible murder too!—that happened in the locked caboose. . . ."

The spring floods that year had washed out most of the back roads between Northmont and the towns to the west, which is why I was forced to take the train to Boughville in the first place. I didn't much like train travel, but my Pierce-Arrow Runabout couldn't forge flood-swollen streams, so I had no choice. The doctor in Boughville, who'd done me some favors in the past, had asked me to take over his patients while he and his wife celebrated their 25th wedding anniversary with a cruise to Europe on the *Mauretania*. The previous year the ship had broken all Atlantic speed records, making the crossing from Ambrose Channel Light Vessel to Cherbourg Breakwater in five days, one hour, and 49 minutes. To sail on the *Mauretania* in 1925 was the height of luxurious travel.

For me, I'd have to be content with a train ride to Boughville.

In order to arrive in time for morning appointments, it was necessary to take the night train from Northmont. Though the trip was less than two hours by car, the circuitous route of the Boston & Western more than doubled that time as it stopped at every little hamlet with the morning's milk and newspapers. But there was a Pullman car on the train so I could catch a few hours' sleep. In those days it was not uncommon for doctors to flag down trains with a lantern to board them at a nonscheduled station—and to depart at their destination by jumping off as the train slowed to five miles an hour. I'd done it just once, landing on gravel and scraping my hand so badly it pained me for weeks.

On the evening of my departure April packed an overnight bag for me an' was waitin' at the office door with all the solicitude of a mother hen. "Be careful now, Dr. Sam. Remember last time—no jumpin' off movin' trains!"

"Don't worry, I'll take care," I assured her.

"Mebbe if you have time you could bring me some o' that good maple syrup they make there."

"This is the time o' year for it. I'll see what I can do." I hefted my overnight bag and decided she'd packed enough for a week's stay. "I don't really need all this stuff, April. I'll just slip a few things into a physician's satchel and travel light."

It was an hour till train time at midnight, and I stopped at the town's lunch counter for a sandwich and a little cup of bootleg Scotch before they closed. Then I went on to the depot.

"You travelin' tonight, Dr. Sam?" the stationmaster asked.

"Just as far as Boughville. Fillin' in for the doc while he takes a cruise to Europe."

"That's where we all should be." He glanced nervously at his big pocket watch. "Wish that ol' train would be early for once!"

"What's the trouble?"

"Got a special shipment of valuables to put aboard."

"Valuables—on that old clunker? How come?"

"Most of our passenger trains don't have cabooses. This one does 'cause it hauls some freight cars too. The caboose is a paymaster's car with barred windows and a good strong safe." He glanced around and lowered his voice. "They're shippin' the Glenworth jewelry collection to Boston for appraisal and auction."

"That should bring a fancy price!" Old Mrs. Glenworth had died of pneumonia during the hard winter, leaving a small fortune in jewelry acquired during four decades of marriage to one of the state's leading industrialists. "You mean they're shipping it to Boston without a guard?"

"The family lawyer is travelin' with it. He should be here any minute now."

"Still, it's a long way around. That train won't reach Boston till mid-morning, after having stopped in every village in the state. My God, the train's goin' west, and you want to ship it east!"

The stationmaster nodded. "I know, but it's the only train that's got a safe, you see. Parsons—that's the lawyer—don't trust himself to just carry the jewelry. He wants it locked up, protected from train robbers."

I had to chuckle at the thought of it. "You think they'll block the track and ride up on horses?"

"Men have done stranger things for a quarter of a million dollars."

I whistled softly. "That much?"

"So Parsons tells me." He glanced over at the door as it opened, and his nervousness transmitted itself to me. I almost expected to see a masked man waving a gun, but it was only the little lawyer, Jasper Parsons, whom I'd seen around town on occasion.

"Who's this?" Parsons asked, as jumpy as we had been. Then, his eyes growing accustomed to the light, he said, "Oh, it's Dr. Hawthorne, isn't it? Are you travelin' tonight, Doctor?"

"Just as far as Boughville, to see some patients. I hope to get a berth and catch a few hours' sleep."

"I'm on my way to Boston," Parsons said. "The long way around." Then, to the stationmaster, "Do you have the strongbox?"

"Right here—and glad to be rid of it!"

From somewhere far down the tracks came the mournful wail of a train whistle. "It's coming," I said.

The little lawyer slipped a small revolver from his jacket pocket. "I'm takin' no chances. I won't rest safely till this shipment is in Boston an' out of my care." He glanced at me and his face lit up with a sudden thought. "Dr. Hawthorne, you can be of assistance if you will. This strongbox won't fit in the train's safe, so I have to transfer the contents. I'd like you to witness the transfer."

"Glad to."

Presently a single glowing headlight appeared down the track, and the night train rolled into the Northmont station with a roar and a hiss of escaping steam. I felt the old thrill that everyone of that era experienced at the arrival of a train—the thrill of being suddenly dwarfed by this massive iron monster that towered above you all smokin' and alive.

We walked quickly to the rear of the train, with Parsons and the stationmaster carrying the strongbox between them. The lawyer's free hand still gripped the revolver, like some modern-day Wells Fargo driver, and I couldn't help chuckling at the melodrama of it.

At the red-painted caboose we were met by a conductor swinging a lantern. He was a German named Fritz Schmidt, and he spoke English with a decided accent. "*Ja*, I am expecting you. Unload your strongbox while I open the safe." His youthful blond features rather surprised me.

I followed them up the steps to the caboose door, standin' on the platform of the adjoining Pullman car. The conductor unlocked the door with a great deal of fanfare, and I had time to study the door itself. It was thick and firmly anchored in its casing, with a small square opening about at chest level. The opening was barred like a teller's window in a bank, and covered with glass.

"They use this car for payrolls," Schmidt explained in his thick accent. "Take it out where the workers are repairing track an' pay them right from here. *Ja*, it is safe."

To my eyes the safe did indeed seem impregnable. It was made of thick steel and bolted to the floor of the caboose. In those dingy surroundings it seemed the sturdiest thing in sight. The conductor swung the safe door wide for our inspection, then motioned for Parsons to produce the jewelry.

At that moment the train gave a sudden lurch forward, throwing us off balance, and began to creep ahead. Out the dirty window of the caboose I saw the stationmaster waving his lantern. We were under way.

"Take this list," Parsons said, thrusting a document upon me, "and check off the pieces as I hand them to the conductor." He opened the strongbox and removed a flat velvet-covered jewel case whose lid he raised for my inspection. "One emerald necklace."

I gaped at the beautiful green and gold ornament and almost forgot to check it off. A country doctor doesn't get to see many treasures like that! And what followed was even more amazing—diamonds an' rubies, all in exquisite settings worthy of a queen. There were nine pieces in all, each more lovely than the others. I wondered if his estimate of $250,000 hadn't been on the low side.

"All there," I confirmed as the final piece was placed in the safe and the steel door slammed shut. The conductor twirled the dial and tried the handle, making certain it was locked.

"Will there be someone in here all night?" Jasper Parsons wanted to know.

Schmidt motioned toward a bunk bed. "I will be sleeping here. It will be safe. Not to worry."

Parsons left the empty strongbox on the floor and we went out, crossing the swaying platform to the Pullman car. Behind us we heard the conductor bolt and lock the inside of the caboose door. I could see his face in the little barred window, looking just the least bit sinister.

In the Pullman car we were greeted by a conductor smoking a long curved-stem pipe while he collected fares. Unlike Schmidt this conductor was obviously American, though with a trace of Irish heritage. "Find your berths, fellas. An' gimme your ticket to punch. Me name's O'Brian, an' I take no sass from drunks or troublemakers. We're here to sleep an' anyone makin' a racket will find themselves off the train at trackside!"

"I'm Dr. Sam Hawthorne. Could you wake me ten minutes before we reach Boughville?"

"Sure will, Doc. You're in Berth Number Nine."

Jasper Parsons was assigned to berth Number Seven, but when the little lawyer attempted to pull back the curtains and climb in, he discovered to his horror that it was already occupied. A burly bald man in paisley pajamas growled out, "What do you want?"

The Irish conductor almost dropped his pipe. "Mr. Apple! I clean forgot you was in there! Sorry to disturb yeh. Here, Mr. Parsons, you take the upper."

"I don't sleep in an upper berth," the lawyer replied with feeling.

O'Brian scratched his head. "Well," he said finally, "I guess that end berth is empty. Take that one."

The commotion brought a response from across the aisle. The curtain of Number Eleven was pushed aside and a young woman's blonde head appeared. "Is this going to go on all night, for heaven's sake? I'm trying to sleep!"

"My apologies," I offered, never one to ignore a pretty face. "I'm Sam Hawthorne, travelin' as far as Boughville."

"That's a coincidence. I'm bound for there myself."

"I thought only doctors arrived in Boughville at four A.M."

She propped herself up on one elbow, careful to remain decently covered. "Doctors and artists. They say the spring sunrise over Boughville Pond is one of the loveliest sights in all New England."

"I hope you enjoy it," I said. "Now I'll let you get back to sleep."

I climbed into my berth and started to undress. It was always a trick in the cramped quarters of a Pullman and I managed to bump my head twice before settling down. A glance at my watch showed it was now almost midnight.

"You all settled in, Doc?" O'Brian asked.

"Sure am." I poked my head out. Down the aisle the little lawyer was filling a paper cup with water before returning to his berth. "Do you and Schmidt change off here?"

"Not tonight. He's worked his shift an' he's sleepin' in the caboose till we hit Boston on the return trip. Havin' a swig o' bootleg Scotch too, if I know him. Want some?"

"No, thanks."

"Have a good rest. I'll wake ye in plenty of time for Boughville."

I rolled over beneath the covers, trying to get comfortable, and listened to the clicking of the wheels on the tracks.

I must have been dozing, but not really asleep, when I felt a hand shaking me awake. "What is it?" I mumbled. "Boughville already?"

O'Brian the conductor was leaning close to my head, whispering. "No, it's only two o'clock. But I think Schmidt is hurt. He needs a doctor."

I mumbled something and groped for my bag. There was no way I could walk through the car in my pajamas, so I quickly pulled on my pants over them. Still feeling a bit naked in my bare feet, I swung out of the berth and followed the conductor toward the rear of the train.

I'd have guessed the train was travelin' at about 20 miles an hour, swayin' just enough so it was necessary to brace myself now and again to keep my balance. With the heavy medical bag in one hand it was no easy chore. And crossing the platform between cars made me jump when my bare feet touched the cold metal.

If I'd expected to find the caboose door standing open, I was in for a surprise. It was still closed just as we'd left it, but the Irish conductor motioned me to peer in the little barred window. "See him in there?"

Fritz Schmidt was sprawled on the floor of the caboose, face down in front of the safe. Little rivulets of blood ran off in all directions from under his body, impelled by the constant swaying of the train. From him my eyes went immediately to the safe. The door of the safe was standing ajar, and I knew we'd find it empty.

"How do we get in here?" I asked, trying the door without success.

"We don't, without breaking in. My keys don't work. He's got it bolted from the inside."

I tapped the glass of the little barred window. "Doesn't this thing open? You must open it for payrolls."

"It can only be opened from the inside. It's got a little spring bolt that snaps shut when it's closed."

I ran my fingers along the edges of the door frame, but there was not even the crack of an opening. I got down on my knees on the cold metal platform and felt beneath the door, but there was no space there either. I realized suddenly that a thin metal edge ran around the door on all four sides, like a modified ship's bulkhead, and I remembered stepping over it when I'd entered the caboose with Parsons earlier.

"We have to reach him," I insisted. "He may be still alive. Isn't there a trap door in the room?"

"Sure, but ye can see from here it's bolted shut on the inside."

"Then how about the back door, to the rear platform? Can you go over the top of the car and try it? We'll never get in this way."

"All right," he agreed. "I'll try it."

He climbed up the metal ladder on our platform and I could hear him going across the roof of the caboose to the far end. I was acutely aware of the cool night air as I stood shivering in my bare feet waiting for him to appear at the opposite end of the car. Finally I could see him through the barred window.

And I could see now that the door on the far end was bolted too. But the window in it was bigger, and the bars set farther apart.

O'Brian smashed the glass and reached between the bars for the bolt. He couldn't see it, but after a few moments of feeling for it he was successful. He unbolted the back door and used his key in the lock. It swung open and he hurried over to Schmidt.

I tapped on the glass at my end, urging him to open up, and he did so. "I think it's too late," he said glumly.

I grunted and went to see for myself. One hand—the right one—was outstretched, and I could see now that Schmidt had written something on the metal floor with his own blood. A single word: *elf.*

"He's dead," I confirmed, lifting the body slightly. "There's a wound in his chest. Looks like a stab wound."

"But there's no knife! What happened to the knife?"

"The killer took it with him, obviously. Along with the Glenworth jewelry."

"But—but ye saw how the caboose was locked up! How could anyone get in?"

"Schmidt could have let them in. I'm more interested in how they got out leaving all windows and doors locked and bolted on the inside."

I walked over to the heavy door by which I'd entered and unlatched the little barred window. It opened easily and when I pushed it shut the lock snapped. I estimated the window was about eight inches high by six inches wide.

"Not even a child could fit through there," the conductor said, "if that's what you're thinkin'."

"No," I agreed. "Buy maybe an elf could."

"What?"

"You'd better wake up Jasper Parsons, and tell him the jewelry is gone."

The little lawyer did not come alone. When he arrived at the caboose, fully clothed, I saw that the girl in the opposite berth had tagged along.

"You'd better stand back," I warned her. "It's not a pleasant sight."

"Is he dead? Was he murdered?" Her eyes were wide with horror.

"Yes, he's dead, and yes, we think he was murdered. Now please go back to your berth."

"I'm staying," she said firmly.

I shrugged and turned toward Parsons. He was kneeling before the empty safe and looked as if he'd just lost his closest friend. "That jewelry was in my care," he muttered, close to tears. "This will ruin me!"

"Let's see what we can do about getting it back," I said.

"Back?"

I turned to the conductor. "Am I correct that the train has made no stops since we boarded it at Northmont?"

"That's right." He consulted his watch. "First stop is Greenhaven, in fifteen minutes."

"And the train was traveling at twenty miles an hour all that time?"

"Mostly faster. We have to slow down over this stretch at night."

"Would you say anyone could jump from a train going this fast?"

"Not a chance! Especially along here—there's all rocks an' stuff. They'd batter themselves somethin' awful."

"So I think we can assume the killer-thief is still on the train. You'd better tell the engineer we'll be stopping at Greenhaven to notify the police. It might cause a delay in the trip."

The blonde girl sighed and sat down. "I just knew I wasn't going to get to Boughville in time to paint the sunrise."

"There'll be others," I assured her. "I guess I don't even know your name. Mine's Sam Hawthorne. Folks call me Dr. Sam."

She smiled and held out her hand. "I'm Dora Winter, from Boston. Please excuse the informal attire. I learned to dress properly at finishing school, but they didn't prepare me for murder."

I gave her lace-trimmed peignoir a passing glance. "Very pretty. Tell me, did you hear anything during the past hour or so?"

She shook her head. "First you awakened me when you boarded the train, and then this man was causing a fuss." She indicated Parsons.

"But you heard nothing in between?"

"No."

The lawyer had given up on the safe and was starin' down at Schmidt's body. "How'd the killer get in here an' out again if the caboose was locked?"

"That's one of the problems," I admitted. "It seems impossible."

"But it happened," O'Brian said.

"Yes. Tell me something—how many people knew the combination of that safe?"

"You mean, on this train? Only two of us—Schmidt an' me. But other conductors who make the run would know it."

"So unless a passenger learned the combination from someone else, the safe must have been opened by you or the dead man. Correct?"

"It sure wasn't me!" he insisted. "How could I have gotten in an' out?"

"Schmidt would have opened the door for you."

The big Irishman looked around, searching for a companion in his misery. "Sure an' he'd've opened it for Parsons here too! They were his jewels. He'd even have opened the safe for him!"

Jasper Parsons growled and threw himself at the conductor. "You're not blamin' me, you murderin' crook!"

"Stop that!" I pulled them apart and used my best voice of authority. "Now look, we won't get anywhere fightin' among ourselves. Schmidt is dead and his killer is still on this train. In a very few minutes we're going to be in Greenhaven, and then we'll have the sheriff an' the state police to answer to. Let's try to straighten this out ourselves."

"Suits me," Parsons agreed. "So long as I get that jewelry back!"

"I would think you'd be more concerned with the dead man," Dora Winter said. "My God, can't you at least cover him up?"

I took a blanket from the bunk bed and spread it over Schmidt's lifeless form. As I did so something stirred in the back of my mind. "This conductor's uniform he's wearing—is it the same one he had on earlier?"

"Sure is," O'Brian confirmed. "We don't bring no change o' uniform on these overnight runs. Hell, we're back home in the mornin'."

"And how many other passengers are on the train?"

"Not many tonight. One other, Mr. Apple, in the Pullman."

I'd forgotten about Apple. "How about the car ahead?"

"Empty."

"Crew?"

"The engineer and fireman. That's all. A freight handler gets on at Greenhaven an' rides the rest o' the way."

I nodded. "Let's go see Mr. Apple."

We trooped back to the Pullman and woke him from a sound sleep. "What is it?" he asked.

"Could you get out o' the bunk, sir?" I'd only seen his head, an' I was anxious to know how tall he was. When he climbed out I could see I needn't have bothered. He was well over six feet—the tallest person on the train.

"Now what's the meaning of this? It's the middle of the night!"

"There's been a murder, Mr. Apple. We need everyone's cooperation."

"A murder? You mean here—on the train?"

"That's right," I confirmed. "In the caboose. Murder and robbery."

"My God, you're not safe anywhere these days! I suppose it was some of those Chicago bootleggers!"

The train began to slow down, coasting to a stop. It was 2:25 A. M. and we were coming into the Greenhaven station.

The sheriff of Greenhaven was a rotund individual named Putnam who was obviously annoyed at having had his sleep disturbed. He glanced at the body, grunted, and ordered his deputies to search the train for the stolen jewelry.

"They're in nine flat jewel cases," Parsons told him. "The largest is about ten inches by eight inches."

"If they're still in the cases," I said.

"What?"

"The thief could have tossed the cases off the train at any point and hidden the jewelry in a much smaller container."

"If they're on this train we'll find 'em," the sheriff assured us. "We'll search everything, including the passengers' luggage."

I didn't expect them to find anything and they didn't. A killer clever enough to escape from a locked caboose would be clever enough to hide the jewelry where it wouldn't be found.

"There's a great deal of money involved here," Jasper Parsons told the sheriff when the hour-long search turned up nothing. "You've got to recover that jewelry!"

"There's money involved in runnin' a railroad too," O'Brian snorted. "We gotta git rollin'."

I could see another battle brewing, so I stepped between them. "Maybe I can be of help. We all seem to be forgettin' that the murdered man left us a dyin' message—a message obviously pointin' to his killer. An elf is a dwarfish being of Teutonic mythology—the sort of myth the Germanic Schmidt would be familiar with. In fact, Schmidt would probably have used the word *elf* if he meant to say *dwarf*."

"Dwarf?"

"Is there—or has there ever been—a dwarf connected with this train? Either as a crew member or recent passenger?"

O'Brian shook his head.

The sheriff was growing impatient. "What's all this business about a dwarf?"

"The conductor," I explained, "was found murdered in a locked room, but I can show you a way in which a dwarf could have killed him."

"Go ahead."

I led them back into the caboose, where the tall Mr. Apple was studying the bloodstained floor. He looked surprised when he saw us, and I was surprised to see him. The sheriff had questioned him earlier, establishing the fact that he was a traveling salesman in plumbing supplies who often rode the night train. He'd indicated then that he had no interest in the murdered conductor or the stolen jewelry. Now he looked up at me and said, "Terrible thing—terrible way to die!"

"That it is," I agreed.

Sheriff Putnam was at my shoulder. "Let's git on with this. Show us how a midget could've killed him an' escaped from this here locked caboose."

"Well, there are a number of hiding places in here for a tiny person. Under the bed covers, behind the safe, down the other end of the car behind those boxes. None of these places would hide a normal-sized man or woman, but a midget or a very small child could go undetected there."

"An' you're sayin' this midget was already hidin' there when the caboose was locked by Schmidt?"

"That's right."

"An' was still hidin' there when you broke in?"

"No, he couldn't have still been in here because O'Brian entered through the back door. He'd have seen anyone hiding behind the safe or those boxes. Besides, we stayed in here till the train reached Greenhaven. I did, at least. At one point I sent O'Brian out to wake Parsons."

"Then how'd the dwarf git out?" the sheriff demanded. I could see he wasn't buying a word of it.

I walked over to the solid door with its tiny barred window. "This window, unlike the others, can be opened from the inside. It's a paymaster's window. No one could fit through it except a midget or dwarf—but once through they could swing the window closed and the lock would snap shut. It's the only possible way the killer could have left the caboose locked after his departure."

Sheriff Putnam unwrapped a chew of tobacco. "How'd the midget git Schmidt to open the safe?"

"I don't know."

"By threatenin' him with the knife?"

"Maybe."

"You don't seem too sure o' things."

"I'm not. No dwarf has turned up in the case. We only have the dead man's message to hint that one even existed."

While the sheriff puzzled over this, Jasper Parsons motioned me aside. "You believe that crazy notion, Hawthorne?"

"No," I admitted. "As a matter of fact, it couldn't have happened the way I described it. If a midget went out that tiny opening, how'd he reach it? The window is chest high for a normal person. And we found no box or chair near enough for him to stand on."

"But—but if you knew it wasn't true why'd you tell the sheriff that?"

"Just to play for time. Relax—I'm tryin' my damnedest to get your jewelry back."

"I think it was that other conductor—O'Brian. He knew the combination o' that safe, an' Schmidt would've opened the door for him. He left through that door at the far end o' the caboose, which he only pretended to unlock later."

I shook my head. "I watched him pull the bolt after he broke the glass. There was no way he could have tricked it up."

The little lawyer was exasperated. "Then the crime is impossible!"

"Maybe. Maybe not."

O'Brian and the engineer were arguing with the sheriff, trying to get permission to continue the interrupted journey. "We've lost an hour already!" the conductor bellowed.

"All right, all right!" Putnam agreed at last, "but I'll ride along with you as far as Boughville. That's still in my county."

Dora Winter came up to me. "Looks like I'm going to miss my sunrise," she said quietly. "But maybe I can paint a portrait of Sheriff Putnam instead."

There was no sleep to be had during the rest of the journey. We sat up in the caboose, drinking bitter coffee from a blue metal pot and speculating about the killing.

"I say it was a common ordinary train robber," the salesman named Apple insisted. "He dropped onto the roof from an overhanging tree and came in through that trap door."

"What was Schmidt doin' all this time?" the sheriff asked, chewing on his tobacco.

"He was taken by surprise. The killer forced him to open the safe, then knifed him an' bolted the trap door so it would look like the murderer was one of us passengers."

"And how'd he leave the caboose?"

"There are tricks you can work with door bolts," Apple answered vaguely.

"But not with these doors," I pointed out. "See the metal rim around them? There's no space where a string or thin wire could be pulled through. True, a string or wire could have been pulled through this little window, but the bolt goes the other way."

"Couldn't the bolt have been pushed shut with a cane or something, through the paymaster's window?"

I shook my head again. "This bolt's hard to work. Try it for yourself. A man's hand couldn't reach it through this window, and anything like a cane or a piece of pipe would probably have left scratches on the bolt—if it could move

it at all from that angle. Besides, it would be a chancy, time-consumin'
operation. Why would the murderer risk bothering about it? Even if the door
was standin'open it wouldn't implicate anybody."

"I think I've got it!" Jasper Parsons cried. "The knife wound didn't kill
Schmidt instantly. We know that because he lived long 'nough to write his
dying word. Suppose the killer stabbed him an' fled. Schmidt staggered to the
door, closed and bolted it, and then fell back to the floor."

"Same objection, in a way," I said. "The bolt works hard, and why would
he do it if he'd already been stabbed? Why not call out for help instead? After
all, we were right in the next car. Besides, it was also locked by key from the
inside. He'd have had to bolt the door, take out his key and lock it, then return
the key to his pocket. If he lived to do all that he was quite a man—especially
since there's only a drop or two of blood near the door."

"Then it's plain impossible," the lawyer said, repeating his earlier judg-
ment.

Sheriff Putnam spit out a glob of tobacco juice. "Elves an' fairies! He was
killed by elves an' fairies."

As the train rumbled on through the night I left them and returned to the
Pullman car. I wanted to inspect the door and walls for possible bloodstains,
remembering how I'd had to balance myself with one hand while walking.

But there were no spots of blood.

Did that mean a killer who could keep his balance—someone like the
conductor O'Brian who was used to swaying trains?

Or merely one with clean hands?

"Conway Falls," O'Brian called into the Pullman. "Coming into Conway
Falls! Next stop Boughville."

"There's no one here but me," I reminded him. "The Pullman is empty."

He shrugged. "Routine."

I nodded and glanced at my pocket watch. It was already after four, and we
were still a half hour away from Boughville. We'd managed to make up some
of the lost time but we were still runnin' late.

The train had started up again, clickety-clackin' along the tracks, when
suddenly I heard a scream from the platform between the cars. I dashed
from the Pullman, recognizing that it must be Dora Winter in some sort of
trouble, and found her strugglin' in Apple's arms.

"What's all this?" I asked. "Let her go!"

He turned on me with a fury. "Mind your own business, Doc! This doesn't
concern you!"

Though he was some inches taller than me, I figured I could take him on. Fellas my age always figure that. I aimed a blow at his jaw which he easily dodged, and before I could recover my footing on the swaying platform he countered with a blow to my solar plexus which took the wind out of me and sent me toppling off-balance. I caught myself before I fell out the door, and he quickly gave me a hand back up.

"Here, I didn't want to kill you," he said, his voice reflecting concern. He was obviously a man of moods.

"I'm okay, Apple."

He glanced at the girl and then back to me. Uncertain, he finally turned and entered the Pullman car without another word.

"Thank you," she said, brushing herself off and straightening her dress.

"Was he tryin' to attack you?"

She hesitated, then nodded. "He wanted me to go with him when we leave the train at Boughville."

"Don't worry, I'll stay with you to make sure you're not bothered." Silently I hoped I'd be more effective the next time.

When the train pulled into Boughville there was no sign of Apple, and I wondered if he'd decided to stay on till the following stop. Sheriff Putnam was there, though, checking those who were leaving the train. "Just an added precaution," he explained, "in case my men missed anything in their search."

I opened my medical bag and Dora Winter opened her case of paints. He grunted and waved us on. Jasper Parsons appeared on the platform next, carryin' his suitcase. "Are you leavin' me, Hawthorne?"

"There's nothing more I can do," I told him.

Apple got off the train then too, accompanied by the Irish conductor. I noticed that O'Brian was countin' out the Pullman tickets, licking his finger at each one.

Countin'.

At my side Dora said something, but I didn't hear it. My mind was somewhere else.

Was it all as simple as that? Could it be? Could it really?

"The sun's just rising," Dora Winter said, pointing toward the glow in the eastern sky. "Maybe I can do some painting after all. Will you walk with me a bit?"

"Sure," I told her. It would be two hours before I could see my first patient. "Just a minute and I'll be with you." I took a prescription blank from my bag and scribbled a brief message for Sheriff Putnam.

"What's this?" he asked when I handed it to him.

"Just an idea I had. It might help you with the case."

O'Brian had hopped back aboard the train and signaled up to the engineer. In a moment the iron horse was pulling out of the station, leaving Apple and the lawyer standing with us on the platform. "How come you got off here?" Sheriff Putnam asked Jasper Parsons. "Weren't you goin' on to Boston?"

"Not without that jewelry I'm not! It was in my care—I'm responsible for it."

Apple gave another glance in Dora's direction and then moved off by himself. "Come on," I said to her. "Let's go catch your sunrise."

"Will you be back?" Parsons called after me.

"Sometime."

Dora was loaded down with her paint case and easel, so I shifted the medical bag to my left hand and took the case from her. We had strolled through the first morning light toward a point overlooking a quiet country pond. It was out of sight of the station, and in that moment we might have been the only people for miles around.

"Do you make this trip often?" she asked, setting up her easel so that it faced the eastern sky.

"I'm just covering for a colleague. How about you?"

She squeezed a bit of oil paint from its tube. The red of it reminded me of blood. "No, I don't come often. Not in the middle of the night, at least."

"What did Apple want with you?"

"The usual things."

"What made him think you'd cooperate?"

"I have no idea."

I decided it was time for a wild guess. "Was it because he'd seen you sometime with Schmidt?"

Her hand froze in midair, holding the red-dipped brush. "What do you mean?"

"Like so many mysteries, this one revolved around *who* rather than *how.* It baffled us because we didn't see that crucial point. We concentrated on the *how* and ignored the *who,* and that's why we couldn't solve it. The question— the pivotal question—was not how the murderer escaped, but rather who opened the safe and stole the jewelry. If we answer that question, the rest becomes obvious."

"And you know the answer?" she asked carefully.

I gazed toward the east, through the trees, shielding my eyes against the rising sun. "Forget Schmidt's death for a moment and you have the answer. He was alone in a locked caboose, one of the only two people on the train who knew the safe's combination. The safe was opened and the jewelry stolen.

You see the answer now? Schmidt—and only Schmidt—could have stolen that jewelry!"

S he made a mark on the virgin canvas, a slash of red that was much too deep for the color of the sky I saw. "Then who killed him? And what happened to the knife—and the jewelry?"

"He had an accomplice, of course. He told us he was going to bed but when we found him dead he was still wearin' his uniform. So he was expectin' someone—not a random passenger who wouldn't have known the jewelry was aboard in the first place, but someone he'd told about it in advance, right after Parsons notified the railroad and requested the safe."

"You asked me if Apple had ever seen Schmidt and me together."

"Yes—because you were the accomplice, weren't you? Once we see Schmidt as the thief, passing the jewelry to an accomplice, the problem of the locked caboose becomes clear. He removed the jewelry from the safe an' passed it out the little paymaster's window to the accomplice waiting between the cars. I don't know what phony story the two of you planned, but he never got a chance to tell it. Because you decided to keep the jewelry all for yourself.

"You stabbed him in the chest through that same little window. He staggered backward, leavin' only a drop or two of blood near the door, and collapsed near the safe. Then you simply pulled the little window closed until the spring lock snapped. It wasn't a matter of the killer escaping from the caboose *because the killer was never inside the caboose!*"

"You think I did that?"

I nodded. "Schmidt named you in his dying message."

"Named me? *Elf?*"

"It came to me when I saw O'Brian countin' tickets just now. Countin'! As an accomplice to a robbery you wouldn't have traveled under your real name. Schmidt didn't know the name you were using, so he couldn't identify you in the usual way—by name. But he did the next best thing: he scrawled the number of your berth—*elf* the German word for eleven. Not the figure 11, which could be mistaken for mere bloody lines, but the word itself. *Elf*—meanin' number eleven, berth eleven. Your berth on the train."

Her eyes were hard now. "And the jewelry?"

"You've been using the wrong color on that canvas ever since you started. Much too dark a red! Maybe because all these tubes of oil paint don't contain what they say?"

I picked up a couple and squeezed them, feeling the hardness inside. "Empty paint tubes, opened from the bottom and then closed again. A clever hiding place, and one the sheriff s men never found. The cases and the larger jewelry pieces had to be thrown off the train, of course—but most of it's right here in your tubes of paint, and the larger pieces of jewelry could be retrieved later."

And that was when she lunged at me with the knife.

"No, no, she didn't even scratch me! That note I gave the sheriff told him to follow me and be ready to arrest her. He was ready, all right—grabbed her before she could do any harm. But I'll admit it gave me a bit of a fright.

"Got to be goin' now? And I was just gettin' warmed up! Come by tomorrow night for a small—ah—libation and I'll tell you about Northmont's big kidnapin'—as impossible a mystery as I ever came across. I always call it the Problem of the Little Red Schoolhouse."

THE PROBLEM OF
THE LITTLE RED SCHOOLHOUSE

"Sure, we had one-room schoolhouses back in my day," Dr.Sam Hawthorne said. " 'Fact, one of my most bafflin' cases involved a kidnapin' at a little red schoolhouse. This was in the fall of 1925, you realize—nearly seven years before the Lindbergh case put kidnapin' on the front pages and got a law passed makin' it a federal crime. Here, let me pour you—ah—a small libation and tell you what happened. . . ."

My position as one of the few doctors in the area (Dr. Sam Hawthorne began) was what got me into the case in the first place. I had a call from Mrs. Deasey, the widow up on Turk Hill, who said her little boy was just home from school and actin' strange. We'd had a bit of polio back in the summer that year, and though I knew the frost had lessened the danger it still seemed like a good idea for me to ride out and see what the trouble was. I told my nurse April where I'd be, then collected my bag and started up to Turk Hill in my yellow Pierce-Arrow Runabout.

Turk Hill had originally been called Turkey Hill, back in the days when there were still wild turkeys to be seen around Northmont. It had always been the back end of town, the area that well-to-do people avoided. Even the farming land was second-rate on Turk Hill, and in that autumn of '25 there were only three houses still lived in up there. Mrs. Deasey tried her best to farm the land her husband had left her, but the other two made no pretense of farmin'. One was a hermit nobody ever saw, an' the other was a young French-Canadian everyone suspected of making illegal whiskey in a hidden still.

As I turned my car into the rutted driveway of her farm, Mrs. Deasey came out to meet me. "I swear I don't know what's got into that child, Dr. Sam. He come home from school today all frightened of somethin'. He won't talk to me about it, whatever it is. I don't know if he's sick or what."

Robert was her only child—an undersized boy of nine who'd already had the usual assortment of childhood illnesses. I found him around the back of the barn, throwing rocks at some target invisible to me. "Hello, Robert," I called to him. "Feelin' a bit under the weather?"

He turned away from me. "I'm okay."

But he was pale, and when I touched the clammy skin of his face he shivered a little. "What's the trouble? You've had a fright, haven't you? Something on the way back from school?" I knew his route home took him past the other two occupied houses on Turk Hill, and there might be something at either place to frighten a lad of nine. Then too, I was remembering his father's mental problems before he died. Was Robert beginnin' to imagine things too?

"It's nothin'," the boy mumbled and went back to throwing stones.

"Did somebody scare you? Threaten you?"

"No." He hesitated. "It's Tommy Belmont."

I tried to touch him again but he broke free and ran away, heading out into the field. I knew I could never catch him, so I turned back to the farmhouse where his mother was waiting.

"He appears to have had a bad fright," I told her. "But he should get over it. Boys his age usually do. See how he is in the mornin'. If there's still some problem, call me on the telephone." The farms on Turk Hill had been linked to town by a party line just the year before, though it was common knowledge Old Josh the hermit had taken a shotgun to the telephone men when they approached his place.

"Thank you for comin', Dr. Sam. It relieves my mind to know it's nothin' serious." She fumbled in her apron pocket. "How much am I owin' you?"

"Nothin' yet. Let's make sure he's all right."

Robert had appeared around the corner of the barn, prob'ly to see if I was gone yet, and I waved goodbye as I climbed into my car. There was nothing more to be done here, but I had the feeling I should talk to young Tommy Belmont.

Unlike Mrs. Deasey and her son, the Belmonts lived in the wealthier part of Northmont, on a hundred-acre dairy farm. Herb Belmont was the town equivalent of a gentleman farmer, spending much of his time with area dairymen and Boston bankers while paid employees fed and milked the cows. The Belmonts had two sons and a daughter, but the older son was away at school in Boston and the girl was only four. There was just Tommy to attend the one-room schoolhouse at the edge of town.

Tommy was a frisky lad of ten, with flaming red hair and freckles to match, who looked for all the world as if he'd escaped from a book by Mark Twain. I almost expected to see him whitewashin' a fence as I pulled up and parked, but instead all I saw was the familiar black police car belonging to Sheriff Lens.

As I went up the walk to the front door, the sheriff himself appeared. "What you doin' here, Dr. Sam?" he asked. "Somebody call you?"

"No. Is something the matter, Sheriff?"

"You'd better come in. Mebbe you can help with Mrs. Belmont."

I walked into the living room and found the woman in tears, hunched in a big flowered chair and being comforted by her husband. "What is it?" I asked Herb Belmont. "Has something happened to Tommy?"

The boy's father stared at me. "He's been kidnaped."

"Kidnaped!"

"He disappeared from the schoolhouse yard, right under the eyes of Mrs. Sawyer. And now there's been a demand for ransom."

"A note?"

"A call on the telephone—a voice I never heard before, sayin' they want $50,000 or they'll kill Tommy!" His voice broke and there was renewed sobbing from Mrs. Belmont.

"Tarnation!" Sheriff Lens thundered. "Ain't nothin' like this ever happened in Northmont afore!"

"When do you have to deliver the money?" I asked, trying to calm them with conversation.

"They said they'd telephone again."

I turned to the sheriff. "It should be no trouble tracin' that call. Jinny down at the switchboard must know who made it."

He nodded agreement. "I'll go check on it."

"And I'll go talk to Mrs. Sawyer at the schoolhouse," I said. "I want to find out more about this disappearance."

S ome neighbors came in to stay with the Belmonts, and I went off in my automobile to the schoolhouse on the hill. I didn't know if Mrs. Sawyer would still be there at four in the afternoon, but her house was within walking distance and I figured I'd find her at one place or the other.

Though there was a newer high school built just after the war at the other end of town, the grammar-school pupils still went to the traditional little red schoolhouse set off by itself on a rise of ground not far from Turk Hill. Mrs. Sawyer, a widow who'd lost her husband in France, presided over the 38 students with a firm grip on the realities of New England life, instructing them on the sort of life that might await those who ventured to Boston or even to New York. She held daily fingernail inspection for all the children, and kept a chart of health chores they had to perform.

When I reached the school she was still there, straining to close a balky window with a wooden window pole bent dangerously close to the breaking point.

"Here, let me do that for you," I said as I entered.

"Dr. Sam! You startled me." She flushed a bit and handed me the pole. She was still an attractive woman, though the years without her husband were beginning to tell on her.

I closed the window and returned the pole to the corner. "I came about Tommy Belmont," I said.

"Tommy! Have they found him?"

"No. Somebody called the Belmont house to say he'd been kidnaped."

"Oh, surely not! Not that—not in Northmont!" She collapsed onto the nearest chair. "I swear he wasn't out of my sight for more than a few seconds. It just couldn't be!"

"Suppose you tell me what happened."

"Nothing happened—that's just it! During the recess Tommy was out playing with the other boys. They avoided the girls—you know how it is at that age—but they seemed to be having a fine old time, just like any other noon recess. They'd been down the hill to Mr. Tilley's wagon for treats and they were back up swingin' and chasin' around as boys will do. I remember seeing Tommy on the swing, going up higher than I'd ever seen him go before. It looked as if he were going all the way to heaven. I glanced away for just a few seconds, when I rang the bell to summon them all back inside, and when I looked back the swing was empty, movin' gently back and forth as if someone had just left it. When they all trooped in, Tommy wasn't among them. He wasn't anywhere, Dr. Sam!"

"Perhaps he went down the hill for more treats."

"No, no. Mr. Tilley had been gone a good ten minutes by that time, and there was no one else on the road. I can see in both directions from up here —look for yourself. There's not even a tree except the big oak the two swings are attached to."

"Was anyone else swinging?"

"No, Tommy was alone. I looked behind the tree, and in the outhouse, and around the other side of the school building. I sent all the children to look for him—but he wasn't anywhere."

"He must have just wandered off."

She stamped her foot. "He couldn't have, Dr. Sam! I tell you he was on that swing an' off it, all in a few seconds. I was here in the doorway. There was no place he could have gotten to without my seein' him! And as for kidnapin', well, who could have taken him? There wasn't another adult on this hill all day, and none of the other children was missin'. He didn't leave by himself and nobody came to get him. He just—vanished."

I walked outside and stared up at the oak tree, then tugged on the ropes that held the swings side by side. "Could he have gone up in the tree?"

"How? The nearest limb is at least fifteen feet up."

"You said he was swinging high."

"He didn't sail off that swing into the tree, Dr. Sam. And he didn't climb the rope, either. I'd have seen him. The other children would have seen him."

"What did you do when you decided he was missin'?"

"When he didn't come back after an hour or so, I sent Mary Lou Phillips over to the Belmont house to tell his folks. We don't have a telephone here."

"What about Robert Deasey?"

"That little boy? What about him?"

"Was he acting strangely?"

"I suppose all the children were very upset. I didn't rightly notice."

"What about strangers? Has anybody been lurking around the schoolhouse lately?"

"No one—no one at all."

"Come on," I said. "I'll give you a ride home."

She accepted with thanks, though her house was no more than a few yards away. I had a reason for wanting to go there, because it was the closest structure of any sort to the red schoolhouse. I thought Tommy Belmont just might be there, but I was disappointed. The place was empty when I escorted her inside, and Tommy Belmont was still among the missing.

S heriff Lens had gotten back to the Belmont farm before me. I parked behind his car and hurried inside. "We traced the call," he told me grimly. "Jinny on the switchboard remembers it came from the Leotard place—that French-Canadian up on Turk Hill. She remembered it especially 'cause he don't make that many calls an' he never made one afore to the Belmont place."

"You think the boy is there?"

"Where else? I don't want to risk goin' up there in daylight, so we'll wait a couple hours till dark. Then me an' my deputies will storm the farmhouse an' rescue the lad."

"Sounds simple," I agreed, but the thought of it troubled me. Could kidnapers be that foolish, to telephone the ransom demand from their own home?

But the news seemed to have bolstered the spirits of the Belmonts, and for that I was thankful. In fact, I was preparing to leave them again when the telephone gave its characteristic double ring.

Tommy's father grabbed the receiver. "Hello? Hello?"

The receiver wasn't quite pressed to his ear, so I could hear the child's terrified, high-pitched voice. I darted forward, reaching Belmont's side before either his wife or Sheriff Lens. But now the child's voice had been replaced by another, harsher tone. "That was to show you we've really got him. We'll deal with him the way Loeb and Leopold did with Bobby Franks, unless you come up with the fifty thousand dollars in a hurry!"

"I—the bank won't be open till morning."

"It'll open special for you. Have the money in your house tonight, and we'll telephone again with instructions."

The telephone went dead. Belmont waited a moment and then replaced the receiver. "My God!" he mumbled. "They'll kill him!"

"We'll see to it they won't, Mr. Belmont," the sheriff told him. "Now, don't you worry none."

I took a deep breath. "You still think they've got him at the Leotard farm?"

"Sure do! But I'll just check with Jinny." He picked up the telephone and had the operator in a moment. "Jinny? Where'd that last call come from?" He listened to her reply and then said, "Fine, Jinny. You done good work."

"Leotard again?" I asked.

Sheriff Lens nodded. "She listened in this time an' heard the boy."

"But did she recognize Leotard's voice?"

"You heard him—he had it disguised."

"I don't know. It all seems too easy."

"He mentioned Loeb an' Leopold, didn't he? And his name's *Leo*tard, ain't it? The guy imagines himself another thrill killer like Leopold."

"Not a killer," Mrs. Belmont gasped. "No, not that!"

"Sorry," Sheriff Lens mumbled. "Figure o' speech."

I could see that Tommy's mother was only moments away from fainting. I led her into the sitting room where there was a couch and got her to lie down. "I've got some sleeping powder here if you think it would help you," I suggested.

"No, no, I have to be awake for Tommy!"

"There's nothing you can do right now, Mrs. Belmont."

Even under extreme stress she was a handsome woman. Her son's flaming red hair had obviously come from her. "There's *surely* nothing I can do if I'm unconscious!"

There was no point in arguin' with her. "Try to rest anyway. You may need your strength later, after Tommy is released."

"Do you think he will be released? Do you think I'll ever see him alive again?"

"I'm sure of it," I said, trying to sound confident. "Now answer a couple of questions for me. What was Tommy wearing today?"

"Brown pants, striped shirt, and a necktie, just like all the other boys. That Mrs. Sawyer insists they wear neckties, 'cept in the hot weather."

"Who were his closest friends at school?"

"There weren't any really close, but sometimes after classes he played with that Deasey boy up on Turk Hill."

"I see." I checked her pulse one more time and then rose to leave. "You take it easy, Mrs. Belmont. We'll get Tommy back for you. I promise you."

I left the Belmont farm and drove around the back roads for a half hour till finally I spotted Mr. Tilley's wagon. Tilley was a peddler who'd become a familiar figure on the county roads hawking household goods and candy for the kids and even doin' a little repair work for farm wives while their husbands were busy in the fields. The sides of his horse-drawn wagon carried only his name—*Tilley*—but everyone knew what he had to sell. Besides, a list of all the things he carried in the wagon wouldn't fit on the sides.

Tilley had a son about Tommy Belmont's age, though no one ever heard tell of a Mrs. Tilley anywhere. As I drove up to the wagon in my car, I could see the Tilley boy up on the seat next to his father. He hopped down when he saw me stop and came runnin' over to examine my yellow Pierce-Arrow, as boys always did.

" 'Evenin', Mr. Tilley," I called out, strolling over to the wagon. It was not yet dark, but anytime after six was considered evenin' in Northmont. "Had a good day?"

"Middlin'," the peddler said, climbing down from his rig. "This time o' year one day's pretty much like another."

"You hear about the Belmont boy?"

He nodded. "I was just up on Turk Hill an' Mrs. Deasey told me. Turrible thing for the town. People come out here to get away from all that big-city crime."

"Your boy is at school with Tommy Belmont, isn't he?"

"Sure is." The peddler scratched his day-old growth of beard. "Frank, come over here an' talk to the man. Did you see Tommy Belmont today before he disappeared?"

"Sure did. So did you—he bought some penny candy off'n the wagon at lunchtime."

"I remember him now. Red-haired boy. Stands out in a crowd."

I turned to Frank Tilley. "Any other redheads in the class?"

"Not like Tommy. His hair's like a fire engine."

"So he bought some penny candy from you?" I asked Tilley.

"Sure did."

"Then what?"

"Him an' Frank went runnin' back up the hill. I watched them a bit till they started swingin'. Then I got old Daisy here movin' along."

"So you weren't there when he disappeared?"

"No, I was long gone."

"Did you see anyone else on the road? Another wagon maybe?"

"Not a one."

"Mr. Tilley, I been up talkin' to the teacher, Mrs. Sawyer. She claims Tommy was swingin' on the swings and then he just disappeared. She claims there was no place he could have gone where she wouldn't have seen him."

The peddler shrugged. "Mebbe he went to the outhouse."

"She looked there. She looked everywhere. And if he'd run down the hill she'd have seen him. She's positive."

"Well, he sure wasn't kidnaped by no aeroplane!"

"No," I agreed. I was staring through the twilight at the houses up on Turk Hill, thinking about Sheriff Lens and his plan to raid the Leotard place. Suddenly I had an idea. "Mr. Tilley, do you ever call on the hermit up there?"

"Ain't seen him in months. Don't think he lives there any more."

"Could we ride up and take a look?"

"Right now?"

"Right now."

I got up on the seat next to Mr. Tilley, while young Frank opened the rear doors and climbed into the back of the wagon. My car would be safe where it was, and I knew I'd attract far less attention approaching Turk Hill on Tilley's wagon.

By the time we reached the hermit's place it was growing dark. Tilley clanged his bell and called out, "Household goods, candy, pots an' pans. Knives sharpened, repairs made, electrical gadgets put in order!"

This last seemed unnecessary, since there were no electrical lines running into the hermit's house. The hermit had a name, Old Josh, but hardly anyone ever called him that. He was just the hermit of Northmont and word was he might have been a deserter hiding out since the Spanish-American War.

Now I ran around the far side of Mr. Tilley's wagon and into the tall grass. I didn't want to get a shotgun blast from one of the windows, either from the hermit or the kidnapers I thought might be there. I made a wide careful circle to the back door and was surprised to find it unlocked. Opening it slowly, I went in on my hands and knees. An odor of rank must hit my nostrils, but there was no sound.

With barely enough twilight left to see my way around, I rose quickly to my feet and made my way through the rooms cluttered with broken-down furniture, dirty plates, and dusty newspapers. One paper I picked up was more than a year old, and it seemed unlikely that the hermit of Turk Hill had received any recent visitors.

I opened the door to the cellar steps, and that was when the odor hit me. I'd been a doctor long enough to recognize it as that of a body long dead. Old Josh was crumpled at the bottom of the stairs, where he'd fallen and died months ago. There were no kidnapers here—only a lonely old man who'd died alone.

Outside, Tilley had started ringing his bell again—as if to summon me. I went out and he came runnin' up. "There's somethin' goin' on at the Leotard place. I thought I heard a shot."

"Stay here," I told him. "I'll go see."

It was only a short distance across the fields to the Leotard house, and before I was halfway there I could make out the sheriff's car in the rutted driveway. There was some sort of commotion, and a good deal of shoutin', but Sheriff Lens seemed to have matters firmly in hand. He was standin' in the light from his car's headlamps, holding a long-barreled revolver pointed straight at Marcel Leotard. The young French-Canadian stood with his hands raised above his head.

"Hello, Dr. Sam," the sheriff greeted me. "You're just in time."

"Did you find the boy?"

"Well, no. But my men are still searchin' the outbuildings. He's gotta be here somewhere. We already uncovered a couple of cases o' bootleg whiskey."

Leotard tried to lower his hands. "This is an insult! I know nothing of any kidnaping. I did not even know the boy was missing!"

"The kidnapers used your telephone," Sheriff Lens informed him.

"Impossible!"

"Why'd you take a shot at me when we drove up?"

"I—I thought it was someone after the whiskey."

A deputy came back from the barn, swingin' a glowin' lantern. "Nothin' back there, Sheriff, 'cept some copper tubing and big vats. Looks like he does a bit o' moonshinin' at times."

Leotard took a step forward and Lens jabbed him with the barrel of his gun. "You just hold it there if you don't want to be a dead man! We're takin' you into town for questioning."

When the deputies had the handcuffs on him, I told Lens about my discovery at the hermit's house. "Think somebody killed him?" the sheriff asked.

"No sign of it. A man his age probably got dizzy and fell down the stairs. Then he couldn't get up. Not a pleasant way to die, all alone like that."

"What took you over there?"

"Leotard's place seemed too obvious. I got to thinkin' the kidnapers could be somewhere nearby, cutting into the Leotard telephone line for their messages. The hermit's place seemed the most likely, but I was wrong."

Sheriff Lens snorted. "Got any other fine ideas?"

"Just one."

"What's that?"

"Maybe Jinny on the switchboard lied about those calls."

S heriff Lens sent a couple of deputies over to the hermit's house, and I retrieved my car and followed behind him as he drove Leotard into town. He locked him in a cell, promising to return soon, and then the two of us walked down the block to the wooden telephone exchange building where Jinny was on duty.

She was one of those stocky middle-aged women given to loud talk and too much beer. I liked her, and she'd been a patient of mine off and on, but right now I had to treat her like a suspect. "We have to know about that call, Jinny," I said. "It didn't come from the Leotard place."

"It darn well did!" she answered indignantly.

"I'm not saying you lied, and neither is the sheriff. But maybe you made a mistake."

"No mistake. It came from Leotard's. Look, it just lit up agin!"

I stared in fascinated disbelief at the switchboard. A tiny red light was glowing above the name *Leotard.* "Answer it."

She plugged in and I picked up the earphones. It was the same harsh voice. "Give me the Belmont house."

"One moment," Jinny said, her hand trembling to make the connection.

I could hear only the breathing of the kidnaper. Then Herb Belmont came on the line. "Hello?"

"Do you have the fifty thousand?"

"Yes, I have it. Is Tommy all right? Let me talk to him."

"I want no more raids by Sheriff Lens, or your son dies. Understand that?"

"Yes."

"Put the fifty thousand dollars—in unmarked bills—into a Gladstone bag or a small suitcase. I want that doctor, Sam Hawthorne, to deliver it at midnight tonight. He's to come alone to the red schoolhouse and leave the bag of money by the door. Then he's to drive away. If anyone tries to interfere, the boy dies. Understand?"

"Yes. But is he all right?"

The connection was broken without an answer from the kidnaper. Sheriff Lens, who'd been listening too, looked at me. "I guess you're elected, Doc."

But at the moment I was more interested in who'd made the call—and from where. "Jinny, is it possible these name tags were switched? Could this be someone else's line?"

"No, it's Leotard's, all right. The only other phone on Turk Hill is at the Deasey place."

I remembered Robert Deasey. I shouldn't have forgotten him for so long. "The Deasey place . . ."

"You want to go up there?" Sheriff Lens asked.

"First we'd better check in at the Belmont farm and tell them what's been happening."

M rs. Sawyer, the teacher, had joined the anxious circle at the Belmont house by the time we arrived. I could see she was trying to comfort the missing boy's mother, but she was having a difficult time of it.

"I hold myself responsible," Mrs. Sawyer said. "Something happened there that I didn't see, didn't notice. The kidnapers got to him somehow."

"You can't blame yourself," I said.

"But I do!"

"Try to think," I said. "Was there anything you forgot to tell me, anything about those last minutes when you saw Tommy on the swing?"

"No."

"Was he looking at you?"

"No, he was facing the other way."

"Is there a cellar under the school where he might have hidden?"

"No."

"A nearby cave where the children played?"

"There's nothing like that, Dr. Sam—nothing at all!"

"And yet the kidnaper wants the money delivered back at the school. He must have some way of getting it."

While we talked, Herb Belmont had been busy packing bundles of currency into a black Gladstone bag. "I'm about ready with this, Dr. Sam."

"It's only ten o'clock. We've got two hours yet."

"You got another idea?" Sheriff Lens asked.

"Just one—the Deasey place."

I drove up Turk Hill as I had that afternoon, stopping in front of Mrs. Deasey's farmhouse. She heard the car and came to the door to see who it was.

"Oh, Dr. Sam! I wasn't expectin' you again tonight."

"How's Robert? Is he asleep?"

"I put him to bed, but he's still awake."

"I'd like to see him again if I could."

"Dr. Sam, you don't think he's been—well, imaginin' things, do you?"

"We'll see." I followed her to the small back bedroom on the ground floor. Robert sat up in bed as soon as we entered the room.

"What is it?" he asked.

"Only Dr. Sam again, honey. He wants to see how you're feelin'."

"Leave me alone with him," I suggested, and she returned to the living room.

"Am I really sick, Dr. Sam?" the boy asked.

"That's something you've got to tell me."

"I can't sleep."

"Maybe if you told me what happened today—"

"No!"

"You said earlier it was about Tommy Belmont, but you couldn't have known then he'd been kidnaped. What was it about Tommy that frightened you so?"

He turned his face to the pillow. "Nuthin'."

"Did you see him disappear?"

"No."

"Well, what then?"

"My mom always says I imagine things. She says if I keep imaginin' things I'll end up in an insane asylum like my dad."

"And that's why you don't want to tell anyone what you saw?"

He nodded, his bobbing head caught by the moonlight streaming through the window. I took his hand and held it tight. "I promise no one's going to send you away for telling me what you saw, Robert. You believe me, don't you?"

"I guess so, Dr. Sam."

"Then tell me. Did you see Tommy disappear?"

"You won't believe me when I tell you."

"Try me anyway."

I could feel his hand tighten in mine. "You see, Dr. Sam, it wasn't that Tommy disappeared at all. It was that I saw two of him."

"Two of him," I repeated.

"Do you believe me, Dr. Sam?"

"I believe you, Robert."

A t ten minutes before midnight I parked the Pierce-Arrow at the foot of the little hill and lifted the Gladstone bag from the seat next to me. In the darkness I could barely make out the shape of the little red schoolhouse ahead. Even the moon had sought shelter behind a cloud, and I dared not risk using the lantern I'd brought in the car.

There seemed to be no one around when I reached the door of the one-room schoolhouse and dropped my satchel. I hesitated only an instant and then headed back down the hill. This was the tricky phase of it, when a rash move on my part could endanger the boy's life.

I climbed back into my car and started the motor. "How'd it go?" Sheriff Lens asked in a whisper. He was crouched down in the passenger's seat, half on the floor.

"No sign of anybody."

"He'll come. He ain't goin' to let that fifty grand just sit there."

Then I saw it—a flash of movement on the hill. The moon had come out from behind the clouds, bathing the landscape in a pale unnatural light. "It's a child!" I said.

Lens was up beside me, his pistol out. "Damned if it ain't the Belmont kid! They sent him to collect his own ransom!"

"Go after him, Sheriff, but be careful."

He jumped out of the car. "What about you?"

"I've got bigger game." I gunned the Pierce-Arrow forward, bumping over the dirt road and rounding a bend.

Ahead of me, targeted in the headlamps, I saw what I'd expected. Pulled up out of sight, under a sheltering willow tree, was Mr. Tilley's wagon. Tilley himself had heard my car approaching. He jumped down from the wagon, taking aim at me with a shotgun.

I jammed the accelerator to the floor and headed straight at him. The roar of the shotgun exploded in front of me, blasting away the right side of my windshield. But then the car hit him, pinning him against his own wagon.

I leaped out and grabbed the shotgun before he could reload.

"Damn!" he screamed. "You near killed me with that car! My leg—"

"Shut up and be glad you're alive. I'll take care of your leg."

Sheriff Lens came over the hill then, gripping the red-haired lad with an iron fist and carrying the Gladstone bag with his other hand. "This ain't the Belmont boy!" he called out.

"I know," I told him. "It's Tilley's son Frank, wearin' a bright red wig. Unless I'm mistaken, we're goin' to find Tommy Belmont tied up in this wagon."

It was one o'clock in the mornin' back at the Belmont farm, but it might as well have been high noon from the number of people around the place. Tommy had been in the wagon, all right, bound and gagged, and drugged with sleeping powders. He was still drowsy, but I knew he'd be okay.

His father and Sheriff Lens and Mrs. Sawyer all had questions. Finally I just held up my hands and quieted them. "Calm down now and I'll tell you the whole thing from the beginning."

"I want to know how he vanished from my schoolhouse yard," Mrs. Sawyer said, "before I go out of my mind."

"Tommy was actually kidnaped about ten minutes before you noticed him missing from the swing. He was kidnaped when he went down the hill with the other children to buy candy from Mr. Tilley's wagon. Tilley drugged him with a piece of candy and put him in the back of the wagon. Then Tilley's son Frank took his place, wearing a red wig and with a few freckles painted on his face."

"And nobody saw this happen?"

"Mrs. Deasey's son Robert saw it, but he was afraid to tell anyone there'd been two Tommy Belmonts, down by that wagon. The false Tommy ran up the hill and began to swing, while the real Tommy was taken away in Tilley's wagon."

"But it was Tommy on the swing!" Mrs. Sawyer protested.

I shook my head. "It was a boy dressed like the others, more or less, and with bright red hair. You saw the hair and not the face. Tommy was your only red-haired pupil, so you assumed the boy you saw was Tommy. But you should have known better. When I talked to you earlier you told me Tommy had been swinging higher than you'd ever seen him go before. Why? Because it wasn't Tommy."

"But how'd he disappear?"

"In the simplest way possible. When you turned your head and called the children back into the schoolhouse, Frank Tilley made sure no one was looking, took off the wig, and stuffed it under his shirt. Maybe he wiped off his painted freckles too, with his handkerchief."

"All right," Sheriff Lens conceded. "But what about those telephone calls?"

"Tilley knew all about electrical repairs, remember? He knew about telephones too. He tapped into the line from near the Leotard place to make his calls. He worked right from his wagon all the time while Tommy was tied up and drugged in the back of it. When he needed a boy to scream into the telephone, he used his son to imitate Tommy."

"How'd you know it was Tilley?" Lens asked.

"His wagon was up around Turk Hill when the ransom calls were made. And I was suspicious when he said he watched Tommy and his son run back up the schoolhouse hill and start swingin' together. Mrs. Sawyer had already told me Tommy was swingin' alone, and she had no reason to lie about it. Once I decided Tommy must have been kidnaped earlier than she realized, Tilley was the only suspect. No one else had come near the school at noon. No one else had a wagon to carry the boy away. The whole business of the mysterious vanishin' was just a ruse to change the *time* of the kidnapin' so we wouldn't think about Tilley, so Tilley could be away from the scene of the crime."

"How'd he expect to get away with it?"

"By tappin' into the telephone lines for his ransom calls, he figured to keep us chasin' around the countryside till he had the money. Then he'd high-tail it out of here fast before Tommy could tell us what happened." I didn't raise the possibility that Tilley might have planned to kill Tommy to keep him from talkin'.

"What'll happen to Tilley's son?" Herb Belmont asked.

"That's for the courts to decide," I replied.

"They found a foster home for the Tilley boy in the next town (Dr. Sam concluded), and with a normal family life he turned out right well. His father drew a long sentence, comin' so soon after Leopold and Loeb, and he died in prison.

"I thought that would be enough crime for the year 1925, but I thought wrong. Next time you come by—another small, ah, libation before you go?—I'll tell you about the strange things that happened at the town church—and on Christmas Day, at that!"

THE PROBLEM OF
THE CHRISTMAS STEEPLE

"**L**ike I was sayin' last time," Dr. Sam Hawthorne began, getting down the brandy from the top shelf, "the year 1925 was a bad one for murder and other violent crimes. And just about the worst one o' them all came on Christmas Day, when the year was almost over. Here, let me pour you a small—ah —libation before I start. . . ."

It had been a quiet fall in Northmont since the kidnaping and recovery of little Tommy Belmont. In fact, about the biggest news around town was that the new Ford dealer over in Middle Creek would soon be selling dark green and maroon cars along with the traditional black ones.

"You see, Dr. Sam," my nurse April said, "pretty soon you won't be the only one round these parts with a bright yellow car."

"Dark green and maroon are a long way from yellow," I reminded her. Kidding me about my 1921 Pierce-Arrow Runabout was one of her favorite sports. My first winter in Northmont I'd put the Runabout up on blocks and driven a horse and buggy on my calls, but now I was gettin' a bit more venturesome. As long as the roads were clear I drove the car.

This day, which was just two weeks before Christmas, April and I were drivin' out to visit a small gypsy encampment at the edge of town. The traditionally cold New England winter hadn't yet settled in, and except for the bareness of the tree limbs it might have been a pleasant September afternoon.

The gypsies were another matter, and there wasn't much pleasant about their encampment. They'd arrived a month earlier, drivin' a half-dozen horse-drawn wagons, and pitched their tents on some unused meadowland at the old Haskins farm. Minnie Haskins, widowed and into her seventies, had given them permission to stay there, but that didn't make Sheriff Lens and the townsfolk any happier about it. On the few occasions when gypsies had appeared at the general store to buy provisions they'd been treated in a right unfriendly manner.

I'd gone out to the encampment once before to examine a sick child, and I decided this day it was time for a return visit. I knew there wasn't much chance of gettin' paid, unless I was willin' to settle for a gypsy woman tellin' April's fortune, but still it was somethin' I felt bound to do.

"Look, Dr. Sam!" April said as the gypsy wagons came into view. "Isn't that Parson Wigger's buggy?"

"Sure looks like it." I wasn't really surprised to find Parson Wigger visiting the gypsies. Ever since comin' to town last spring as pastor of the First New England Church he'd been a controversial figure. He'd started by reopening the old Baptist church in the center of town and announcin' regular services there. He seemed like a good man who led a simple life and looked for simple solutions—which was why so many people disliked him. New Englanders, contrary to some opinions, are not a simple folk.

" 'Mornin', Dr. Sam," he called out as he saw us drive up. He was standin' by one of the gypsy wagons, talkin' to a couple of dark-haired children. "'Mornin', April. What brings you two out here?"

"I treated a sick boy a while back. Thought I'd see how he's coming along." I took my bag from the car and started over. Already I recognized my patient, Tene, as one of the boys with the parson. "Hello, Tene, how you feeling?"

He was around eleven or twelve, and shy with non-gypsy *gadjo* like myself. "I'm okay," he said finally.

"This the boy who was sick?" Parson Wigger asked.

I nodded. "A throat infection, but he seems to be over it."

At that moment Tene's father appeared around the side of the wagon. He was a dark brooding man with a black mustache and hair that touched the top of his ears, leaving small gold earrings exposed. Though Parson Wigger was the same size and both men looked to be in their mid-thirties, they could hardly have been more different. Except for an old arm injury which had left him with a weak right hand, Carranza Lowara was the picture of strength and virility. By contrast Wigger gave the impression of physical weakness. The Parson's hair was already thinning in front, and he wore thick eyeglasses to correct his faulty vision.

"You are back, Doctor?" Tene's father asked.

"Yes, Carranza, I am back."

He nodded, then glanced at April. "This is your wife?"

"No, my nurse. April, I want you to meet Carranza Lowara. He is the leader of this gypsy band."

April took a step forward, wide-eyed, and shook his hand. "Pleased to meet you."

"I'm trying to help these people get settled for the winter," Parson Wigger explained. "These wagons are hardly good shelter for twenty people. And the two tents are not much better."

"We have lived through the winters before," Carranza Lowara said. He spoke English well, but with an accent I hadn't been able to place. I supposed it must be middle European.

"But not in New England." The parson turned to me and explained. "They came up from the south, as do most gypsies. I've encountered them before in my travels. Spain deported gypsies to Latin America hundreds of years ago and they've been working their way north ever since."

"Is that true?" I asked Lowara. "Do you come from Latin America?"

"Long, long ago," he replied.

I happened to glance back at my car and saw a gypsy woman in a long spangled skirt and bare feet. She was examining my car intently. I'd seen her on my previous visit, and suspected she was Lowara's wife or woman. "Is she of your family?" I asked.

"Come here, Volga." The woman came over promptly and I saw that she was younger than I'd first supposed. Not a child, certainly, but still in her twenties. She was handsomer than most gypsy women, with high cheekbones and slightly slanted eyes that hinted at a mixture of Oriental blood. I introduced her to April and they went off together to visit the other wagons.

"She is my wife," Lowara explained.

"Tene's mother?"

"Yes."

"She seems so young."

"Gypsy women often marry young. It is a custom. You should come to a gypsy wedding sometime and see the groom carry off the bride by force. It is not like your Christian weddings, Parson."

"I imagine not," Parson Wigger replied dryly. "But I will come to a gypsy wedding only if you honor me with your presence at my church."

The gypsy shook his head. "Your townspeople do not like us."

"They might like you more if they saw you attending Christian services."

Lowara shrugged. "We have no religion. We would as soon go to your church as any other."

"Come, then, on Christmas Day. It's just two weeks away. Once you know the people and are friendly with them, you might even find an old barn to stay the winter."

"Would a barn be any warmer than our tents? I think not."

"Come anyway," the Parson pleaded. "You won't regret it."

The gypsy nodded. "I will talk to the others. I think you will see us in two weeks."

Parson Wigger walked me back to my Runabout. "I think their appearance on Christmas morning will have a good effect on the townspeople. No one can hate a fellow Christian on Christmas."

"Some call them beggars and thieves. They say the women are good for nothing but telling fortunes."

"They are human beings with souls like the rest of us," Parson Wigger reminded me.

"I agree. You only have to convince a few hundred of your fellow citizens." I didn't have to remind him that his own popularity in Northmont was not too high at that moment.

April came back from her tour of the wagons and we drove away with a wave to Parson Wigger. "He's really tryin' to help those people," she said. "That Volga thinks highly of the Parson."

"She's Lowara's wife. She must have been a child bride. I treated her son and never even knew she was the mother."

"There's an old woman in one wagon who tells fortunes," April said with a giggle.

"She tell yours?"

April nodded. "Said I was gettin' married soon."

"Good for you." April was some years older than me, in her mid-thirties, and not the most beautiful girl in town. I figured the old gypsy woman was a good judge of human nature.

On Christmas mornin' it was snowin' gently, and from a distance down the street Parson Wigger's church looked just the way they always do on greeting cards. I wasn't that much of a churchgoer myself, but I decided I should show up. Last Christmas I'd spent the entire day deliverin' a farm woman's baby, and an hour in church sure wouldn't be any harder than that.

Parson Wigger was out front, bundled against the cold and snow, greetin' the people as they arrived. I waved to him and stopped to chat with Eustace Carey, who ran one of Northmont's two general stores. "How are you, Doc? Merry Christmas to ye."

"Same to you, Eustace. We've got good weather for it—a white Christmas but not too white."

"Folks say the gypsies are comin' to the service. You heard anything about it?"

"No, but it is Christmas, after all. Nothin' wrong with them comin' to church."

Eustace Carey snorted. "What's wrong is them bein' here in the first place! I think they hexed old Minnie to get permission to camp on her land. These gypsy women can hex a person, you know."

I was about to reply when a murmur went up from the waiting churchgoers. A single crowded gypsy wagon pulled by a team of horses was comin' down the center of the street. "Looks like they're here," I remarked to Carey.

It was obvious then that Parson Wigger had been standin' in the snow for exactly this moment. He hurried out to the wagon and greeted Lowara and the others warmly. It seemed that all the gypsies had come, even the children, and after the Parson shook hands with them, they filed into church.

"I don't like 'em," Carey said behind me. "They look funny, they smell funny, they got funny names."

"Oh, I don't know about that, Eustace."

We followed the gypsies into church and took our seats in one of the front pews. I glanced around for April, then remembered that she'd be at the Catholic church on the other side of town.

After a few moments' wait Parson Wigger came out wearin' his traditional long black cassock and white surplice. He carried a Bible in one hand as he mounted the pulpit and then began to speak. "First of all, I want to wish each and every one of my parishioners—and I feel you are *all* my parishioners—the very merriest of Christmases and the happiest of New Years. I see 1926 as a year of promise, a year of building our spiritual lives."

I'd never been a great one for listening to sermons, and I found my eyes wandering to the double row of gypsies down front. If the sermon was boring them too, they were very good at masking their feelings. Sitting right behind them, and none too happy about it, was old Minnie Haskins who'd given them permission to use her land.

Later, when Parson Wigger had concluded his sermon and prayer service, and we'd sung the obligatory Christmas hymns, I sought out Minnie Haskins in the back of the church. Despite her years she was a spry little woman who moved about with remarkable agility. "Hello there, Dr. Sam," she greeted me. "Merry Christmas!"

"Merry Christmas to you, Minnie. How's the leg?"

"Fit as a fiddle!" She did a little kick to show me. "A touch o' rheumatism can't keep me down!" Then she pulled me aside as the others were leaving and whispered, "What're all them gypsies doin' here, Doc? I'm in enough trouble with folks for lettin' them camp on my farm. Now they come to church!"

"It's Christmas, Minnie. I think they should be welcomed at church on Christmas Day."

"Well, lots o' folk are upset with Parson Wigger for invitin' them, I'll tell ye that!"

"I haven't heard any complaints yet except from Eustace Carey."

"Well, him an' others."

Carey joined us then, still grumbling. "Soon as I can get the Parson alone I'm goin' to give him a piece o' my mind. Bad enough fillin' the church with gypsies but then he takes 'em right down front."

"Where are they now?" I asked.

"Would you believe it? He's taken them up in the steeple to show them the view!"

I followed them out to the sidewalk and we looked up through the fallin' snow at the towerin' church steeple. Though each of its four white sides had an open window for the belfry, no bell had rung there since its days as a Baptist church. The Baptists had taken their bell with them to a new church in Groveland and Parson Wigger hadn't yet raised enough money to replace it.

As we watched, the gypsies began comin' out of the church and climbin' back onto their wagon. "They can't read or write, you know," Carey said. "No gypsies can."

"Probably because they haven't been taught," I replied. "A little schoolin' for the youngsters like Tene would help."

"Well," Carey said, "I'm still goin' to talk with the parson about this, soon's I can catch him alone."

I glanced around for Minnie but she'd disappeared, swallowed up by the fallin' snow. We could barely see across the street now as the fat white flakes tumbled and swirled in the breeze. I could feel them cold against my face, clingin' to my eyelashes, and I decided it was time to go home. Just then Volga Lowara came out of the church and climbed into the wagon. The driver snapped the reins and they started off.

"I'm going in to see the parson now," Carey said.

"Wait a minute," I suggested. I could have been wrong but I didn't remember seeing Carranza leave the church. He might have stayed behind to talk with Parson Wigger.

"The heck with it," Carey decided at last, his hat and coat covered with fat white snowflakes. "I'm goin' home."

"I'll see you, Eustace. Wish the family a Merry Christmas." It was somethin' to say, avoidin' obvious mention of the fact that his wife hadn't accompanied him to Christmas services.

I decided there was no point in my waitin' around, either. As Carey disappeared into the snow I started in the opposite direction, only to encounter Sheriff Lens. "Hello there, Dr. Sam. Comin' from church?"

"That I am. A snowy Christmas, isn't it?"

"The kids with new sleds'll like it. Seen Parson Wigger around?"

"He's in the church. What's up?"

"Funny thing. I'll tell you about it." But before he could say more the familiar figure of Parson Wigger appeared in the church doorway, still wearin' his long black cassock but without the white surplice. For just an instant a stray beam of light seemed to reflect off his thick glasses. "Parson Wigger!" the sheriff called out, startin' through the snow for the church steps.

Wigger turned back into the church, bumpin' against the door jamb. It was almost as if the sight of Sheriff Lens had suddenly terrified him. The sheriff and I reached the back of the church together, just in time to see Wigger's black cassock vanish up the stairs to the belfry.

"Damn!" Lens exploded. "He closed the door after him. Is he running away from us?"

I tried the belfry door but it was bolted from the other side. "He'd hardly run up there to get away from us. There's no other way out."

"Lemme at that door!"

It was an old church, and a powerful yank by Sheriff Lens splintered the wood around the loose bolt. Another yank and the door was open.

Lens led the way up the wooden steps. "We're comin' up, Parson," he called out.

There was no answer from above.

We reached the belfry and pushed open the trap door above our heads. The first thing I saw was Parson Wigger outstretched on the floor a few feet away. He was face up, and the jeweled hilt of a small gypsy dagger protruded from the center of his chest.

"My God!" Sheriff Lens gasped. "He's been murdered!"

From the trap door I could see the entire bare belfry and the snow swirling around us outside. It seemed there was not another living creature up there with us.

But then somethin' made me turn and look behind the open trap door.

Carranza Lowara was crouched there, an expression of sheer terror on his face.

"I did not kill him," he cried out. "You must believe me—*I did not kill him!*"

I t was the damnedest locked-room mystery I ever did see, because how could you have a locked room that wasn't even a room—that was in fact open on all four sides? And how could you have a mystery when the obvious murderer was found right there with the weapon and the body?

And yet—

First off I'd better tell you a bit more about that belfry itself, because it was the first time I'd ever been up there and some things about it weren't obvious from the ground. The big bell was gone, all right, though the wooden frame from which it had hung was still in place. There was also a round hole cut in the floor, maybe four inches in diameter, through which the heavy rope for ringing the bell had passed.

But the thing that surprised me most about Parson Wigger's belfry was the thin wire mesh fencing tacked up over all four open windows. It was like chicken wire, with gaps of a couple inches between the individual strands. Since it obviously wasn't meant to keep out flies it took me a moment to figure out its purpose.

"Birds," Sheriff Lens explained, noting my puzzlement. "He didn't want birds roosting up here."

I grunted. "You can't even see it from the street, the wire's so fine."

Wigger's body had been taken away, and the gypsy had been arrested, but we lingered on, starin' through the wire mesh at the street below. "The news has really spread," Lens observed. "Look at that crowd!"

"More than he had for services. Tells you somethin' about people, I guess."

"Think the gypsy did it, Doc?"

"Who else? He was alone up here with Wigger."

Sheriff Lens scratched his thinning hair. "But why kill him? God knows, Wigger was a friend o' theirs."

There was a sound from below and Eustace Carey's head emerged through the open trap door. "I just heard about the Parson," he said. "What happened?"

"He was showin' the gypsies the view from up here. They all came down except Lowara, an' I guess he musta hid in here. We saw Parson Wigger down by the front door, lookin' out at the gypsies gettin' ready to leave, and I wanted to talk to him. He seemed to run away from us, almost, an' bolted the steeple door after him. By the time Doc Sam and I got up here, he was dead with the gypsy's knife in his chest."

"No one else was up here?"

"No one."

Carey walked over to the west side of the belfry, where the wind-driven snow covered the floor. "There are footprints here."

"He had a lot of gypsies up here lookin' at the view. Footprints don't mean a thing." Sheriff Lens walked over to the open trap door.

Suddenly I remembered something. "Sheriff, we both agree that Wigger looked as if he was running away from you. What was it you were so anxious to see him about?"

Sheriff Lens grunted. "Don't make no difference, now that he's dead," he replied, and started down the stairs.

The next mornin' at my office I was surprised to find April waitin' for me. It was a Saturday, and I'd told her she needn't come in. I'd stopped by mainly to pick up the mail and make sure no one had left a message for me. Most of my regular patients called me at home if they needed me on a weekend, but there was always the chance of an emergency.

But this time the emergency wasn't the sort I expected. "Dr. Sam, I've got that gypsy woman, Volga, in your office. She came to me early this mornin' and she's just sick about her husband bein' arrested. Can't you talk to her?"

"I'll see what I can do."

Volga was waitin' inside, her face streaked with tears, her eyes full of despair. "Oh, Dr. Hawthorne, you must help him! I know he is innocent! He could not kill Parson Wigger like that—the Parson was our friend."

"Calm down now," I said, taking her hands. "We'll do what we can to help him."

"Will you go to the jail? Some say he will be lynched!"

"That can't happen here," I insisted. But my mind went back to an incident in Northmont history, after the Civil War, when a black man traveling with a gypsy woman had indeed been lynched. "Anyway, I'll go talk to him."

I left her in April's care and walked the three blocks through snowy streets to the town jail. Sheriff Lens was there with an unexpected visitor—Minnie Haskins.

"Hello, Minnie. Not a very pleasant Christmas for the town, is it?"

"It sure ain't, Dr. Sam."

"You visitin' the prisoner?"

"I'm tryin' to find out when they'll be off my land. I was out there to the caravan this mornin' and all they'd say was that Carranza was their leader. They couldn't go till Carranza told 'em to."

"I thought you gave them permission to stay."

"Well, that was before they killed Parson Wigger," she replied, reflecting the view of the townspeople.

"I'd like to speak with the prisoner," I told Sheriff Lens.

"That's a bit irregular."

"Come on, Sheriff."

He made a face and got out the keys to the cell block. We found the gypsy sitting on the edge of his metal bunk, staring into space. He roused himself when he saw me, somehow sensing a friend. "Doctor, have you come to deliver me from this place?"

"Five minutes," Sheriff Lens said, locking me in the cell with Lowara.

"I've come, Carranza, because your wife Volga asked me to. But if I'm going to help you, I have to know everything that happened in the belfry yesterday."

"I told the truth. I did not kill Parson Wigger."

"What were you doing there? Why didn't you leave with Volga and the others?"

He brushed back the long raven hair that covered his ears. "Is it for a *gadjo* like yourself to understand? I stayed behind because I felt a kinship for this man, this parson who had taken the *roms* unto himself. I wanted to speak with him in private."

"And what happened?"

"He went down after the others had left the belfry and stood in the doorway looking after them. Then he came back upstairs, quite quickly. I heard him throw the bolt on the door below, as if he feared someone might follow him. When he came up through the trap door my back was turned. I never saw what did it. I only heard a slow gasp, as of a deep sigh, and turned in time to see him falling backward to the floor."

"You saw no one else?"

"There was no one to see."

"Could he have been stabbed earlier?" I asked. "Down in the church?"

"He could not have climbed those steps with the knife in him," Lowara said, shaking his head. "It would have killed him at once."

"What about the knife? You admit that jeweled dagger is yours?"

He shrugged. "It is mine. I wore it yesterday beneath my coat. But in the crowd after services I was jostled. The knife was taken from me."

"Without your realizing it? That's hard to believe."

"It is true, nevertheless."

"Why would anyone want to kill Parson Wigger?" I asked.

He smiled and opened his hands to me. "So a gypsy would be blamed for it," he said, as if that was the most logical reason in the world.

The snow stopped falling as I walked back to the church. In my pocket, neatly wrapped in newspaper, was the jeweled dagger that had killed Parson Wigger. The sheriff had given up any hope of finding fingerprints on the corded hilt with its imitation ruby, and had allowed me to borrow it to conduct an experiment.

It had occurred to me that the knife could have been thrown or propelled from some distance away, and that it might be slender enough to pass through the chicken-wire barricade. To test my theory I entered the unguarded church and climbed once more to the belfry in the steeple.

But I was wrong.

True, the knife could be worked through the wire with some difficulty, but coming at it straight ahead or even at an angle, the width of the crosspiece—the hilt guard—kept it from passing through. It simply could not have been thrown or propelled from outside.

Which left me with Carranza Lowara once more.

The only possible murderer.

Had he lied?

Remembering that moment when Sheriff Lens and I found him standin' over the body, rememberin' the terror written across his face, I somehow couldn't believe it.

I went back downstairs and walked around the pews, hopin' some flash of illumination would light up my mind. Finally I stuffed the dagger back in my coat pocket and went outside. It was as I took a short cut across the snow-covered side yard that somethin' caught my eye, as white as the snow, and half buried in it.

I pulled it free and saw that it was a white surplice like the one Parson Wigger had worn during the Christmas service. There was a dark red stain on it, and a tear about an inch long.

I stood there holding it in my hand, and then turned to stare up at the steeple that towered above me.

❝I reckon we gotta ship the gypsy over to the county seat," Sheriff Lens was saying when I returned to the jail and placed the dagger carefully back on his desk.

"Why's that, Sheriff?"

"Eustace Carey says there's talk o' lynchin'. I know damn well they won't do it, but I can't take no chances. It happened fifty years ago and it can happen again."

I sat down opposite him. "Sheriff, there's somethin' you've got to tell me. That man's life may depend on it. You sought out Parson Wigger on Christmas Day for some reason. It was somethin' that couldn't even wait till after the holiday."

Sheriff Lens looked uneasy. "I told you—it don't matter now."

"But don't you see it *does* matter—now more than ever?"

The sheriff got to his feet and moved to the window. Across the square we could see a small group of men watching the jail. That must have decided him. "Mebbe you're right, Doc. I'm too old to keep secrets, anyway. You see, the Hartford police sent through a report suggesting I question Parson Wigger. Seems he wasn't no real parson at all."

"What?"

"He'd been passin' himself off as a parson down Hartford way for two years, till somebody checked his background and they run him outta town. Some said he was runnin' a giant con game, while others thought he was more interested in the parish wives. Whatever the truth, his background was mighty shady."

"Why didn't you tell me this before?"

"Like I said, the man's dead now. Why blacken his character? He never did no harm in Northmont."

The door opened and Eustace Carey came bargin' in, followed by a half-dozen other local businessmen. "We want to talk, Sheriff. There's ugly words goin' around. Even if you keep that one safe, there might be an attempt to burn the gypsy wagons."

I knew then that I had to speak out. "Wait a minute," I said. "Settle down and I'll tell you what really happened to Parson Wigger. He wasn't killed by the gypsy, and he wasn't killed by any invisible demon, unless you count the demon within himself."

"What do you mean by that?" Carey demanded.

I told them what I'd just learned from Sheriff Lens. "Don't you see? Don't you all see? The Parson was standin' there in the doorway and he saw us comin' for him. It was the sight of the sheriff that frightened him, that told him the jig was up. Why else would he run into the church and up the belfry stairs, boltin' the door behind him? It was fear that drove him up there, fear of Sheriff Lens and the truth."

"But who killed him?"

"When he heard that bolt break, when he heard us on the stairs and realized his masquerade was about to be uncovered, he took the gypsy's dagger and plunged it into his own chest. There was never any invisible murderer or any impossible crime. Parson Wigger killed himself."

I t took a lot more talkin' after that, of course, to convince them it was the only possible solution. You see, I had to get Carranza out of his cell and demonstrate that he couldn't have stabbed the parson with his right hand because of that old arm injury. Then I showed, from the angle of the wound, that it had to be done by a right-handed person—unless he'd stabbed himself.

"There was no one else up there," I argued. "If Carranza Lowara didn't kill him, he must have killed himself. It's as simple as that."

They released Lowara the next mornin', and Sheriff Lens drove him out to the gypsy encampment in the town's only police car. I watched them go, standin' in the doorway of my office, and April said, "Can't you close that door, Dr. Sam? Now that you've solved another case can't you let the poor man go home in peace?"

"I have something else that must be done, April," I told her. "See you later."

I got into the Runabout and drove out over the snow-rutted roads to Minnie Haskins' place. I didn't stop at the farmhouse but continued out around the back till I reached the gypsy encampment. When Volga saw the car she came runnin' across the snow to meet me.

"How can we ever thank you, Dr. Hawthorne? You have saved my husband from certain imprisonment and even death!"

"Go get him right now and I'll tell you how you can thank me." I stood and waited by the car, venturing no closer to the wagons where I could see little Tene playing in the snow. Presently Carranza joined me, with Volga trailing him.

"I owe you my thanks," he said. "My freedom."

I was starin' out across the snowy fields. "I owe you somethin' too. You taught me something about the different types of deception—deception as it is practiced by the *gadjo* and by the *rom.*"

As I spoke I reached out and yanked at his long black hair. It came away in my hand and Volga gasped. He was almost bald without the wig, and seemed at least ten years older. I stripped the mustache from his upper lip too, and he made no effort to stop me.

"All right, Doctor," he said. "A little deception. Will you have me arrested again because I wear a wig and false mustache? Will you say after all that I killed Parson Wigger?"

I shook my head. "No, Carranza. This doesn't tell me that you killed Wigger. But it does tell me that Volga killed him."

S he gasped again, and fell back as I'd struck her. "This man is a demon!" she told her husband. "How could he know?"

"Silence!" Carranza ordered. Then, turning to me, he asked, "Why do you say these things?"

"Well, I proved for myself that you didn't kill Wigger. But I didn't for a minute believe that such a man would kill himself simply because the sheriff wanted to talk to him. And yet he had run away from us. That was the key to it—the key to the crime and the key to the impossibility. I was lookin' around in the church yard and in a snowbank I found this." I drew the bloodstained surplice from under my coat.

"And what does that prove?"

"See the tear made by the knife goin' in? And the blood? Parson Wigger had to be wearin' this when he was stabbed. Yet Sheriff Lens and I saw him without it in the church doorway. Are we to believe he went up to the belfry, put on his surplice, stabbed himself, removed it somehow, stuck the knife back in his chest and died—all while we were breakin' in the door? Of course not!

"So what is the only other possibility? If the body in the belfry was Wigger's, then the person we saw in the doorway was *not* Wigger. He fled from us simply because if Sheriff Lens and I had gotten any closer we'd have known he was not Wigger."

Volga's face had drained of all color, and she stared silently as I spoke. "If not Wigger, then who? Well, the man in the cassock ran up into the belfry. We were right behind him and we found two persons up there—the dead Wigger and the live Lowara. If the man in the cassock was not Wigger—and I've shown he wasn't—then he had to be you, Carranza."

"A good guess."

"More than that. I'd noticed earlier you were both the same size. At a distance your main distinguishing feature was your black hair and mustache. But I remembered that day two weeks ago when I was out here and noticed your earrings under your short hair. When I visited your cell, your hair was long enough to cover your ears. It couldn't have grown that fast in two weeks, so I knew you were wearing wigs. If the hair was false, the mustache could be too—mere props to add to your gypsy image. A bit of deception for the *gadjo*."

"You have proved I was Wigger for a fleeting moment. You have not proved Volga killed him."

"Well, what did you accomplish by posing as Wigger? From a distance with our vision blurred by the falling snow, the sheriff and I saw only a tall man in a black cassock, wearing Wigger's thick glasses. If we hadn't come after you we'd have gone away convinced that Wigger was still alive after Volga and the others had left the church. You did make two little slip-ups, though. When you turned away from us in the church doorway you bumped into the frame because you weren't used to his thick glasses. And yesterday in the cell you told me how Wigger had stood in the doorway—something you couldn't have seen if you'd really been in the belfry all that time, as you said."

"That does not implicate Volga!" the gypsy insisted.

"Obviously you weren't doing this to protect yourself, because it gave you no alibi. No one saw you leave the church. The only possible purpose of your brief impersonation was to shield another person—the real killer. Then I remembered that Volga was the last gypsy to leave the church. She'd been alone in there with Wigger, she was your wife, and she was the most likely person to be carrying your little dagger. Where? In your stocking top, Volga?"

She covered her face with her hands. "He—he tried to—"

"I know. Wigger wasn't a real parson, and he'd been in trouble before because of his interest in parish wives. He tried to attack you up there, didn't he? You were only a handsome gypsy woman to him. He knew you could never tell. You fought back, and your hand found the dagger you always carried. You stabbed him up there and killed him, and then you found Carranza in the church and told him what you'd done."

"It would have been a gypsy's word against a parson's reputation," Carranza said. "They would never believe her. I sent her back with the wagon and tried to make it look as if he was still alive."

I nodded. "You put on his cassock because at a distance the bloody rip in the cassock wouldn't show on the black cloth. But you couldn't wear the white surplice without the blood showing. You barely had time I to get the cassock back on Wigger's body, stuff the surplice through the chicken wire, and push it out so it wouldn't be found in the belfry. You couldn't put that back on the body because you hadn't been wearing it downstairs."

Carranza Lowara sighed. "It was hard work with my weak hand. I got the cassock back on the body just as the lock gave way. Will you call the sheriff now?"

I watched his son playing with the other gypsies, and wondered if I had the right to judge. Finally I said, "Pack up your wagons and be gone from here by nightfall. Never come near Northmont again."

"But—" Carranza began.

"Wigger was not a good man, but maybe he wasn't bad enough to deserve what he got. I don't know. I only know if you stay around here I might change my mind."

Volga came to me. "Now I owe you more than ever."

"Go. It's only a Christmas present I'm giving you. Go, before it fades like the melting snow."

And within an hour the wagons were on the road, heading south this time. Maybe they'd had enough of our New England winter.

"I never told anyone that story," Dr. Sam Hawthorne concluded. "It was the first time I took justice into my own hands, and I never knew if I did right or not."

He emptied the last of the brandy and stood up. "It was in the spring of '26 that a famous French criminal sought shelter in Northmont. He was called the Eel because of his fantastic escapes. But I'll save that story till next time. Another—ah—libation before you go?"

THE PROBLEM OF
CELL 16

"**S**ure," Dr. Sam Hawthorne began, filling the glasses, "there was a time when Northmont made the front pages of papers all across the country. Another small—ah—libation? And some of the stories even mentioned my name. They called me a young New England doctor and that's what I was, back in the late spring o' 1926 when The Eel came to our town. . . ."

It was a warm day for May (Dr. Sam remembered), and I'd gone out to Jeff Whitehead's farm to treat a gunshot wound. That in itself was unusual because we didn't get many gunshot wounds in Northmont 'cept durin' huntin' season. Jeff and Mrs. Whitehead had 40 acres of good farmland that he worked with their two teen-age sons. I'd never treated the family for anythin' more serious than the flu, though I'd visited the farm the previous summer to see some giant mushrooms that had sprouted in a back pasture. I wasn't an expert on the subject—mycology, I think it's called—but I was able to confirm they were safe to eat.

This day Matt, the older son, met me at the farmhouse. He was the one who'd telephoned me, and he called out, "This way, Dr. Sam. He's bleedin' bad!"

"Who is?"

"Eustace Carey. He's been shot in the left thigh." Carey owned one of Northmont's two general stores and he was somethin' of a troublemaker. Still, that didn't explain what he was doin' bleedin' from a gunshot wound in Jeff Whitehead's pasture. "How'd it happen?"

"Don't know, Dr. Sam."

I left my yellow Runabout parked by the house and walked back through the fields carryin' my medical bag. We came over a slight rise and there they were—Jeff Whitehead and a man from town named Henkle, both standin' over Eustace Carey. They'd tried to fashion a maskeshift tourniquet around his upper thigh, but it hadn't done much good. I could see at a glance that the wound itself wasn't too serious, though he'd lost a good deal o' blood and that was always dangerous.

"I think I'm dyin', Doc," he said to me.

"Nonsense, Eustace!" I started cuttin' away the trouser leg. "How in hell did this happen?"

"I was walkin' with that gun an' I tripped over a root."

The gun, a long-barreled Colt revolver, lay on the grass nearby. "This is hardly the huntin' season," I commented, going to work on the wound.

"We were shootin' at woodchucks," Jeff Whitehead volunteered. I turned to look at his son Matt and at Rudy Henkle. "All four of you? Where's your wife an' younger boy, Jeff?"

"In town, doin'the shoppin'."

"You know I gotta report gunshot wounds to the sheriff."

"Sure," the wounded man said. "Report it."

When I finished patchin' him up the best I could, I suggested we ride into my office where I could try to probe for the bullet. "We may have to put you in the hospital over in Felix for a few days, but you'll pull through all right."

As I was talkin' I picked up the revolver and took it along, and while the other three were busy carryin' Eustace to my car I broke open the weapon and examined the cartridges. The gun was fully loaded. It hadn't been fired.

Whoever shot Eustace Carey, it wasn't Eustace himself.

On the way back to town fate played one of its crazy tricks. I was just approachin' the county road intersection, castin' a glance at my patient to see how he was managin' the trip, when a tan Packard traveling at high speed cut across my path. I tried to slam on my brakes, but it was too late. The front of my Pierce-Arrow hit the right front fender of the Packard with a crunch.

I was out of the car in an instant, runnin' to see if the other driver was injured. He was a short slim man wearin' a drivin' cap to shield his eyes from the sun. He lifted his head as I approached and muttered somethin' in a language that sounded like French. I had the distinct impression he was cursin' me.

"Sorry about this," I told him. "I'm a doctor. I have an injured man in the car."

Without a word he tried to back his car and go around me, but his front fender was so badly crumpled that the wheel wouldn't move. Jeff and his son and Henkle were followin' me in the Whitehead car and now they piled out to see if they could help. The arrival of these others seemed to further disturb the driver. "Look here," he said finally, speakin' English with a thick accent, "get me out of this. I must be on my way!"

I turned to Jeff Whitehead. "My car will still run. Can you tow him into town with yours while I get Eustace to my office? I'm concerned about his leg."

"Sure, Dr. Sam. You go ahead."

I left them at the crossroads, and it was obvious the Frenchman didn't like the idea at all. I figured they'd tow him to Russell's Garage and look over the damage. Meanwhile, I drove Carey to my office and did a better patch job on the wound, but couldn't remove the bullet. I told April to report the gunshot wound to Sheriff Lens, and before long the sheriff hobbled down the street to my office.

I'd grown quite friendly with Sheriff Lens durin' my four years in Northmont, and just a few weeks earlier I'd had to treat him for a sprained ankle suffered when he slipped on a wet spot and fell durin' the ceremonies openin' the new jail. It had been an embarrassin' moment for the sheriff, and the embarrassment was goin' to last till he could walk without that slight limp to remind everyone of his accident.

But the new jail had opened on schedule, the best and biggest in the county, and Sheriff Lens was as proud as he would have been of a new daughter. "Fifteen cells," he'd bragged the day of the openin'. "That's more than the jail at the county seat. You need 'em these days with all the bootleggers around."

Now, as April showed him into my treatment room, he took one look at Eustace Carey and exclaimed, "My God, Eustace! Shot yourself in the leg! You sure the woodchuck didn't pot you from its hole?"

"It ain't funny, Sheriff! I lost a lot o' blood out there—mighta bled to death!"

"You're too mean to bleed to death. Hell, the way you an' Jeff Whitehead been fightin' I'm surprised you'd even set foot on his property." The sheriff squinted. "You sure you weren't trespassin' and Jeff took a shot at you?"

"I shot myself," Carey insisted. "It was an accident."

I finished rewrappin' his bandages and remembered the gun I'd picked up. There was no point in keepin' it quiet. I'd brought it in from the car and now I handed it to Sheriff Lens. "Here's his gun. Don't look to me as if it's been fired."

The sheriff sniffed the barrel and then broke open the cylinder. "Oh, sure, Doc. Here's an empty cartridge. And you can still smell the powder."

"Let me see that." I couldn't believe my eyes. Where there had been six unfired bullets before, now there was a recently fired cartridge under the firin' pin. "I don't understand this. I could swear it hadn't been fired when I first examined it."

Sheriff Lens chuckled. "You leave the firearms to me, Doc. You just patch 'em up."

"I'm not crackin' up, Sheriff. I know what I saw." But we were interrupted by the arrival of Jeff Whitehead's older boy, Matt.

"Doc, Sheriff," he said, "I think you should come down to Russell's Garage. That fellow you ran into is causin' quite a rumpus. Hank Russell says he can't fix the car before tomorrow an' the fellow wants another car. Says he's in a hurry. Mebbe he's a gangster or somethin'."

"Never heard of a French gangster," I commented, and Sheriff Lens perked up.

"You say he's French?"

I shrugged. "Seems so to me, but I wouldn't swear to it."

"Let's go see."

I left Eustace in April's care and we accompanied Matt back to Russell's Garage. The Frenchman was arguin' vigorously with Hank Russell when we entered, apparently tryin' to rent a car with which to continue his journey. But cars weren't all that plentiful in Northmont and big Hank Russell just kept shakin' his head.

"What seems to be the trouble here?" Sheriff Lens asked.

The little Frenchman turned and saw the badge pinned to the sheriff's chest. It seemed to throw him into a momentary panic and he looked as if he was about to take off. Then, to my complete amazement, Sheriff Lens had his gun out, pullin' back on the hammer and aimin' it at the little guy in dead earnest.

"Guess you'd better stand right there," he said in a soft voice I hardly ever heard him use.

"What's all this, Sheriff?" Hank Russell asked. "Who is this fella?"

"Unless I'm very much mistaken, he's the notorious Georges Reme, otherwise known as The Eel, a confidence man wanted by the police of two continents. An' I've got him, right here in Northmont!"

It was a moment of triumph for Sheriff Lens, but it was to be short-lived.

As I learned later from the sheriff and from newspaper articles, Georges Reme was a con man who'd worked various swindles in Europe before comin' to America. But the exploits that had earned him the nickname of "The Eel" involved several daring escapes from police captivity. He boasted that no jail could hold him, and he seemed well on the way to provin' it.

The exploit that made the front page of *The New York Times* involved his most recent arrest in Paris. Transported to the Palais de Justice with a dozen other offenders, he managed to separate himself from the adult criminals and hover by a bench where a number of juvenile delinquents were waitin' to be questioned. When one of them was called, Reme took him by the arm and marched him out of the room, posin' as a detective. Once in the Juvenile Court he abandoned the youth and passed a police guard by claimin' he was a secret-service inspector.

The Eel had dropped from sight after that, only to reappear in Boston several weeks later. Posing as a French count with a collection of valuable paintings, he'd fleeced a leading museum out of a large amount of cash. And just a few days ago, according to Sheriff Lens, the Boston police had cornered him in an apartment house where he was staying. Though every exit was guarded, he escaped by posin' as a mailman, after he'd knocked out the real mailman and stolen the uniform.

"Sounds like something out of G. K. Chesterton," I commented.

"Who?"

"A writer. You wouldn't know him, Sheriff."

"Well, I know about The Eel, sure 'nuff! The Boston police say he stole a car from a salesman of carnival supplies an' high-tailed it outa town. They alerted every police department in New England."

Georges Reme merely looked at me and the sheriff an' said, "I will be gone from this town by morning."

"Darned right!" Sheriff Lens agreed. "I already called Boston an' they're sendin' two detectives to take you back tomorrow. I'll just have to put up with you overnight."

"No jail can hold The Eel," he boasted, soundin' very French.

"We'll see." The sheriff took a ring of keys from his pocket and motioned toward the stairs leading up from his office. "Come on."

I followed along, through a heavy barred door that Sheriff Lens unlocked and left open, and then down a passageway lined with empty cells. These cells occupied the entire second floor of the jail, with 11 of the 15 bein' along three outer walls. The buildin' was almost square and the jail corridor ran in an inner square, with the center portion containin' four holdin' cells for overnight drunks and the like. These inside cells, without windows to the outside world, were numbered 1 through 4, with the other numbers alternatin' left and right till they reached, number 16 in the far outer corner.

Sheriff Lens unlocked the door and motioned Reme inside. "This'll be your home till mornin'. I'll bring your supper later."

The cell was about ten feet deep by six feet wide, with a single cot bolted to the wall. There was a toilet and sink and stool, but nothin' else. The glass was raised on a small barred window some six feet off the floor, lettin' in the warm May air. I knew it looked out on the back of Russell's Garage where the blacksmith shop used to be.

As Sheriff Lens pulled the cell door shut and the lock clicked into place, I asked, "How come number 16? You've only got 15 cells."

"Well, yeah, but I skipped 13 'cause it's unlucky."

"Seems to me any cell would be unlucky to a man in jail."

"Yeah, but 13 is unluckier than most. People are funny."

"There was a story by a man named Jacques Futrelle called 'The Problem of Ceil 13'."

"Another of your author fellas! You do a peck o' reading, Doc."

"It was about a professor who escaped from a prison cell in a bafflin' manner."

"Huh! 'Nother good reason for not havin' a cell numbered 13!"

I couldn't beat that logic, so I didn't try.

B ack at the office my nurse April was all ears. "Tell me what happened, Dr. Sam. I hear tell Sheriff Lens captured a master criminal."

Somehow the idea of little Georges Reme bein' a master criminal brought a chuckle out of me. "Well, it wasn't all that excitin'," I said, but I went on to tell her the details of the automobile accident and the trouble they'd had towin' Reme's car into town with that dented fender. Russell was goin' ahead with the repairs, even though no one knew who'd be payin' the bill.

Later that day I sent Eustace Carey over to the hospital in Felix so they could remove the bullet. I was still puzzled about that revolver, though I thought I had an idea. I was thinkin' it through later that night in my apartment when the telephone rang just after midnight. I thought about Mrs. Hitchins pregnant out at her farm, and about old man Aarons hovering near death. Whoever it was, a phone call that late usually meant a trip out.

But it was Sheriff Lens, more excited than I'd ever heard him before. "Doc, can you come over to the jail right away? I just went back to check the cells an' The Eel is gone!"

"You mean escaped?"

"I don't know what I mean, Doc—he's just gone!"

"I'll be right over," I told him.

When I arrived he had every light in the jail on, and had summoned his two deputies to help in the search. But it was a hopeless task from the beginnin'. There was only one other prisoner in the jail that night—Rudy Henkle, Carey's friend. After Carey had gone off to the hospital Rudy had started drinkin' heavily. He'd broken a window at Dixie's, where they served bootleg whiskey in coffee cups, and generally made a nuisance of himself till Sheriff Lens was forced to arrest him.

Rudy had been given Cell 1, at the opposite end of the building from Cell 16, and he'd slept through the whole thing anyway. Now, sobering up, he called through the bars, "What's goin' on? How's a man to sleep with all the lights on in the middle of the night?"

"Calm down, Rudy," I said. "I'll be in to talk with you later." Then I followed Sheriff Lens along the corridor between the cells to the one where I'd last seen Georges Reme. Cell 16 was empty now like the others, without any evidence that it had ever been occupied, except for a wrinkled blanket on the floor.

"There it is, Doc. He's just vanished!"

"All right," I said. "Now tell me everything that happened since I left you this afternoon."

"Well, not much of anything happened, to tell the truth. I had some food sent in for the prisoner at suppertime and I took it up to him myself 'cause all my deputies had gone home. I tried talkin' with him, but all I got was more of the same—about how he'd be gone by mornin'."

"Exactly how did you bring him the tray? Get one and show me just what you did."

Sheriff Lens grumbled but he went back downstairs for the metal tray on which he brought the food. "I set it on the floor here an' unlocked the cell door. Then I picked it up again and went in."

"Did you lock the cell again once you were inside?"

"No, I left it standin' open. He wasn't goin' anywhere. I had my hand on my gun the whole time an' besides, the barred door at the top of the stairs was locked."

"He could have overpowered you and taken your keys."

"That little squirt?"

"He could have thrown food in your face and been on top of you before you knew it."

"He'd of ended up dead for his trouble, I'll tell you that!"

"All right," I said. There was no use speculatin' on it, since The Eel hadn't escaped that way anyhow. "Then what did you do?"

"Sat there an' watched him eat. Oh, he was a slippery one, all right! No doubt about that! Once when he edged too near the cell door I had to draw my pistol. But he settled back down and finished his food."

"And then?"

"Hell, then I picked up the tray with both hands, swung the cell door shut behind me, and left. These cell doors lock automatically when they're closed, with a latch bolt, but they need a key to re-open 'em. The door at the top o' the stairs has a dead bolt, and I had to unlock it and then lock it again."

"All right. Then what happened?"

"Nothin' much. I already told you about arrestin' Rudy Henkle."

"Tell me again. Tell me about bringin' him to his cell."

"Well, that's just what I did. I had to half carry him up the stairs an' dump him on the cot. I s'pose that's why I put him in the first cell inside the door, so I wouldn't have to lug him too far."

"And The Eel was in Cell 16 at that time?"

"Sure! I didn't turn the lights on down that end because it was after ten an' I figured he was sleepin'. But after I had Rudy stowed away an' locked up tight I took a stroll down there. I could I see him huddled under his blanket."

"But he didn't move or speak?"

"No. I told you he was asleep. Anyway, I went back an' snapped off the light an' locked the door at the top o' the stairs. And then I stayed in my office the rest of the evenin'."

"Is there any other way out of the cell block except through your office?"

"No, sir! Fire Department wanted a back stairs for emergencies, but I told 'em the building is fireproof—it's all brick outside. Besides, a back stairs would have to be locked all the time, so it wouldn't much help in a fire."

I walked to the window and reached up to tug at the bars. They were all firmly in place, and even a man as small as Georges Reme couldn't have wiggled between them. I stooped to pick up the blanket from the floor. "You say he was sleepin' under this?"

"That's right."

An idea struck me. "When you went back to check on him, did you try the cell door to make sure it was locked?"

" 'Course I did! It was locked, all right, and he was inside."

"All right. When did you go up again?"

"Henkle started raisin' a fuss about a half hour ago. I could hear him 'cause he was right at the top of the stairs. I went up and he said he'd been havin' a nightmare. This time when I checked The Eel's cell it was empty."

"Let's look outside," I said.

The second-floor cell overlooked the lot behind Russell's Garage, but this late at night there was no one around. I found a lantern sittin' on a barrel and lit it, throwin' an eerie glow on the hard earth.

"One thing, Sheriff," I said. "Was the cell door still locked when you noticed that Cell 16 was empty?"

"Sure was!"

"Any chance Reme was hiding under the bunk?"

"Impossible. I turned on all the lights right away, and I made sure the cell was empty before I unlocked the door. That blanket was on the floor and he was gone."

I bent and picked up something from the ground directly under Reme's cell. "What is it?" Sheriff Lens asked.

"A long piece of string."

"String?"

"It's as if The Eel made himself small enough to fit between those bars and then lowered himself to the ground on this piece of string."

"That's crazy!"

"You got any better idea?"

"No," Sheriff Lens admitted.

"Did he have any string in his pockets when you arrested him?"

"He might have," the sheriff said. "I frisked him for weapons, but I didn't make him empty his pockets. I figured he was only bein' held overnight."

"Then he might even have had some picklocks."

"No, no—anything metal like that I'd have felt when I searched him. Besides, these new jail locks are supposed to be pickproof."

I rolled up the string and slipped it into my pocket. "Then what are we left with? The Eel was in Cell 16 at ten o'clock with two locked doors between him and freedom. Two hours later he was gone, with the doors still locked and the window undisturbed. No one else was even on the same floor with him except Rudy Henkle, and he was asleep in his own locked cell."

"That story you mentioned, Doc, about Cell Number 13—how did the guy escape in that one?"

"It was a complicated method, but basically he managed to get a message to a friend on the outside who helped him."

"Think The Eel had friends on the outside?"

"I don't know what to think right now," I admitted. "Ask me in the mornin'."

"By mornin' The Eel will be halfway to Chicago!"

"I don't think so," I said, studying the back end of Russell's Garage.

April came bustlin' into the office a little after eight the next mornin'. "My, aren't we early this morning!"

"I didn't get much sleep," I told her.

"Did you hear the news about The Eel escapin'? Sheriff Lens will be laughed outa town."

"It'll be too bad if he is. I like the sheriff. He's a good man."

"His spankin'-new, escape-proof jail with fifteen cells! The first real prisoner he gets walks away like the jail was made of paper."

"Do I have any patients this mornin', April?"

"Mrs. Bassett's stoppin' by to get a new prescription, that's all."

"I'll write it out and you can give it to her. I'm goin' out."

"Down to the jail?"

"No. To Russell's Garage."

Though the hour was early, Hank Russell was already smeared with axle grease and crankcase oil. His father before him had been a blacksmith, and when he died Hank had seen the handwritin' on the wall and turned the shop into a garage. He was a good mechanic for a town like Northmont, and it made us feel we were keepin' up with the automotive age.

"Hello, Dr. Sam. How's your patient doing?" he asked me as I entered the garage.

"Which one?"

"Eustace Carey, o' course!"

Carey's wound had completely left my mind. "Oh, I'm sure he's comin' along. They'll probably let him out of the hospital today."

"That's good. Foolish accident."

If it was an accident, I thought. Aloud I asked, "How soon will you have that car repaired?"

"Just finishin' it up. Guess The Eel won't be needin' it now, though. He's probably far away from here."

I walked over and looked at the car. Russell had hammered out the dented fender and the wheel turned freely now. "Anybody else been around?" I asked. "Whitehead's son, maybe?"

"Haven't seen him since yesterday."

I walked over to the jail and found Sheriff Lens on the telephone to the Boston police, tryin' to explain what had happened to his prisoner. When he'd finished, sputterin' and embarrassed, I asked, "Have you released Rudy Henkle yet?"

"Hell, no, Doc. If I have my way he'll stay there till he rots."

"The judge might have somethin' to say about that."

"I been thinkin' about it all night, and I figured out how The Eel escaped. It's the only way he coulda got out! It was like that Cell 13 story you told me about. He took the string from his pocket an' lowered a note out his cell window. Hank Russell saw it from his garage an' come over to read it. The Eel promised money in return for help. So Hank got Rudy Henkle, who was still hangin' around, to help. Rudy pretended to be drunk an' smashed that window so I'd have to arrest him. Once in his cell he managed to get a picklock to The Eel, an' that Frenchman used it. I know our locks are supposed to be pickproof, but who in hell knows what Frenchmen can do?"

"How did Rudy get the picklock to The Eel?" I asked.

"Well, I suppose he slid it along the floor," Sheriff Lens answered, a bit uncertainly.

"But The Eel's cell was in the opposite corner of the building. It was down the corridor and a sharp left turn from Henkle's. There's no way Henkle could have reached it or even seen it from his cell."

"Yeah," the sheriff muttered. "I suppose you're right. But I still think Henkle's involved."

"Suppose you let me talk to him, Sheriff. I might learn something."

He took me up and opened the cell door. Rudy Henkle was seated on the cot, holding his head in his hands. "Hello, Rudy," I said. Behind me, Sheriff Lens had relocked the door.

"When are they goin' to let me outa here, Doc? I don't know nothin' about The Eel's escape."

"But you got drunk and broke a window, Rudy."

"Well, sure . . ."

"Why?"

"What do you mean, Doc?"

"Why'd you get drunk? It's not like you."

He looked away. "I don't know."

"Want me to tell you, Rudy? Want me to tell you what happened out at Whitehead's farm yesterday?" Sheriff Lens had walked around the corner to look into Cell 16 again, but I dropped my voice anyway so he wouldn't hear.

"How do you know?"

"I know. When I looked at that Colt revolver it hadn't been fired. But when Sheriff Lens examined it later, after the car accident, it smelled of gunpowder an' there was an empty cartridge in it. Now I know I wasn't blind, so that only left one explanation—there were *two* Colt revolvers out at Whitehead's farm yesterday, and you guys switched 'em on me while the car was parked right after the accident."

"I don't know what you're—"

"And what do *two* long-barreled revolvers suggest?"

"What?"

"A duel."

His shoulders slumped, but he said nothin'.

"Those crazy fools fought a duel out there yesterday, didn't they? Whitehead and Eustace Carey, settlin' their old grievances with pistols! Jeff Whitehead's son was his second and you were Carey's second. Only Carey never even got a shot off, did he? Jeff Whitehead plinked him in the leg and then you all suddenly decided you needed a doctor."

"We were damn' fools," Rudy admitted, lifting his head to look at me. "It's a wonder one o' them wasn't killed. When I had sense enough to think it through last night I went out and got good and drunk! But even that didn't help —I passed out here in the cell and dreamed about it all over again. I even heard the shot."

"Shot?"

"It woke me up durin' the night. It was as if a real shot had been fired. But I know I musta been dreamin' about the duel."

I patted his knee. "Don't worry, Rudy. I'll speak to the sheriff about gettin' you out of here."

Sheriff Lens returned and unlocked the cell door for me. I led the way through the second door and waited while he locked it behind us. "What did you find out?" he asked.

"It's just an idea—but I think I know how The Eel did it. I'm goin' to come back here tonight and show you what happened."

The rest of the day dragged on interminably. All the talk in town was about the escape, and even the State Troopers came by to question Sheriff Lens. There was talk of usin' bloodhounds to pick up The Eel's trail, figurin' he'd lit out across country, but as near as I could tell nothin' much was accomplished.

I went back to the jail at dusk and led Sheriff Lens down the street to Russell's Garage. "What we comin' down here for?" he asked. "We should be out chasin' The Eel!"

"I don't think The Eel ever left Northmont, Sheriff, and I'll try to prove it."

"Never left—"

"Keep your voice low," I warned as we moved through the gatherin' darkness at the side of the garage. On our right I could see the jail, and the barred window of The Eel's cell.

"I still say Henkle was in on it," Lens grumbled softly. "An' now I had to let him go."

"Henkle wasn't involved."

"Then how was it possible? There's no other answer!"

"There are at least two other answers, Sheriff."

"What?"

"You see, the whole impossibility is based solely on your testimony. If your story collapses, the impossible escape collapses."

"But—"

"Rudy Heinkle was awakened by what sounded like a shot. He thought it was part of a dream he was havin', but what if it wasn't? What if you went back to serve Reme his food and he tried to jump you? You pulled your gun and shot him, Sheriff. Then, terrified at what you'd done, you carried the body out and buried it back here in these weeds. And made up the whole story of The Eel's impossible escape."

Sheriff Lens was staring at me in the near darkness, and I could see that his hand had dropped to the gun he carried. "You believe that, Doc?"

"No, I don't. If that was what happened, you'd have told the truth. Shootin' a prisoner who's tryin' to escape is a lot less damagin' to your reputation than lettin' one escape! Besides, I told you there were two possible answers."

It was then that we heard the noise—somewhere nearby, not 50 feet away —a gentle movement that might have passed unnoticed. Someone was at the side door of Russell's Garage, workin' on the lock.

I sprang forward. "Come on, Sheriff, it's him!"

Georges Reme turned and tried to run, but we were on him in an instant. I held him down while Sheriff Lens got the handcuffs on him. "This time we'll take better care of you," I promised.

He was cursin' in French when we took him inside, and I settled down in the sheriff's office to explain the correct answer to the problem of Cell 16.

While Georges Reme smoked a cigarette with his cuffed hands, I said, "It was a complex escape method worthy of Futrelle's 'Cell 13.' The Eel didn't rely on outside help but simply worked from minute to minute, taking advantage of existing conditions. It's a way of life for him, I imagine, and other criminals could duplicate it if they had skill and daring."

Sheriff Lens was growing impatient. "How'd he get out of that locked cell?"

"Well, I suppose he had to start with the cell door. You showed me it had a latch bolt that snapped shut when the door closed. But you left the cell door open while he ate, and you even told me you had to draw your gun once when he got too close to it. In that instant, when he was at the open door, Reme managed to jam something—maybe a piece of bread or even a toothpick— into the bolt hole, preventing the bolt from latching completely when the cell door was closed. You were carryin' the food tray with two hands, Sheriff, and you didn't have a free hand to try the door and make sure it was locked properly."

"But I tried it later," Sheriff Lens insisted.

"I'll get to that later. My point is that yesterday evening just after supper-time Georges Reme was free of his cell. Only the barred door at the top of the stairs stood between him and freedom."

"But I was down here in the office. Even if he managed to get that door open somehow, he couldn't of got by me!"

"He didn't manage to open the door, Sheriff—you opened it for him."

"I—"

"When you brought in Rudy Henkle. Remember, Henkle was in Cell Number 1, nearest the stairs. It's one of that center block of four cells, and it's at the opposite end of the floor from Cell 16. In fact, as I pointed out earlier, you couldn't even see Cell 16 from Cell 1. I can assume you left the door at the top of the stairs open, because you would have had your hands full with Rudy and because I've seen you leave that door open two times now when I was with you. You have to turn the key to lock it and you just didn't bother. But for Reme here, hiding in the darkness around the corner of those center cells, it was the chance he was waitin' for. While your back was turned gettin' Rudy onto the bunk, he slipped past and went down the stairs to freedom."

"But I saw him after that in his locked cell!" the sheriff protested.

"You saw somethin' bulky under a blanket, and with the lights at that end of the floor off you just assumed it was Reme. But The Eel was clever. He couldn't know you'd be comin' up with a prisoner at ten o'clock. In fact, for all he knew he'd be alone up there till you checked him in the mornin' and brought his breakfast. So he thought up an idea to give himself a few precious seconds of time. If you came up in the mornin' and saw the cell empty, you'd raise the alarm instantly, probably even run back to the stairs before The Eel could escape down them. He needed you at the cell for thirty seconds to a minute while he sneaked around that center cellblock, through the open door and down the stairs."

"So *you* knew I left it open. But how did *he* know?"

The Eel merely smiled, so I answered the question. "He saw you leave it open when you took him up to the cell yesterday, Sheriff."

"Oh."

Anyway, before he left his cell after dinner he prepared a dummy under the blanket and then locked it in the cell by simply removin' the obstruction he'd put into the bolt hole and lettin' the bolt snap shut."

"What dummy? You've told me how The Eel could escape from a locked cell—now tell me how the dummy could escape!"

"Sheriff, the stolen car Georges Reme was drivin' belonged to a salesman for carnival supplies. Of all the samples he might have had in that car, what would be the most likely?"

Sheriff Lens looked blank, but Georges Reme smiled. "I compliment you, Doctor," he said. "I never expected such perception in a town like this."

"Balloons," I said simply. "You had a couple of balloons in your pocket, along with the string for them. You inflated them, placed them under the blanket, and dropped the string out the window. Once you were outside the jail, you tugged at the string, pullin' the balloons through the bars. At least one of them burst, makin' a noise that sounded like a gunshot to the half-sleepin' Rudy Henkle."

"Why'd he bother to pull the balloons out?" Sheriff Lens asked. "Why not leave them there?"

I shrugged. "I suppose he considered it a good trick he might want to use again. And with the balloons gone his escape was all the more bafflin'. That's why he took the balloons with him, though he dropped a piece of the string."

"I never saw the string runnin' out that window."

"It was dark, and you hadn't turned on that light, remember? You had only the light by Henkle's cell."

Sheriff Lens shook his head. "A lotta things coulda gone wrong with it."

"I told you The Eel worked from minute to minute. All his escapes have depended on luck and darin'. That's why I figured he wouldn't set out on foot across country. He'd already established there were no other cars available here, and if he stole one he might be unfamiliar with its operation. A car like mine is a bit tricky, for instance. So I took a chance that he was hidin' somewhere nearby, waitin' for Russell to fix his car so he could steal it a second time."

"I'll be damned," Sheriff Lens said.

Then I turned to The Eel. "Tell me, Georges, where were you hidin' for almost twenty-four hours?"

At first I didn't think he'd answer, but then he did. Maybe he was proud of havin' fooled me that much. "I was inside the barrel beside Russell's Garage," he said with a smile. "The one from which you lifted the lantern."

"Well," Dr. Sam Hawthorne concluded, "that's how I solved the mystery an' made the front pages of the New York papers. But it was all for nothin', of course. Six months later The Eel escaped from a Boston jail and made his way back to France. He was always a slippery fellow. What about Whitehead an' Carey and their duel, you ask? That part of the story was far from over. It led to an impossible crime involvin' an old country inn. But the hour is late, and that'll have to wait till next time. A small—ah—libation for the road?"

THE PROBLEM OF
THE COUNTRY INN

"Yes, come in," Dr. Sam Hawthorne urged, holding wide the door. "You're just in time for—ah—a small libation and a story. I think I promised to tell you about the old country inn this time, and about the masked bandit who just might have been a ghost. It was in the early summer o' 1926, just after that affair with the Eel, and at a time when the feud between Whitehead and Carey was still heatin' up. They'd fought a sort of duel, you'll remember, out at Jeff Whitehead's farm, and Eustace Carey, owner of one of Northmont's two general stores, had ended up with a bullet in the thigh. . . ."

After Eustace was released from the hospital in Felix (Dr. Sam went on), I checked him over about once a week. The bullet wound in his thigh was healing well, though there was still the possibility of a secondary infection.

I'd just returned from seeing Eustace when my nurse April met me at the door with a message. "Sheriff Lens phoned. He wants you out at the Ferry House. He says there's been a shootin'!"

"Thanks, April," I said, turning on my heel toward the waiting Pierce-Arrow. It was beginning to look like a busy day.

The Ferry House was the nearest thing Northmont had to a genuine country inn. It was located out on the Post Road at the point where the ferry used to cross Snake Creek. The ferry never ran at night, of course, and travelers used to stop at the inn for food and lodgings before continuing their journey in the morning. The Ferry House had been built in 1802, and it survived into the twentieth century, even though Snake Creek is a lot narrower now and a bridge replaced the ferry long ago.

The inn was owned and run by William Stokes, a retired lawyer who'd moved to Northmont with his wife about five years earlier. She'd died of the influenza during my first winter in town, causing a bit of a scare that we were going to have another epidemic like the one in 1919. But except for a few isolated cases nothing came of it. Stokes, a vigorous man still in his mid-sixties, buried his wife out behind the inn and kept right on operating it.

This day, a sunny Monday in June, William Stokes wasn't lookin' vigorous any more. I reached the inn and parked my Runabout behind the sheriff's car, and the first thing I saw as I entered was Stokes' body sprawled on the rug by the front desk. There wasn't much blood.

"When did this happen?" I asked Sheriff Lens.

"About two hours ago. I been tryin' to reach you."

"You don't need me. The man's dead."

"That's for sure!" the sheriff said, covering the body again with a sheet. "Shot right through the chest at close range."

I glanced in at the dining room off to the right, where I recognized the inn's room clerk, little Benny Fields, hunched over a shot of bootleg whiskey. There were others in the room too, but I didn't recognize any of them. "What happened?" I asked.

Sheriff Lens tugged his pants up over a spreading stomach. "Benny was gettin' the weekend receipts ready for the bank when a holdup man came in through the front door. Benny says he was wearin' a fringed leather jacket and carryin' an' old western revolver. An' he had on a black mask like an outlaw or a highwayman."

I grunted at that. "Benny must have been hittin' the bottle."

"Anyways, Stokes was upstairs and came down right in the middle of this. The bandit took one look an' shot him clean through the chest. Then the bandit heard some people comin' up the front walk, so he hightailed it down that hall to the back door."

The hall ran under the stairs leading to the second floor. At one time there had been doors off the hall to the kitchen and a back bedroom, but these doors had been boarded up and papered over long ago. Now the hall led nowhere except to the back door, which opened on a gravel parking area that could accommodate three or four automobiles.

I glanced back at the room clerk's counter where a sack of currency still rested. "He got away without the money?"

"Without the money, but he didn't get away."

"You caught him?"

Sheriff Lens nodded with just a trace of pride. "Benny says the killer ran down that long hall, an' you can see for yourself it leads only to the back door. Trouble is, the door's bolted on the *inside*. Nobody coulda gone out an' left it like that."

"What do you mean?"

"I mean Benny's lying. And I'm arrestin' him for the murder of William Stokes."

I went in to the table where Benny sat and pulled out the chair opposite him. "How you feeling, Benny?"

He glanced up with the frightened look of a trapped animal. "Not so good, Dr. Sam. It's not every day I get accused of murder."

"Tell me what happened, will you? Everything, from the minute you came on duty this morning."

"It was like I told the sheriff. This masked man—"

"Everything. From the beginning."

Benny sighed and started over. "Well, you know we don't do much of a business here any more, 'specially since Prohibition an' all. But we generally have one or two rooms occupied upstairs, and on weekends we do a fair food business. Stokes lived upstairs—alone since his wife died—and so does the housekeeper, Mrs. Adams. I got me a place the other side o' Snake Creek, just across the bridge. Anyways, when I come on at eight on Monday mornings my first job is to open the safe and total up what we took in from dinners over the weekend. Sometimes in the summer like this it's a tidy sum. You get people drivin' out all the way from Boston—"

"How tidy?" I asked.

"It was over five hundred dollars this weekend."

"How many guests upstairs right now?"

"Just one—a Mr. Smith."

"So the only people in the inn at the time of the robbery—or the attempted robbery—were you and Stokes, plus Mrs. Adams and this Mr. Smith upstairs."

"That's right. The kitchen help don't come in till late afternoon on Mondays." His gaze shifted to a nearby table. "Mrs. Adams tends to us if we need anything to eat before then."

I glanced around, following his eyes, and saw a tall woman with vaguely masculine features. She was drinking a cup of tea and talkin' to one of the sheriff's deputies. "Go on with your story," I said.

"Well, I was just countin' the money when the front door bursts open and in walks this masked man. He was dressed like a reg'lar bandit—fringed leather jacket, black mask, western hat, and a revolver."

"What did he look like?"

"He was medium height, maybe a little taller than me, and he had a bushy mustache that showed under the mask. That's about all I can tell you. Oh —and a little beard too. Coulda been fake."

"Fat? Thin?"

A shrug. "Medium."

"Go on."

"He pointed the revolver at me an' motioned towards the money." Benny trembled as he took another sip of whiskey. "I got his message right off."

"He didn't speak?"

"No."

"Odd. Sheriff Lens said that Stokes came downstairs in the middle of this. What attracted him?"

"I s'pose he heard me talkin', asking this guy what he wanted. Anyways, as soon as he saw Stokes the bandit turned and fired one shot straight at his chest. I ducked behind my counter and then almost at once I heard voices from outside. There were a couple of delivery men comin' in with the week's supply of meat."

"Did they see the killer?"

Benny shook his head. "I wouldn't be in this jam if they had. He turned and ran down the hall to the back door."

"Did you actually see or hear him go out?"

"Well, no—but he musta! I shouted to the meat man that there'd been a shootin' and I started down the hall. But I could see he was gone, so we all ran outside. There was no trace of him, and we figgered he'd made it into the woods along the creek."

"See any footprints?" I asked.

"No, but it's all gravel out there, and there hasn't been any rain lately. We wouldn't expect footprints."

"So you called the sheriff?"

"Right. He was here within ten minutes, and he poked around good. I hadn't looked at the back door that close, an' I was as surprised as anyone when he said it was bolted shut from the inside."

"Is it usually kept bolted?"

"Just at night. Stokes generally unlocked it first thing in the mornin', so I just assumed it was open. He must not 'a gotten to it before he was killed."

"So the sheriff thinks you did it."

"Sure! He says where could this masked highwayman have gotten to, and he's right—there's no place!"

"Let's go look at that hall."

The body had been removed, and Sheriff Lens was outside supervising its loading into the town ambulance, a converted World War model that had seen service with the army. I glanced out at the sheriff, then led the way down the back hall. It was a corridor about three feet wide and 20 feet long, with a single wooden door at the end.

As Fields had indicated, it was impossible to see the door from behind the room clerk's desk at this end. The hallway walls were papered with a pattern of faded flowers, water-stained at some spots near the ceiling. The floor was covered with a long single unbroken piece of brown linoleum, effectively ruling out the possibility of a trap door.

I tested the floor anyway, and tapped on the walls with my knuckles. Near the far end I heard hollow sounds in both walls. "What's this?"

"The old door on the right led to the kitchen, and the one on the left to a bedroom converted into a storeroom. Around the turn of the century they were both boarded up and papered over. We use the entrances around the other side for both rooms. This hallway now is just for guests who want to park in the rear."

I could see that the door bolt was in place, and it didn't slide back and forth too easily. The screws holding the bolt to the door, and the screws holding the bolt's metal receiver to the door frame, were all tightly in place. I tapped the door panels, but there was no trick exit. The door jamb itself was thickly weatherstripped, so the door opened and closed quietly. Outside there was only the gravel parking area.

I turned to stare at the ceiling. "What's right above this?" I asked.

Fields thought for a moment. "The upstairs hall, with Mrs. Adams' room at the end of it."

"I'll have a look." I returned to the dining room and introduced myself to Mrs. Adams. Her strong features were quite handsome close up, accentuated by the lipstick she wore—she was one of the few women in town who used lipstick and rouge. "You treated my sister-in-law over on the ridge," she said.

I remembered the case—a middle-aged woman with female trouble. Unfortunately I hadn't been able to help her much. "I'm assisting Sheriff Lens in his investigation," I said. "I wonder if you could show me around upstairs."

"All right," she answered, rather coldly.

On the way up the creaky front steps I asked her about their single paying guest. "Was he down in the dining room?"

She shook her head. "Hasn't stirred out of his room. Got the *Do Not Disturb* sign out. Sleeping through all the excitement."

"Seems a bit odd."

A shrug was her only reply. At the top of the stairs she asked, "What did you want to see?"

"Just a general look around. Which is your room?"

"Here." She made no move to open the door.

"Would it be possible to look inside?" I asked.

She eyed me with distaste, then unlocked the door. The room was perfectly ordinary, done in a pseudo-colonial style like the rest of the Ferry House. "Satisfied?" she asked.

"This would be directly over the downstairs hall?"

"I suppose so. I never thought about it."

"You know the killer vanished down there?"

For the first time her grim face relaxed into something approaching a smile. "You think he came up through the ceiling?"

"I've seen things almost as strange." As I walked out of the room I spotted the *Do Not Disturb* sign still in place on the opposite door. "I think it's time Mr. Smith was awakened."

I knocked gently on the door.

No answer.

I tried knocking harder.

"You'll wake the poor man!" Mrs. Adams protested.

"Did it ever occur to you, Mrs. Adams, that the late-sleeping Mr. Smith could well be the masked killer who vanished so mysteriously?"

"What?" My words seemed to confound her. "But how could that be possible? He was up here!"

I knocked again on the door, and this time a muffled voice answered. "Go away, I'm trying to sleep."

"Mr. Smith, I must talk to you. There's been a murder downstairs."

"Go away!"

But I kept up the pounding, growing more suspicious by the second. If Smith didn't want to be seen, that was all the more reason for seeing him.

Finally I heard the lock turn and the door swung open an inch. That was all I needed. My shoulder hit the door and forced it open the rest of the way.

The man in the room, the mysterious Mr. Smith, was none other than our erstwhile duelist-farmer, Jeff Whitehead.

"Well, Jeff, I'm surprised to see you here," I said, not acting half as surprised as I felt.

"I—I'm glad it's you, Doc. Ever since I heard Carey was outa the hospital I been afraid he'd come gunnin' for me."

"You mean because of that foolish duel?"

Whitehead nodded. "There's been bad blood between us a long time. Even after I shot him he was yellin' the duel was unfair 'cause he didn't get a chance to fire. He swore he had a shot comin', and he said he'd be lookin' for me as soon as his leg was better."

"So you been hiding out here? It's hardly very far away."

"I didn't want to leave the family. I figured if I could just stay here a few days, till Carey got tired of lookin' for me, I'd be safe."

"Does anyone know you're here?"

He shook his head. "I told my son I'd be away for a few days, that's all."

I sat down on the bed, careful not to disturb the smooth spread. "You know, Jeff, you and Carey are both middle-aged men with grown children. It's about time you started acting like adults instead of children. This whole business of the duel was foolish, and your hidin' out here is just adding to the foolishness. Go back home to your family, or you'll likely end up in a peck of trouble."

He looked puzzled. "What do you mean? What's been going on downstairs?"

"Didn't you hear the shot?"

"Shot? No—I must have been sleeping. But I thought there was a lot of comings and goings for this place. And I did see the ambulance."

"The owner, William Stokes, was shot dead by a masked bandit who was tryin' to rob the place."

"My God!"

"How well did you know Stokes?"

"Hardly at all. That's why I picked this place to hide out. The clerk didn't know me, either."

"Then you know nothing about the killing?"

"No. I haven't been out of this room since last night."

"All right," I said. "Look, stay here for now. Sheriff Lens is downstairs and I know he'll want to question you, but outside of him I won't tell anyone you're here."

I left him in his room and went back downstairs. Mrs. Adams was standing in the upstairs hall, watching me as I went, but she didn't speak.

Downstairs I told the sheriff about Jeff Whitehead. "Think he's involved in this somehow?" Lens asked.

"I doubt it. I don't see how." But there was another thought stirring in the back of my brain. "What about these men who were delivering the meat, the ones who came in just after the killing? Are they still around?"

Sheriff Lens shook his head. "I questioned them and let 'em go on their way. They had other deliveries to make and their ice was meltin' fast today. I know 'em both anyway—Tommy Bay and George Kraft from Northmont Packers. You know, they drive that red wagon around with the big picture of a steer on the side."

"I'd like to talk to them," I said.

"You agree Benny Fields musta killed Stokes? Or do you think this is another one of your impossible crimes?"

"I don't know yet. But would you hold off arresting Fields till tomorrow? He's not going anywhere and maybe by that time I'll have a better idea of just what happened."

Sheriff Lens wasn't happy, but he finally agreed. "All right, Doc, I've trusted you before and I'll do it again. I'll admit that was a pretty crazy story for Fields to make up if it's not true. But I can't explain that door bolted on the inside."

"Neither can I."

I drove back to town, following the most likely route of the meat delivery wagon. Finally I saw it parked ahead of me, off the road in front of the pavilion at North Park. I stopped my Runabout in front of the horses, trying not to startle them. Then I walked over to where Bay and Kraft were chatting with the pavilion manager. I could tell from the drift of the conversation that they'd been talkin' about the killing of William Stokes.

"Why'd anyone want to shoot him?" the manager asked.

Tommy Bay spit out a wad of tobacco juice. "Hell, when a man's stickin' up a place he ain't about to need any more motive. I figger old Stokes was just unlucky."

I intercepted the men as they started back to the meat wagon and asked, "Did you see anything of this masked bandit?"

Both men shook their heads. "Not a trace," George Kraft said. "And we ran around the back for a look."

"Why didn't you run after him down the hall?"

Tommy Bay spit again. "Hell, we wasn't askin' for trouble. The man had a gun! We figgered we'd just see where he run to. But we never did catch sight of him."

"Thanks a lot, boys," I told them. I got back in my car and drove off while Tommy Bay held the nervous horses in check.

That evening I paid another call on Eustace Carey. He was hobbling around in the back room of his general store, doing more work than I liked to see him tackle, and he greeted me a little sheepishly. "Hello, Doc. Checkin' up on me?"

"You shouldn't put too much weight on that leg, not quite yet."

"I know, I know. But there's work to be done."

"What about Whitehead?" I asked.

"What about him?"

"I'd hate to see you gunnin' for him."

"I'm not doing anything like that."

"He thinks you are. He's in hiding." I decided to settle the thing once and for all. "Look, would you go with me to see him, shake hands, and bury the hatchet?"

Eustace Carey thought about it. "Sure," he said finally. "Why not."

"Fine. I'll take you to him first thing in the morning."

Next I went over to the sheriff's office and told him what I proposed to do. He snorted at the idea. "Doc, peacemakers never make it far in this here world."

"Would you rather I let them shoot each other?"

"No, no, of course not. But right now I'm more interested in who shot William Stokes."

"It still looks to you like attempted robbery? There's no chance the robbery was just a stunt to camouflage the murder?"

"Well, Doc, that's where you an' me differ. I didn't buy the robbery story to start with. I think Fields shot his employer an' made up the whole story of a masked outlaw."

"Did you question the other people at the Ferry House? That housekeeper, Mrs. Adams, for instance?"

Sheriff Lens nodded. "Says she was just gettin' dressed in her room when she heard the shot."

"Is there a Mr. Adams?"

"She's a widow. He was killed in the war."

"What about Jeff Whitehead?"

"I talked to him."

"You believe his story about hiding out from Eustace?"

"Seems likely."

"But do you believe it?"

"Mebbe." The sheriff leaned back in his chair. "When you takin' Carey to meet with him?"

"First thing in the morning."

"Good luck."

I telephoned the Ferry House and told Jeff Whitehead I'd be bringing Carey over first thing in the morning. He was reluctant, but he finally agreed.

Early the next morning I phoned April at home and told her I'd be out at the Ferry House till late morning. "You can reach me there if there's an emergency," I said.

"You're the one likely to have the emergency when Carey an' Whitehead get together."

"I'm hopin' things will go smoothly."

I picked up Carey in my Runabout shortly after eight o'clock, noticing with satisfaction that his limp seemed better today. "You'll be dancin' a jig before long," I assured him.

"Yeah."

He was wearin' a hunting jacket that seemed heavy for June, and I noticed the right-hand pocket was weighted down. I brushed against it, felt the hard steel of the revolver, and yanked it out. "Damn it, Eustace, you can't go seein' him with a gun in your pocket! What kind of peacemakin' would that be?"

"It was only to defend myself, in case he tried somethin'."

"Well, he's not going to! So I'll just keep this gun."

I locked the gun in the side luggage compartment, then started the motor. Eustace was grumbling about going unarmed to the Ferry House, but by the time we reached our destination his mood improved.

"Whitehead's got a room upstairs," I said. "We'll go right up there. He's expecting us."

I led the way up the walk and opened the front door of the inn. At first glance I saw no one behind the clerk's desk and I wondered where Benny Fields might be. Then, as Carey limped in behind me, I suddenly saw a face appear from behind the counter. It was a masked man with mustache and beard, wearing a cowboy hat and a fringed leather jacket. He'd been trying to open the safe when we walked in.

I saw the gun in his hand and I yelled to Carey, "Hit the floor!" There was a deafening roar as the masked man fired directly at us.

I felt the bullet tug at my sleeve as it went by. Then I heard Carey gasp and go down hard. I turned and saw him on the floor, bleeding from a wound in his side near the waist.

The masked man raised the gun for another shot but thought better of it. He turned and ran down the long hall to the back door, just as he'd done the previous morning.

I wanted to go after him, but I had a bleeding, possibly dying, man on my hands. I knelt by Carey's side, wadding my handkerchief against the wound to stem the flow of blood. His eyes were open but he seemed to be going into shock.

Then, from that kneelin' position, I turned and looked down the hallway. It was empty.

And even from this distance I knew the bolt was still in place on the back door.

I had to shout for assistance, but it was some moments before Jeff Whitehead appeared from his upstairs room.

"What is it?" he asked, seeing Carey on the floor. "What happened?
"Didn't you hear the shot?"
"No. I must have been dozin'."
"Call the ambulance, quick! He needs a hospital."
"Is he bad?"

I'd had time to examine the wound, which wasn't as deep as I'd first feared. "Not as bad as it could have been. This heavy jacket probably saved his life."

Whitehead hurried off to call the ambulance, and Fields and Mrs. Adams appeared from the dining room. "Where've you two been?" I asked. There was a redness about Fields's mouth that might have come from lipstick.

"I was in the kitchen having my morning coffee," Fields said. "Mrs. Adams just joined me and asked if I'd heard a shot."

"It was your bandit friend again, and he disappeared in the hallway the same as yesterday."

"My God!" Mrs. Adams looked as if she were going to faint. "Is it a ghost?"

"Let's take a look at that door," I said to Fields.

We went down the hall and examined it. The heavy bolt was still in place, locking the door from the inside. There was no way anyone could have gone through that door and left it bolted.

Benny Fields put his left hand on the bracket and pulled the bolt open with his right. "Still works as hard as ever," he said. Then he swung open the door and we looked outside. It was the same as it had been the day before. The gravel parking area was empty and undisturbed. The woods in the distance were gently peaceful.

I turned and retraced our steps down the hallway. The wallpaper was still faded and stained, but all of it was still firmly in place. Even where the former doors had been boarded up and papered over, there was no sign of a tear, crack, or hinge. This time I got a broomstick from the kitchen and poked at the ceiling, but there was no opening.

The masked bandit had vanished again, and this time I'd seen it with my own eyes.

I went back to tend to my patient while Mrs. Adams and Whitehead hovered nearby. Soon I could hear the ambulance bell approaching.

It was a puzzle, all right—as impossible a crime as I ever encountered.

Was I dealing with a murderous bandit who recklessly returned to the scene of his crime, or was I somehow part of an elaborate plot in which Eustace Carey had been the intended victim all along?

They told me at the hospital that Eustace Carey would live, and that was the best news I had all day. They'd probed for the bullet, removed it, and Carey was out of danger.

When I got back to my office, Sheriff Lens was waitin' to talk to me. "You actually seen this masked bandit, Doc?"

I nodded. "He was hidden behind the counter when we came in, apparently working on the safe. He fired one shot that just missed me and hit Carey. Then he took off down that same hallway and vanished."

"Did he look like Fields said?"

"Exactly." I went on to describe him.

"Why'd he be dumb enough to come back a second time? 'Cause he left the money the first time?"

"Could be. Or he might have been waitin' there by the safe just to get a shot at Carey."

"You said the bullet almost hit you first."

"That's true. If he was aimin' at Carey he was a poor shot."

"So where does that leave us, Doc?"

I thought about it. "He didn't get the money today either. Maybe he'll be back again tomorrow."

"You believe that?"

"No," I admitted.

"Until this mornin' I was ready to lock up Fields. Now I don't know what to do. You think it's a ghost, Doc?"

"No more than the bandstand 'ghost' was last summer."

"You mean it's more trickery? But how'd he work it? How'd he vanish from that hallway? I can't think of a single way it coulda been done."

"I can think of two ways," I told him, "and that's my trouble. Both of them would work once, but neither one would work twice."

"Two ways!"

"Look, Sheriff, I want to try an experiment. I want you to round up those two meat delivery men and bring them out to the Ferry House tonight. Can you do that?"

"You mean Tommy Bay and George Kraft? Sure, I can find 'em all right."

"Good. I'll see you there at eight o'clock and maybe we'll catch our phantom."

In some ways it's harder to solve a mystery with two solutions than one with none. I spent the remainder of the afternoon pondering the two possible explanations before setting out on the drive to the inn. Finally I knew what had happened, and I knew how to prove it.

I arrived at the Ferry House a little before eight o'clock. Benny Fields was sweepin' the front hallway, looking unhappy. I asked what the trouble was and he replied, "The lawyer was here. He said Stokes's heirs might sell the inn. I'd be out of a job."

"If Sheriff Lens arrests you, you'll be out of a job too," I pointed out.

"But how can he arrest me now?"

"Just pray that he doesn't. Is Jeff Whitehead still upstairs?"

"I think so, yes."

I went up and knocked on his door at the top of the stairs, imagining that I saw Mrs. Adams peeking out at me from her room across the hall. Whitehead answered at once and showed me in. "Has there been any break in the case, Doc?" he asked. "Can I go home now?"

"There'll be a break tonight, I think. And you've been free to go from the beginning."

"I was afraid with Carey prowlin' around—"

"Balderdash!" I snorted. "You've never been afraid of Eustace Carey in your life! I know the real reason you're here, so you can stop lyin' to me. I know all about—"

I was interrupted by the slamming of the front door downstairs, followed by the voice of Sheriff Lens calling my name. "Let's go downstairs," I said to Whitehead, "and we'll try to wind this thing up."

"I don't want to go," he muttered.

"Should I bring them all up here?"

"No . . ."

"Then come on."

I went down the hall to summon Mrs. Adams, then led the way downstairs to where the sheriff was waiting with the two deliverymen.

"What'd you drag us out here for?" Tommy Bay was muttering. "We don't know nothin' about these shootings!"

I glanced at Benny Fields as he took his position behind the desk, and then at Mrs. Adams standing tall and grim at the foot of the stairs. I even looked down the long hallway to make certain I could see the bolted door at the end. This time the masked bandit would not escape.

"Let me tell you a story," I began. "It's the story of how William Stokes could have been killed yesterday mornin' by a masked bandit who escaped through a bolted door."

"Get on with it," George Kraft said. "I gotta get back to work."

"Well, Stokes was upstairs, just gettin' ready to come down, when he saw the meat delivery truck pull up out front. Only instead of Bay and Kraft he saw a masked man wearin' a fringed jacket and carrying a western revolver."

"*What?*" Tommy Bay gasped. "What in hell is this?"

"One of them—it doesn't matter which—entered first with the gun and held up Benny. The other one came up the front walk with the meat, chatting to himself so that Benny would think he heard two people talkin'. Then Stokes appeared and got himself shot, and the killer ran down the hall, unbolted the door, and went out. The one carrying the meat enters, helps Benny with the dyin' man, and then manages to slip down the hall to rebolt the door from the inside. Meanwhile, the killer ditched his costume and reappeared as a delivery man. With the confusion and all, Benny never realized that both delivery men weren't here all the time."

"Say," Benny Fields said, "it coulda been like that, now that I think of it."

"That's plumb crazy!" George Kraft exclaimed. "Even if it was true, why'd we bother to rebolt the door?"

"To frame Benny Fields for the killing," I said. "To make it appear that his story was impossible."

"You got any proof o' this?" Sheriff Lens asked quietly, his right hand resting on the butt of his gun.

I took a deep breath. "No, Sheriff, I don't—because none of it is true. I only said it *could* have happened this way."

"But it didn't?" He looked exasperated.

"Kraft and Bay weren't even on the scene of this morning's shooting. And I could see that bolted door before anyone went near it to fool with the lock. The method I've outlined couldn't have been used today, therefore it wasn't used yesterday. We can't believe that *two different* bandits would duplicate their crimes that exactly. No, it was the same person yesterday and today— and since Bay and Kraft couldn't have done it today, that makes 'em innocent of yesterday's killing too."

"I'm sure glad o' that!" Tommy Bay said.

Sheriff Lens wasn't satisfied. "Then what in hell'd I drag 'em down here for?"

"So I could dispose of the wrong answer before gettin' to the right one."

"Damn it, there's *no* other way it coulda been worked, Doc."

"Yes, there is."

"If the door was really bolted from the inside, an' if there's no other way outa that hall—"

"There's no other way. The walls, floor, and ceiling were examined by me personally."

"The killer entered the hallway, he didn't go through the bolted door and he didn't get out any other way. Then what happened to him?"

I glanced around at the others and started talking. "I was put off the track by the second shooting this mornin'. I even thought for a while that Eustace Carey was prob'ly the intended victim all along, that I'd been snookered into bringing him here for that purpose." I stared hard at Jeff Whitehead. "Jeff could have been the masked and bearded bandit. There was something about his being on the scene that didn't ring true anyhow. With all the commotion yesterday mornin' he stayed hidden in his room till I forced my way in. Why? Not because he feared Eustace Carey. That just didn't hold water."

"You think Whitehead killed Stokes to lure Carey out here somehow?" Sheriff Lens asked.

"The thought crossed my mind—until I remembered the bed. It was the bed that told me of Whitehead's guilt, and also of his innocence."

Jeff Whitehead stepped forward, starting to protest, but I held up a restraining hand. "No, no, I know you didn't kill anybody, Jeff. You're not the masked bandit."

"Then who in hell is?" Sheriff Lens demanded. "You've eliminated every man in the place!"

I glanced sideways at Mrs. Adams. "The killer never spoke. It could have been a woman."

"Mrs. Adams?"

"No. I happen to know she's innocent."

"Then *who*? And *how*?"

"I hate to admit it, Sheriff, but you were right all along. There never was a masked bandit. Benny Fields made up the whole story, after he murdered his employer."

A trapped scream came from Benny's throat and he turned to run, dashing, once more down that long hallway.

But this time Sheriff Lens had his revolver out. "Stop or I'll shoot, Benny!" he shouted.

Fields kept running. He was almost to the bolted door when the sheriff fired.

This time Benny Fields didn't disappear.

"You could have killed him, Sheriff."
     "I only aimed for his legs."

Mrs. Adams was hysterical, her face pressed against Whitehead's shoulder. Kraft and Bay merely stood there. I told one of them to call for an ambulance.

"I should've arrested him yesterday mornin'," the sheriff said. "He had guilt written all over him."

"I guess he did," I had to agree. "I suppose Stokes caught him with his hand in the cash, or else they just had a violent argument. Anyway, Benny pulled out a revolver and shot his employer. I don't think any of it was planned in advance, and he must have been horrified when Bay and Kraft came in the front door moments later.

"He managed to hide the pistol behind the counter, and he made up the first story that popped into his head—about a masked bandit who was tryin' to rob the place and killed Stokes. His story was possible, until you noticed that the hall door was still bolted on the inside. Then Benny Fields was in big trouble."

"Okay, I saw all that the first day," Sheriff Lens spouted. "But what about the shootin' this mornin'? You *saw* the masked bandit! You *saw* him disappear down this very hallway!"

"Well, what would you have done in Benny's shoes? He's free but likely to be arrested durin' the next day or two. His only chance is to stage another appearance of the masked bandit—to convince everyone his story is true. Carey and I were just unlucky enough to arrive at the wrong moment. The victims could just as well have been Bay and Kraft makin' another meat delivery. He didn't mean to kill Eustace—in fact, it was better not to, 'cause that would give him two witnesses to the bandit's existence."

"But he did vanish in the hallway! You tol' me so, Doc!"

"Indeed he did. But even that had to be part of his plan. When he thought of a masked bandit, he described him as dressed in clothes he already owned —I'm sure you'll find them hidden somewhere, along with the gun—and the rest of his description fit too. Benny was fairly short, but he said the bandit was just a little taller than him. Cowboy boots would add that extra inch or two. So he waited there, crouched behind the desk in his disguise."

"What if one of the other employees—like Mrs. Adams—had spotted him first?"

"I'm sure he'd have shot anyone—he didn't care where his witness came from, so long as there was somebody to back up his story." I led the sheriff back down the hall to the bolted door. "He gimmicked this bolt in a simple way. You remember I examined the lock yesterday and all the screws were tight. But look—now you can see the ends of wooden toothpicks around these two screws holdin' the bolt receiver to the door frame.

"Sometime last night he removed these screws and slightly enlarged their holes. The result was that though the door *looked* bolted, a turn of the knob and a tug pulled these two screws out of the door frame and the door opened.

"When Fields was through the door he simply pulled it closed behind him. The loose screws went back in their holes and the door looked as if it were *still* bolted. Later he put the ends of toothpicks in the holes to tighten the screws."

Sheriff Lens scratched his head. "How'd you tumble to this?"

"Two things. When I saw Fields after this morning's shooting, there was a little redness around his mouth. He'd yanked off the false beard and mustache too fast in disposin' of his costume. Then, when he and I went down to examine the door, he held his left hand on the receiver bracket to keep the screws from comin' out again when he pulled the bolt."

"Hell, you mighta *seen* the bandit go through the door! Or ran down an' tried it right away. Or the screws mighta fallen on the floor instead 'a going back in their holes!"

"Sure, any of those things could have happened, Sheriff—but none of them would have been fatal to his plan. He'd just have said the screws musta been loose all along and that's how the bandit escaped yesterday too. We'd know he was lyin' but we couldn't have proved it. When the trick did work, he was content to go along with the seeming impossibility."

"It was a simple killin' and he sure made it complicated!"

"He invented a lie about a crime that unexpectedly became impossible and then had to invent a method for bringin' it off, just so people would believe him."

"What about Jeff Whitehead an' the bed? What was all that about?"

Jeff and Mrs. Adams were still standing together and I lowered my voice. "When I found him hidin' in his room yesterday morning, the bed was all made up with the spread on it. Now he hadn't been outa the room, and he'd had the *Do Not Disturb* sign on the door. Nobody makes up their own bed at an inn— not when there's a housekeeper on duty. I think Mrs. Adams made up the bed because she shared it with him. That's the real reason he was here in the first place. The made-up bed told me they were guilty of a crime—but not of murder."

Sheriff Lens could only scratch his head and say, "I'll be doggoned!"

"Well," Dr. Sam Hawthorne concluded, "they found Benny's disguise and the gun hidden behind the big old kitchen stove. And a check of the books showed he had been stealing small amounts from the inn for years. So the case was all wrapped up.

"Another—ah—small libation? Next time I'll tell you about that November's election—an election in which a man was murdered while he was alone in a voting booth. Now, *that* was an impossible crime!"

THE PROBLEM OF
THE VOTING BOOTH

"**W**ell, it's another Election Day," Dr. Sam Hawthorne said, pouring the drinks. "Elections always remind me of the voting booth murder back in Northmont. It was November of 1926, and Sheriff Lens was runnin' for re-election. I suppose it was about the most impossible-seemin' murder I ever came up against. A little—ah—libation before I start? . . ."

I remember it rained on Election Day that year and Sheriff Lens was worried the weather might keep a lot of his supporters at home. He'd waged a hard-fought campaign against a challenger named Henry G. Oatis—a newcomer to Northmont who'd had some law-enforcement experience down south but then moved north after the death of his wife. Of course we still used paper ballots in those days. Only a few of the big cities had voting machines back in '26, though they'd been authorized for use in elections since 1892. You know, it was Thomas Edison who invented the voting machine back in 1869—the first invention he ever patented—though it was lots different from the machines they use today.

Anyway, Northmont still used paper ballots. You gave 'em your name, signed the voting book, and they handed you a ballot. You went into the curtained booth to make your marks, then deposited the ballot in a slotted box just outside the booth. It was a simple system and it worked just fine, 'cept when the polls closed it sometimes took half the night to count all the ballots accurately and come up with a winner.

This day, as I said, it was raining. Not a gentle spring-like rain, but the sort of drivin' New England rain that comes so often in the fall, bringin' down what's left of the leaves and being generally unpleasant. Because of the rain I'd driven April, my nurse, to the polling place in the back of Whitney's Barber Shop. Truth to tell, even if it hadn't been rainin' she'd have wanted me to come along.

"Imagine it, Dr. Sam! They give women the vote and then make us go to a barber shop to cast our ballot!"

"I smiled and tried to calm her down. "Well, April, it's not that bad. The north end of town's votin' in the schoolhouse, and we'd be votin' in the Town Hall if it wasn't for all the repairs going on. Will Whitney's a selectman and it was mighty nice o' him to let the town use his barber shop for a polling place."

"It's not just here, Dr. Sam. I read in the papers that women in New York and Chicago often have to vote in places like barber shops."

"At least they don't have to vote in saloons. Prohibition took care of that."

We pulled up in front of Will Whitney's shop and April put up her umbrella against the driving rain. I drove around back and parked in a lot already pockmarked with puddles. Then I ran for the back door, hoping I wouldn't get too wet.

"Need an umbrella this mornin'," a voice greeted me as I came through the door. It was Sheriff Lens himself, looking fat and happy and trying not to show his nervousness.

"What you doing here, Sheriff?" I asked. "A little illegal electioneerin'?"

"Naw, this fella from the newspaper wants a picture of me and Oatis shakin' hands outside the votin' booth. Silly idea, but I gotta go along with it."

The fella from the newspaper was a young photographer named Manny Sears, recently come to town, whom I'd encountered of late taking pictures of everything from prize steers to Mrs. Kelly's triplets. I shook his hand and watched while he went about the business of loadin' flash powder into its holder. It reminded me of the bandstand killin', where flash powder had played so important a part. "Don't you ever get tired of snapping pictures, Manny?"

He grinned boyishly at me. "Sure don't, Dr. Sam. Photographs in newspapers are the coming thing. Even *The New York Times* is using them on their front page sometimes, in place of drawings."

"So you're going to have the winner and the loser shakin' hands."

"That's right. Friendly enemies, you might say."

April had taken off her raincoat and was shaking the moisture from her umbrella. Both the party workers behind the desk were friends of hers, and she was settling down for a chat. One of them, Mrs. Morgano, was an occasional patient of mine. I knew she was a Republican like Sheriff Lens. The other woman, Ida Fry from the dry-goods store, must have been the Democrat.

We seemed to be the only ones who'd arrived to vote, though Will Whitney was busy cutting the hair of a customer in the front of the shop. The customer was a man I didn't know, and I wondered what brought a stranger to Northmont on a rainy Election Day.

"Well, I'm gonna vote," April said, accepting a lengthy ballot from the ladies behind the desk. Besides the candidates for sheriff and selectmen, there were a number of local ordinances to be voted on. And at the top of the ballot, ahead of everything, were the statewide offices. It wasn't a presidential year, but we were electing a governor and a senator, as well as our local congressman.

Reading and marking the paper ballot was time-consumin', and April was in there a full two minutes before emerging to drop her folded paper into the slotted box on her left. "Did you vote the right way?" I asked with a smile.

"I voted against everyone who was in now—'cept Sheriff Lens, of course."

The sheriff beamed and started to thank her, but was interrupted by the arrival of his opponent. Henry G. Oatis stormed in like the wind-driven rain behind him, stampin' soggy shoes on the barber-shop floor. He removed his glasses to wipe them, squinting nearsightedly at the gathering.

"I'm here to take your picture, Mr. Oatis," the young photographer announced, holding his camera and flash high. "I want the two of you together here by the booth."

For the moment Henry Oatis ignored him, turnin' instead to Will Whitney by his barber chair. "Don't let that razor slip, Will. I can't afford to lose a single vote today." But when he replaced his glasses and saw the man in the chair more clearly, he seemed startled. "You're not from Northmont!"

"Just passin' through," the man mumbled, with what sounded to me like a southern accent.

Oatis turned away quickly and I wondered vaguely if he knew the man. Will Whitney flayed the air with his razor and bent once more to his task. And Ida Fry broke off a gossipy conversation with April to wave a ballot in the candidate's direction. "Henry, you come over here this instant and do your votin'! There's plenty of time for picture-takin' afterwards."

He gave a little bow in response. "Always willin' to bend to the will o' the party, Ida. How are you, Sheriff? Enjoyin' your last week in office?"

Sheriff Lens sputtered a bit. It had been a rough campaign, with Oatis charging Lens was "a do-nothin' country hick," and the Sheriff responding by branding Oatis as a carpetbagger in reverse. I could see their tempers hadn't mellowed any at the voting booth. The whole scene embarrassed me because I considered myself a good friend of the sheriff's and hated to see the degradation the campaign had brought upon him. Maybe it happened to all politicians when they had to go out and scrounge for votes, but it hit home with Sheriff Lens. He was a man afraid of losin' his job. It was as simple as that.

Oatis had slipped off his raincoat for the picture, but he still held the ballot that Ida Fry had handed him. The photographer was fussing at the booth, gettin' everything ready, but Oatis merely brushed by him. "Like I said, votin' first, pictures later."

He drew the heavy black curtain closed behind him and I could imagine him bending over the ballot, pencil in hand. "You want some coffee, Dr. Sam?" Mrs. Morgano asked, already pouring a cup.

"Don't mind if I do. It'll take the chill out of my bones."

Manny Sears had posted himself about ten feet in front of the voting booth, waiting with his camera and flash for Oatis to come out. Up front, Will Whitney left his barber chair and walked back to watch, leavin' his customer unattended for a moment. Sheriff Lens tried to ignore the whole thing by chatting with April and the other ladies. Outside, a shift in the wind had brought the rain beatin' against the barber-shop windows.

I could see Henry Oatis' legs beneath the black curtain as he marked his ballot, and after a few minutes it seemed he was taking unusually long with it. "How you comin' in there, Henry?" Ida Fry called out at last, when nearly five minutes had elapsed. "Need any help?"

"I'm just about finished," he called back. "Damned long ballot!"

There was another moment's wait and then he pushed the curtain aside to come out. He was holding the folded ballot in his left hand and the pencil in his right, and there was a look of immense surprise on his face.

He took two uncertain steps forward and I saw the blood on his shirt front. "Oatis, what is it?" I asked, springing forward to catch him as he started to fall. Behind me, young Manny Sears ignited his flash powder and got the picture.

I lowered Oatis gently to the floor and started rippin' open his shirt. "Murderer . . ." he managed to gasp. "Stabbed . . ."

Then he relaxed and his head fell to one side. I knew he was dead.

"Everyone keep back," I said. "This man's been murdered."

D espite his dying words, my first thought was that he'd been shot, maybe by one of those guns equipped with a Maxim silencer. But as soon as I uncovered the wound I saw that he'd been stabbed without doubt. The hole in his shirt front, and in the flesh beneath it, was nearly an inch long and quite narrow. It was a typical knife wound, in the region just below the heart. If the thrust was upward, the blade could easily have reached the heart.

"He was alone in the booth!" Sheriff Lens exclaimed. "No one coulda killed him in there!"

"I know." The others were crowding around and I motioned them back. "We have to find the knife," I said, "and I'd better do the lookin'. Sheriff, you stay at the front o' the shop with the others."

"Why can't I—?"

"Because somebody might think you killed him," I explained.

That shut him up, and I pulled the curtain wide to examine the voting booth. There was nothing inside except a wooden shelf with a couple of pencils on it—identical with the pencil Oatis still clutched in his right hand. I looked under the shelf and on the floor. I felt the black curtain to make sure a knife wasn't concealed in it, and then went around the back of the booth to look for a hole through which a knife blade could have thrust.

There was nothing.

The booth was solid wood on three sides, with the curtain on the fourth side, facing everybody. Inside there was nothing but the shelf for marking the ballot.

"All right," I said finally, stepping around the body on the floor. April had covered it with an extra piece of black curtain, but even that did not prevent Mrs. Morgano from drifting off into sobbin' hysterics. "You'd better take her out to my car," I told April, "till she recovers. The rain's let up now."

April helped the woman to her feet and Sheriff Lens lent a hand. "April," I said, calling her aside. "Sort of go over her dress and make sure she doesn't have the knife on her."

"You think—?"

"No, no! But we have to cover everything." After they'd gone I said to the others, "We've got to search every inch of this place for the knife that killed him. We're not goin' to know who or how till we find that knife."

"This is a barber shop," Will Whitney reminded us. "It's full o' razors an' scissors and the like. I couldn't work without 'em."

I agreed. "But I don't think any of 'em would have a blade wide enough to make this wound. Let's take a look."

We searched the place for twenty minutes, pulling open every drawer, measurin' the width of every pointed instrument we could find. We searched each other and we searched the corpse. We even looked in the hamper where Whitney threw his used towels after giving customers a shave, but there was no weapon hidden among the linens.

In the meantime voters were arriving again now that the rain had stopped. We had to keep them waiting outside, at least until the body could be removed, but the news of the candidate's death was soon spreading across town. There was a call from the mayor, and another from the county's election commissioner, and for a time the ringing of the telephone was like a discordant hymn in the background.

"He musta committed suicide," Sheriff Lens announced at one point. "There was nobody near him."

"If he did he had to stab himself with this pencil," I said. "It's the sharpest thing he had on him. Besides, it's hardly likely he'd kill himself on the day he might be elected sheriff. He didn't enter that booth like a man in a state of depression."

"Okay," the sheriff agreed, "but, then how'd anyone get near enough to stab him? We were all out here—Will Whitney with his customer, Mrs. Morgano and Ida behind their table, you and me and April in front of the booth, and that photographer waitin' to take his picture. None of us was anywhere near the booth."

"Knives can be thrown," I pointed out, "though it beats me how a thrown knife could have remained invisible to us all."

"Mebbe he was stabbed before he ever entered the votin' booth," Will Whitney volunteered, wipin' the dried soap from one of his razors. "Knew a fella over in Shinn Corners once got knifed in a brawl an' didn't even realize it at first."

But I couldn't go along with that. "Oatis stood in that booth almost five minutes markin' his ballot. He couldn't have lived that long with a wound to the heart—and besides, there'd have been a lot more blood than there was. No, he was stabbed either just before or just after leavin' that booth. He didn't live more than a minute."

"We was all lookin' right at the booth, though!" Sheriff Lens argued. "Sears here was even goin' to take a picture."

I suddenly remembered something. "You *did* take a picture, didn't you? Just at the instant he started to fall!"

The young photographer nodded. "Sure, I got one. That was before I realized he'd been stabbed."

"How long would it take you to develop it?" I asked.

"Oh, I could have a print in an hour or so."

"Then why don't you do just that? The picture could contain a valuable clue."

"You really think so?" He seemed excited for the first time since the killing. "I'd better get back to the paper with it."

April signaled me from the other side of the shop, where she was picking through the wet umbrellas lined against the wall. "I was just thinkin' the knife coulda been dropped in a folded umbrella, Dr. Sam."

"I already thought the same thing, but there's no knife there."

"You looked?"

"Sure. Now what was the signal for?"

"You're lettin' Manny Sears walk outa here without checkin' his camera."

"Camera? You mean—?"

"Couldn't he have a spring device to fire a knife through the lens openin'? Somethin' like that?"

"Then what happened to the knife?"

"It coulda been made of ice and melted."

"Not in two seconds, it couldn't. And no ice would be sharp enough to go through his shirt and skin like that. My God, April, what have you been readin'?"

"Nothing more violent than *Show Boat,*" she insisted.

"Sounds more like Fu Manchu to me."

"No, really, Dr. Sam—haven't you noticed Manny's odd behavior?"

"He's done nothing that I could see."

"Exactly!" she exclaimed. "And *that* is his odd behavior!"

"Now I know what you've been reading—Sherlock Holmes!"

"Seriously, wouldn't he have raced back to his paper with that picture right away? Why's he hangin' around here?"

I had to admit she had a point. I went over and checked out his camera, but it was real enough—no openings for darts or knives. And when I asked him why he'd hung around this long he had an answer for that. "I thought Sheriff Lens might want some photographs of the scene of the crime, before they took the body away."

The sheriff heard him and nodded agreement. "Yeah, sure, take me a couple of pictures, son. They might come in handy."

I'd talked to everybody in the place except Will Whitney's strangely silent customer, and I wandered over to the barber chair where he was still sitting. "What'd you say your name was, mister?"

"Didn't say." He was maybe 35 or 40, with the look of an outdoorsman about him. "But it's Crocker. Hy Crocker."

"You live around here?"

"Nope."

"Just passin' through?"

"Might say that."

"You didn't know the dead man, did you? Henry Oatis?"

"How'd I know him? I only just got to town this mornin'."

"Most people like to be home to vote on Election Day."

"Never paid much mind to politics down my way."

"And where would that be, Mr. Crocker?"

"South o' here."

"You in business?"

He nodded. "Dogs. I raise and train dogs."

"For hunting?"

"Yeah. And watchdogs. Keeps trespassers off your land." He took out a thin foreign-lookin' cigar and lit it, making no effort to leave the barber chair though Whitney had finished with him long ago. "Bloodhounds too. Maybe Sheriff Lens could use a bloodhound."

"I'll ask him, Mr. Crocker."

But I had more important things to ask the sheriff just then. They were finally removing the body, carefully edgin' the stretcher through the narrow front door, and the people waiting outside were crowdin' close. "Better clear them out of there, Sheriff," I warned. "This isn't a sideshow."

But when Lens yelled at one of the farmers from the hill, the man yelled right back. "That's one way to win an election—right, Sheriff?"

Lens was not a man to let an implication like that go unchallenged. "I'll find the man that killed Oatis, never you fear!"

"What if you lost the election, Sheriff?" another heckler joined in.

"If I lost the election I'll resign and let them call a new election to fill the spot. I don't want the job if the people don't want me."

That seemed to quiet 'em for the moment, and the ambulance pulled away with the body of Henry G. Oatis inside. With its departure the place returned to a semblance of normality. The voters, impatient from their long wait, crowded into the shop, keeping Ida Fry and Mrs. Morgano busy with the registration-books.

April came up to me holding a pencil. "You want this, Dr. Sam? I pried it outa the dead man's hand before they took him away. No sense his bein' buried holdin' a pencil."

"No sense indeed." I turned it over between my fingers, but it was just an ordinary wooden pencil identical to the one I'd used to mark my own ballot. It could not have been used to stab a man to death.

"Who do you think killed him?" April asked. "An' how?"

"An invisible man with an invisible knife."

"Sheriff Lens?"

"No. Lens wouldn't commit murder. He may not be the smartest sheriff in the state, but he stands for law and order above all else. Besides, I think he honestly expects to be reelected today."

"Who else is there?"

"The mysterious dog trainer, Mr. Hy Crocker."

"Why him?"

I shrugged. "He's a stranger in town. There had to be a motive for Oatis' murder and the most likely time for that motive is in the past. Oatis hasn't been here long enough to make enemies in Northmont—not the sort of enemies who'd kill him in such a devious way, anyhow."

April took up the suggestion of Crocker's involvement enthusiastically. "Should I follow him an' see where he goes?"

"Don't we have any patients today?"

"Only old Mrs. Foster an' when she saw the rain this morning she called in to postpone it for a week. Said her wagon would get stuck in the mud."

"All right," I agreed. "Keep an eye on Crocker and see where he goes. I'm going to stroll over to the newspaper and see if Manny Sears has those pictures developed yet."

Though the rain had stopped, the skies that Tuesday afternoon were a long way from clearing. Great gray clouds hung on the horizon, thrustin' their thunderheads at us from the west. It would rain again, I knew, and soon.

The office of the *Northmont Bee* was busier than I'd ever seen it. Men were on the phones, spreading details of the murder to the big-city dailies in Boston and New York. The publisher, Ed Andrews, was looking over the headline for the evening edition. Generally the *Bee* appeared only three times a week, on Monday, Wednesday, and Friday, but the murder of a candidate for sheriff in a town voting booth rated a special edition.

"Howdy, Doc," Andrews said. "You were on the scene agin, weren't you? Gonna come up with a solution this time?"

"We'll see."

"Manny says he got a flash picture."

"I hope he did. Is it ready yet?"

"They're developing it now."

I remembered Hy Crocker and my theory of something from the past. "Tell me about Oatis, Ed. What's his background?"

The publisher shrugged. "Come up here from North Carolina 'bout a year ago. He was police chief down there, in a town a little bigger than this. His wife died and he wanted a fresh start, wanted to get away from his old memories."

I grunted. Oatis hadn't seemed too old. "How'd she die?"

"Who?"

"Mrs. Oatis. Professional curiosity. If she was his age she wasn't very old."

"You're right," he agreed, consulting a printed obit. "She was thirty-eight. Killed in a house burglary two years ago. They caught the guy—a tramp passin' through—and hanged him. He broke into the house lookin' for food and stabbed her."

"Did the tramp confess?"

"How the hell do I know if he confessed? I'm just readin' you what's here, Doc."

I saw Manny Sears coming across the room with a couple of wet prints, holding them gingerly by the edges. "Here are the pictures."

I glanced casually at the one he'd taken at Sheriff Lens's request, showing the sprawled body of Oatis, then turned my attention to the picture taken as Oatis left the voting booth. The black splotch of blood on his chest was just beginning to form, and his face was frozen into that surprised look I remembered so well. The knees seemed to be saggin' just a bit, and the fingers of his left hand were thrown wide as if he was grabbin' for support.

It was the moment before death, the moment just after the knife had penetrated—and yet there was no knife visible anywhere in the picture.

Our eyes had not deceived us. Henry G. Oatis had been stabbed to death while alone in the voting booth, with no less than eight people watching from outside, and with a knife that seemed to have vanished into thin air.

I went back to Will Whitney's barber shop and waited till there was a lull in the voting. Then I asked Ida Fry and Mrs. Morgano if I could examine the voting booth again.

"Don't know what you expect to find in there," Ida Fry said, pulling the curtain open for me. "We even mopped up the blood so's it wouldn't upset anybody."

I bent to examine the wooden shelf on which the ballots were marked. It was about the height of my stomach, and I could imagine a knife blade springing out of it to stab Henry Oatis and then being pulled back into its secret slot by some mechanical device.

It was a good idea but a wrong one. The shelf was solid wood.

I was leavin' the barber shop by the back door when I heard the growling of dogs and a woman's scream. I couldn't be sure, but it sounded like April.

I ran across the rutted parking area, jumping puddles of muddy water, and came out of the back street. April was on the ground about halfway up the block, tryin' to fight off two ugly German shepherds.

I yanked off my raincoat and wrapped it around my left arm as I ran, then waded into the thick of it, using my padded arm to ward off the lunges of the dogs. April had all but given up the fight, crawling away to protect herself from the snapping jaws. I dragged her free, fighting back the dogs, until suddenly a sharp whistle called them off.

April lifted her tear-streaked face from the ground and I saw the marks of the dogs' savage attack. "I have to get you to a hospital."

"It was Crocker's truck, Dr. Sam! I was tryin' to see what was inside and the dogs got loose."

"I'll take care of Crocker later," I told her. I could see him standin' across the street, putting a leash on the dogs.

I helped her to her feet and washed off the teeth marks, treatin' them with an antiseptic till I could get her to the hospital. My first thought was for April, but then I wanted to get back and take a look at Hy Crocker's truck.

By the time I returned from the hospital the rain had started again—a fine annoying drizzle that seemed to soak through to the bones. April was restin' comfortably at the hospital, where they'd decided to keep her overnight in case she had any bad reaction to the treatment. I was sure the dogs weren't rabid, and I hated to subject her to the long and arduous series of inoculations with Pasteur serum unless it was necessary. But I did want to have another look at those dogs, preferably when they were standin' still.

Crocker had made no effort to leave town after his dogs attacked April, and I found him over at Dixie's lunch counter drinkin' a cup of coffee. The coffee at Dixie's was often spiked with some good Canadian whiskey, but I couldn't tell about his cup.

"Hello there, Dr. Hawthorne," he greeted me. "Sorry about your nurse. How is she?"

"Alive, no thanks to those hounds of yours."

"They're trained to guard my property. I called them off as soon as I saw what was happening."

"I'd better take a look at them. They could be rabid."

"*My* dogs?" He laughed at me. "Healthiest animals around. But come on, look all you want."

He finished his coffee and went outside, leading me around the corner to the lot where the truck was parked. The dogs were back inside now, growlin' and snappin' as I approached.

"What's in the truck that's so valuable?" I asked.

"Nuthin'." But he made no effort to unlock the door.

I was losing my patience with him. "Look here, Crocker, I could have Sheriff Lens arrest you on an assault charge right now! My nurse is in the hospital thanks to those dogs of yours. She could have been killed."

"No, no, these dogs aren't trained to kill."

"But maybe their master is. Maybe you followed Henry Oatis up here from the south and killed him."

"He wasn't killed by no dogs. He was killed by a knife." He smiled slyly at me. "And don't forget I was sittin' in that there barber chair all the time."

"I'm rememberin'." I was rememberin' something else too— about Henry Oatis' murdered wife. She'd been stabbed like him, and I wondered if today's crime was tied in somehow with that one two years back. "Open up the truck," I told Crocker. "I still need to examine your dogs."

"They got no rabies."

"I'll be the judge of that. Open up or I'll have the sheriff arrest you and shoot both your dogs."

He opened the door reluctantly, bringing out the two big German shepherds. They gave a couple of low growls in my direction, but I could see he knew how to control them. I could also see, with a sudden flash of illumination, the reason for Hy Crocker's mysterious behavior. The front end of the truck was piled high with cases of bootleg whiskey, thinly disguised in boxes marked *Maple Syrup*.

"Wrong time of the year to be runnin' maple syrup," I told him with a knowing smile.

"What you goin' to do about it?"

"Nothing."

The dogs seemed healthy enough, and I was no defender of the 18th Amendment. As long as the attack on April hadn't been intentional I saw no reason to involve myself in his affairs. Besides, the sight of that whiskey had just about flip-flopped me on the subject of Crocker's involvement in the murder. A man arriving in a strange town to do a killin' doesn't run the risk of fillin' his truck with bootleg hooch.

I'd have to look elsewhere for Oatis' killer.

The rain fell in a maddening drizzle throughout the early evening hours, discouraging many voters who'd delayed their trip to Will Whitney's barber shop. There was no way of knowin' how many stayed away because of the killing, but when the polls closed at nine o'clock and Ida Fry unlocked the ballot box in the presence of Mrs. Morgano and the county elections inspector, there were only 197 ballots.

"That's less than last year," Mrs. Morgano remarked, checking the number against the voter list she'd been keeping.

"Bad weather," Sheriff Lens suggested.

"And murder," Ida Fry added. Her face had gone suddenly white, as if the memory of the day's events had finally drained the life from her.

"Count 'em," the sheriff urged. "I want to see if I got beaten by a dead man."

"We'll need the votes from the schoolhouse too," Mrs. Morgano reminded them. "They usually get a bigger turnout from the north end o' town."

Though the barber shop itself had been closed since six o'clock, Will Whitney had come back after dinner to lock up the building after the women completed their ballot counting. He stood now near the front of the shop, leaning on the barber chair where Hy Crocker had been seated during the killin'.

Certainly Will couldn't have done it. Not from that far away.

I tried to focus my mind on the problem. Forget the invisible knife, forget everything else except who was closest to Oatis at the moment of death. And hadn't Will Whitney taken a few steps toward the booth?

Manny Sears, raising his camera and flash.

Ida Fry and Mrs. Morgano, behind their table.

Sheriff Lens with April and me.

Will Whitney givin' a shave to Hy Crocker.

"Here's the results," Ida Fry announced. "It's 133 for Sheriff Lens, 61 for Henry Oatis, and 2 invalid."

I remembered the photograph Sears had taken of Oatis as he emerged from the booth and started to fall.

"That's only 196, Ida," Mrs. Morgano said,

I remembered the thing that was missing from the photograph, the thing I should have noticed at once.

"Sure, 196." And I knew in that instant how Henry G. Oatis had been killed.

"But there were 197 voters. We've got them all numbered."

"I don't care," Sheriff Lens said. "I'm just happy I won. I'd 'a been spooked if Oatis come out ahead of me!"

The election commissioner reached for the telephone to check with the other polling place while Ida Fry and Mrs. Morgano disputed the missing ballot. "I think I can help you find it, ladies," I said.

"You can?" Mrs. Morgano said, seeming surprised.

I turned to Ida Fry. "Ida—"

"It's official!" the election commissioner shouted. "Final totals are 345 for Sheriff Lens and 228 for Oatis!"

"Ida," I said, repeating her name. "You've got to give us the knife. You can't protect him any longer. There's no reason to protect him any longer."

"I—" Her face had gone dead-white again as I spoke, and I could see she was near to breaking.

Sheriff Lens was by my side, and every eye in the place was on me. "You mean Ida killed him?"

"Of course not. I mean that Henry Oatis committed suicide, and hid the knife in the one place we never looked."

"We looked everywhere!" Sheriff Lens insisted. "In fact, we looked everywhere twice!"

"We looked everywhere except one place—a place where we were forbidden by law to look."

"Where in hell was that?"

"The ballot box."

Sometime in the midst of it all Manny Sears returned to take pictures. Everybody was talkin' at once, trying to sort out what must have happened, and Ida Fry brought a moment of silence when she reached under the table to produce a short, wide-bladed hunting knife with a flat hilt covered by tape.

"Ida!" Mrs. Morgano screeched. "Where'd you get that?"

I answered the question for her. "Out of the ballot box. I saw Ida's face go white as she was takin' out the ballots, but it didn't occur to me that she'd felt the knife inside one of 'em and realized what had happened."

"Just what *did* happen?" Sheriff Lens asked.

"Henry G. Oatis went into that booth and stabbed himself, and maybe we'll never be sure of the real reason for it. Maybe he thought he was goin' to lose the election and couldn't face it. Anyway, he stabbed himself and slipped the knife inside his folded ballot. You'll notice the thick handle had been removed from the knife and the hilt covered with tape. And the long ballot was big enough, even when folded, to hide the length of this fairly short knife."

"And we never saw it?"

"We never *noticed* it," I corrected. "Everyone came out of that booth and dropped their folded ballot in the box. We saw Oatis with the ballot in his hand, but then our attention was distracted by the blood on his chest. We never saw what happened to the ballot, but since Manny Sears's photograph clearly shows the open fingers of his left hand an instant later, he could only have dropped it into the ballot box, along with the knife.

"Actually we should have known there was something suspicious about Oatis right away. He came out of that votin'booth with the pencil in one hand and the folded ballot in the other. Now he had to put down the pencil to fold the ballot, so why'd he pick it up again? It could only have been to make it seem both his hands were occupied—to get us away from the idea he could have stabbed himself."

Manny Sears flashed his powder again, taking a picture of the knife.

"He musta known we'd find the knife when the votes were counted," Sheriff Lens said.

"I think he counted on Ida here behaving just the way she did. For the good of the party she hid the knife and said nothing. With Ida and Mrs. Morgano both removin' the ballots, he had a fifty-fifty chance she'd find the knife first.

But he forgot one thing—his ballot had bloodstains from the knife on it, and Ida had to hide it along with the knife itself. This made the count come out wrong—one too few."

"So there was no murderer," the sheriff said. "Just a bizarre suicide. But what about that Hy Crocker?"

"A bootlegger passin' through town. He had no connection with it."

They settled down after that, Ida Fry to a soft sobbing sound, the others trying to comfort her, Sheriff Lens to the quiet celebration of his victory. I left them and walked down the street with Manny Sears.

"You got some good pictures today," I said.

"You bet!"

"I have to ask you somethin', Manny."

He glanced up at the sky. The rain had stopped and I suppose he was searchin' for stars. "What's that, Doc?"

"Did you know he'd kill himself when you left the knife there for him to find?"

"Huh?"

"A man doesn't commit suicide for no reason while in the act of voting for himself for public office. He commits suicide if he suddenly realizes his secret's been found out. That knife with its taped handle was a very special one, wasn't it? Without even checkin' the newspaper files I'll bet it's the knife that killed Oatis' wife two years ago in North Carolina—or one made to look just like it."

Manny Sears was silent for a time. Finally he said, "Oatis did it, Doc. He killed his wife and blamed it on a passing tramp who'd broken into the house looking for food. They hanged the tramp. He was my brother."

It was my turn to be silent. When I spoke, I said, "So you came up north after Oatis and confronted him with it on Election Day—the day he hoped to start a new career and a new life."

"How'd you know, Doc?"

"Oatis took a long time in that booth, decidin' what to do after he found the knife. It was unusual-lookin' with its taped handle and I figured it had a special meaning to him. If I was right and the knife was left on the shelf in that voting booth for him to find, only you could have left it there. I remembered you fussin' with the booth just before Oatis went in. And it explained why you were so anxious for a picture of Oatis as he emerged from the booth. The picture of guilt."

"I didn't think he'd kill himself, Doc. I was hopin' he'd go to pieces and confess."

"He almost did. The surprise of dying brought the words *murderer* and *stabbed* to his lips. He was talkin' about killing his wife." I shook my head wonderingly. "But his pride still made him hide the knife. He couldn't face the accusations, but even in death he tried to disguise his final despairing act."

"What will you do, Doc?"

The stars were coming out now. I could see them overhead. "Me? Nothing. Go to the hospital and see April. There's no need to tell the whole story to anyone."

"And so it never got told till now," Dr. Sam Hawthorne said. "It was one of our little secrets, up in Northmont. I see your glass is empty and it's gettin' late. Another little—ah—libation? No? But come by again next week and I'll tell you about another crime—an honest-to-goodness murder this time. It didn't happen till the summer after the voting booth affair, and I was just beginning to think crime had passed Northmont by at last. But then there was the county fair, and a time capsule with a body inside it. . . ."

THE PROBLEM OF
THE COUNTY FAIR

"**S**ay, now, I was gonna tell you about the county fair this time, wasn't I? Pull up a chair while I pour us a small—ah—libation. Close to the fire where it's warm. This here's a summer story, but it's liable to chill you to the bone. . . ."

It was in the summer of '27 (Dr. Sam Hawthorne went on), and I was settling into my medical practice nice and steady. We hadn't had a killing in Northmont since that Election Day mystery the year before, and for the first time I was thinkin' the Grim Reaper had gone and forgotten about us. Even my nurse April remarked on it as we were leavin' for the county fair that warm August morning.

"It's almost a year since the last killing, Dr. Sam. You think law an' order has finally come to Northmont?"

"I try not to think about it at all," I told her. "Afraid I might break the spell."

She piled into the yellow Pierce-Arrow Runabout and I took the wheel. It was a short drive down Main Street and out the River Road to the fairgrounds. Usually it was a deserted place, on a slight hill not far from the river. The first thing we saw as it came into view was the grandstand surrounded by a high board fence painted a bright yellow. That and the little Ferris wheel off in the distance.

We parked the Runabout in a great dusty field at the rear of the grandstand, and I could see from the number of cars that as usual the fair was attractin' visitors from all the surrounding counties. It was a big fair, a good fair, with lots of crowd-pleasing attractions. Though April shied away from the sideshow—the snake charmer, the fat lady, the scantily clad dancing girls, and the two-headed calf—they were popular with the men and boys who always found a way to separate themselves from the womenfolk.

There were gamblers too, working their seedy con games, and they seemed to mostly prey on the young who knew no better. The older men, perhaps tired of the hootchy-kootchy girls after all these years, generally drifted down to the cattle show to inspect the animals. There they stood around while their women went to the sheds where the cakes and pies and needlework were on display. The smaller children, tired and dusty-faced, usually accompanied the women unless they could be palmed off on some willing older brother or sister.

"It's just so wonderful, Dr. Sam!" April exclaimed, her face alight with childish joy. "I wish the fair lasted the whole year long."

"But then it wouldn't be so wonderful," I argued logically. "In fact, I expect we'd all get bored with it quite soon."

"Look, there's Mayor Chadwick."

I never saw Felix Chadwick without remembering how his predecessor had been murdered at a Fourth o' July celebration three summers earlier. But it was doubtful that the same fate would ever befall Mayor Chadwick. He was a chicken farmer who had little use for even the ceremonial aspects of politics. I was surprised he'd even shown up—until I remembered about the time capsule.

The time capsule was Emma Thane's idea. She was the closest thing we had to a town historian, and she'd come up with some obscure evidence that in 1627 merchants and adventurers from William Bradford's Plymouth Colony had set up a trading post near the present site of Northmont. "In a way it's our tercentennial," she'd announced at a meeting of the town council early that year, "and it should be celebrated properly."

Since Northmont had always been eager to fill the sky with fireworks on the Fourth o' July, there was some debate as to what form our tercentennial celebration should take. More fireworks? Bigger ones?

"No," said Emma Thane, pounding her knobby walking stick to be heard above the others. "We should bury a time capsule, to be opened a hundred years from now."

Well, the idea caught on right away, especially after Gus Antwerp from the Metal Works said he could make us a capsule out of sheet steel and even bury it for us, all at no cost to the town. It would be his contribution to the celebration, and Mayor Chadwick was quick to accept the offer.

So here was the mayor himself bearin' down on April and me, trying to put aside chickens for a day of politics and pageantry. "Don't mean to horn in on you two. Mighty fine day, ain't it? Beamin' sun, not a cloud in the sky! It would be really goin' some to top a day like this."

"A fine day," I agreed. "And there's a goodly turnout for the fair. I see a lot of cars from outside the county."

"The bettin' attracts 'em," he confided, as if he was revealing some dark secret known only to the town council. "Are you ridin' in the afternoon races, Doc?"

It was a custom of our county fair to hold harness races on the oval track in front of the grandstand, with local citizens driving the sulkies. But it was not a sport that had ever appealed to me. "Not this year, Felix," I replied. I just never could bring myself to address him as Mayor.

"Well, I'll see you later at the time capsule. You brung somethin' to put in it?"

"Oh, sure."

He smiled at April and moved on, immediately swallowed up by the crowd headin' for the sideshow attractions. "That man!" April exploded when he was out of earshot. "I wonder if he'll go around passin' out free chickens again next election day. That's the only way he won last time."

"Oh, Felix isn't so bad. He's not up to the job, but does Northmont really need a mayor who's up to the job?"

April ran into some young women she knew and they went off to the needlework exhibit. I wandered toward the sideshows, promising to meet her at the grandstand in an hour for the time-capsule ceremonies.

I was lingering near one of the gambling tables, watching a quick-fingered three-card Monte operator, when a voice behind me said, "Dr. Hawthorne, I've had the most wonderful news!"

I recognized her voice even before I turned to accept the peck on the cheek with which she always greeted me. Gert Friar was a good friend, one of the livelier and more intelligent of Northmont's eligible young women. I'd made an effort to court her myself the previous summer, but it was obvious even then that her heart belonged to a fellow named Max McNear.

"The news must be about Max," I said at once, looking into her laughing blue eyes and hiding my disappointment that she still refused to even call me by my first name.

"He's coming home! He telephoned me from Cleveland three days ago. He should be here today."

"It'll be good seein' him again," I lied, smilin' all the time. Max McNear was something of an itinerant musician and troublemaker. He'd organized a small group to play country music for local square dances, and Gert had even sung with them a few times. That was how she met Max in the first place. But after a few dances where he'd gotten drunk on bootleg hooch and beaten up some local lads, he found himself pretty much ostracized by the community. By the end of last summer, Gert Friar was the only defender he had left. His return to Northmont now would bring a few grimaces to some of the townsfolk.

"I told him about the time-capsule ceremony and he said he'd be here in time for it."

"That's fine, Gert."

She fell into step beside me, the smile suddenly faded. "You've never really liked Max, have you, Dr. Hawthorne?"

"When you call me that I feel like your father. Please call me Sam."

"All right." The smiled returned fleetingly. "Sam."

"Good! You know, I'm really not much older than you are."

"It seems you've been here forever, though. I remember you nursing me through the measles."

"I was right out of medical school then. It was the winter of '22 when I came here."

"Only five and a half years?"

"They were important years to you, Gert. You grew into a woman."

"I'm only twenty."

"And Max is—how old?"

"Thirty-one. I know—I've heard it all from my folks plenty of times. He's too old for me. He's no good. He drinks." Her voice grew softer. "But I love him, Sam."

"I remember you were pretty broken up when he left town."

"I guess it was the suddenness of it. One day he was here, the next day he was gone. He didn't even leave me a note."

"The police were after him. Sheriff Lens was going to throw him in jail after he beat up Mayor Chadwick's boy."

"I know. The drinking was no good for him. But he told me on the telephone that he's reformed now. He hasn't had a drink in months."

"Good for him!"

"You will be friendly to him, won't you, Sam? He has so few friends here. It would mean a lot to me."

"For you I'll be friendly to him." I glanced at my pocket watch and saw that it was almost noon. "But we'd better be gettin' over to the grandstand for the ceremonies or you might lose your job." Gert worked as a secretary for Gus Antwerp, and it seemed likely he'd want her on hand for the burying of his sheet-metal time capsule.

We joined the flow of the crowd toward the yellow-walled grandstand as the barkers made one last effort to lure folks into the hootchy-kootchy tent. But even the kids were deserting temporarily the pleasures and thrills of the Ferris wheel and the other rides to witness this moment of history. The first person we saw as we entered the grandstand was old Emma Thane, leanin' on her knobby walking stick and breathin' fire. She spotted Gert at once and blocked our path.

"Well, young lady, your man is back, I see."

"Max! He's here?"

"Darn near ran me off the road with that truck o' his! You tell him to be more considerate to people. If he's back in Northmont to make more trouble you tell him we'd just as soon he stayed away."

"I'm sure he wasn't trying to harm you," Gert Friar murmured. I could see she was mainly interested in gettin' past this woman and flyin' into Max McNear's arms.

But Emma Thane wasn't yet ready to release us. "Folks hereabouts got to have the gumption to stand up to the likes of Max McNear. They got to tell him he has to live as part of the community. The law says we don't drink intoxicatin' beverages, and that law is the same for you and me and Max McNear."

"I'm sure he understands that, Miss Thane."

"Don't know that he does! Drove all over that road like he was drunk again. Just like the old days." But now she'd stepped aside and we were finally able to get by her. I made a parting comment on the beautiful weather and we entered the grandstand, where I got my first look at Gus Antwerp's time capsule.

He'd dug a hole for it in the very center of the oval field, around which ran the harness-racing track that would be put to use later in the afternoon. From my angle the capsule looked like a great silver cigar suspended upright from a block and tackle, its bottom already hidden by the piles of dirt around the hole. At the top of its eight-foot length, a hinged metal door stood open to receive the mementos of the community.

Mayor Chadwick, still tryin' to shake off his chicken-farmer's image, stood up and said a few appropriate words through a static-filled loudspeaker just purchased at county expense. Then Emma Thane came forward to be honored for her idea. The mayor helped her up the dirt pile so she could reach the door in the top of the erect capsule and deposit her memento— the day's newspaper. A line of school children followed. Some of the smaller ones had to be held in the mayor's arms to reach the door of the time capsule where they deposited a selection of their textbooks.

I left Gert Friar in the stands, still searching for Max's familiar face, and made my way onto the field. Gus Antwerp, looking almost clean in his neatly pressed suit, shook my hand with vigor.

"Good to see you here, Doc! Got a smidge o' something for my capsule?"

I pulled a booklet from my inside pocket. "Medical records for last year from the grammar school. A hundred years from now they might be interested in what made our kids sick."

"Great!"

I stared up at the sheet-metal capsule. "How long did it take you to build this thing?"

"Just part o' one night is all. I rolled the sheet and welded the seam, then fixed a flat piece to the bottom and put the door in the top."

Mayor Chadwick motioned me forward, announcing my name almost inaudibly over the faulty loudspeaker. It didn't matter, though. Just about everyone knew me and a little cheer went up. I could see April at the edge of the crowd, waving to me.

I climbed up the dirt pile with my record book, taking time to peer down into the time capsule, inspectin' the thing out of sheer curiosity. The hinged door itself was round like the top of the capsule, and about two feet in diameter. With the sunlight from overhead I could see all the way to the bottom of the capsule, where the papers and books and other mementos were beginning to form a small pile. The capsule seemed too big for what little we were putting into it, but I was never one to criticize another man's labors. Besides, the thing looked great hangin' there from its ropes—almost like one of those spaceships on the cover of *Amazing Stories* magazine, pointed toward the stars.

I tapped the thin metal wall with my knuckles, wondering if it would really last a whole century, then I dropped my record book in among the other things and climbed down. A few small kitchen and farm implements went in next, together with some prizewinning recipes from the fair's baking contest. A picture of a prize bull, a Sears Roebuck catalogue, and Mayor Chadwick's copy of the town charter completed the collection.

As we all watched, the mayor closed the top of the capsule and Gus Antwerp sealed it with his bulky welding equipment. Then, like a ship's captain guiding his vessel through a narrow strait, Gus pulled out the metal support beneath the upright capsule and signaled for it to be lowered the rest of the way into the earth. There was a screeching of metal as it disappeared from view. Then the mayor handed Emma Thane a shovel decorated with a red ribbon and helped her throw in the first symbolic bit of earth.

I went to join April. "You were fine, Dr. Sam," she announced. "The whole thing was so moving! I wish I could be here a hundred years from now to see it dug up."

Before I could reply, Gert Friar joined us. Her deep blue eyes were wide with fright. "Dr. Haw—Sam, you've got to help me!"

"What is it?"

"I've been looking all over for Max and I finally found his truck, but he's not in it!"

"He's probably in the crowd somewhere."

"Sam, I think there are bloodstains on the front seat of the truck."

April and I exchanged glances, "I'll go look," I said quietly

The truck was a Ford and its canvas sides were painted with the words *Max's Music Makers*. It had been a familiar sight on the back roads of Northmont during the previous summer, before Max McNear's sudden disappearance. Now it had brought him back here—to what end?

"They're bloodstains," I confirmed. "But there could be lots of explanations. He might have cut his finger. Or it could even be animal blood."

"Do you believe that?" Gert asked.

I didn't answer directly. "We'll go look for him."

"I *have* looked. I've looked everywhere."

I tried to make a joke of it. "Bet you didn't look in the hootchy-kootchy tent."

"Sam, please."

"All right, I'll help you. April, you know Max McNear, don't you? We'll fan out over the fairgrounds and meet back at this truck in thirty minutes."

I took the sideshow route, checking the dancing girls' tent and the fat lady's booth. But there was no sign of the missing Max McNear. Near the end of the half hour I came upon Emma Thane and I questioned her about the truck. "You said it nearly hit you, Miss Thane. What time was that?"

"Mebbe about eleven. Or a bit earlier. Did you see him?"

"We're looking. He seems to have disappeared again."

Just like a year ago, I couldn't help thinking.

Back at the truck, I learned that April and Gert had been no more successful. "I have to find him," Gert insisted. "Those bloodstains mean he's hurt."

Or dead, I added silently. But then another thought came to me. "Gert, are you sure it was Max you talked to on the telephone the other night? Long-distance lines can sound garbled at times, you know."

I saw her hesitate. "Well, of course it was Max. Why would he say he was if he wasn't?"

"I don't know," I admitted.

"I'd be in a sorry state if I couldn't recognize Max's voice."

I watched some children running in and out of the crowd by the cake booth. Off in the distance the men were assembling for the afternoon's weight-hauling contest with teams of draft horses. Everything seemed as it should be, except for Max McNear's bloodstained truck. "Look," I said, "maybe Max didn't come back today."

"Didn't come back? Of course he came back!"

"Only Emma Thane saw him, and in truth she really saw just the truck. Gert, this is going to be very hard on you, but I have to say it. Maybe Max never came back because he never went away. He had a lot of enemies a year ago. Maybe one of them killed him."

Her sharp intake of breath was almost like a scream. "No, no, it was Max on the phone, I tell you!"

"All right," I agreed with a sigh. "Let's keep looking."

This time we agreed to meet at the grandstand for the harness races. April stayed with me and as soon as we were alone she asked, "Do you really think he's dead, Dr. Sam?"

"I don't know what to think, April. Can you remember how things were a year ago? Who were Max's enemies?"

"All I know is what the talk was at the time. He beat up Mayor Chadwick's son awfully bad, you know."

"I remember that."

"Heck, anybody he met might have disliked Max McNear. He was that sort. Even Gert Friar mighta disliked him if she caught him with some nineteen-year-old out behind somebody's barn."

"Some gal was hornin' in on Gert?"

"No one gal, but I know there were some. With Max McNear you could tell by just lookin' at him."

"Gert was already out of high school then. Was she working for Gus Antwerp?"

April shook her head. "Remember? Gus didn't move here till the fall, after Max was long gone. Gert was at loose ends and Gus needed a girl around the place, so he hired her."

I had one more place to look—the stables where the trotters were being prepared for the afternoon races. April came with me and we went through the stalls—but there was no Max McNear.

"Change your mind 'bout racin'?" Mayor Chadwick asked, encountering us there.

"No chance," I said. "I don't even drive buggies any more. Horseless carriages for me."

He walked with us out to the grandstand where most of the people at the fair were once again assembled. Even the gamblers and con artists had closed up their games and were busy taking bets on the races. Out in the center of the oval Gus Antwerp and a few others were finishing the burial of the time capsule. The block and tackle still hung over them—like an empty scaffold awaiting its next victim.

A cheer went up from the crowd as the first of the sulkies appeared on the oval track. But somethin' else had caught my eye—something white that fluttered in the afternoon breeze on the ground near the buried capsule. "Go find Gert," I told April. "I'll be right back."

I dashed across the dirt track and onto the grassy oval, headin' toward the men with their shovels. Gus Antwerp waved as he saw me approaching.

The thing on the ground was a book, its white pages flappin' open. It was one of the books the school children had brought to deposit in the time capsule —a seventh-grade arithmetic.

Its pages were splattered with blood.

I found Mayor Chadwick in the reviewing stand, watchin' the parade of the sulkies. "You're just in time, Doc. Got your bets down? You know Sheriff Lens is drivin' one o' them things?"

"Mayor, I want you to order the time capsule dug up."

"The—what did you say?"

"The time capsule. You have to dig it up."

"What in tarnation for? You forget to put some love letters in it? Ha, ha!"

"I'm serious, Mayor. Max McNear has disappeared."

His face hardened. "McNear disappeared a year ago."

"And now he's disappeared again."

"Well, he sure ain't in that time capsule!"

I held out the blood-splattered arithmetic book. "*This* is supposed to be in the capsule and I found it out in the field. I think the capsule was opened again after it was buried."

"Impossible!"

"I know it's impossible, but impossible things have happened in Northmont before this. I should know—I'm becoming something of an expert on them."

"You're serious, ain't you, Doc?" he asked, squinting at me.

"Damned serious."

He sighed and started for the steps. "Let's see what Sheriff Lens thinks."

The sheriff was sitting in his sulky trying to button the checkered silk shirt over his ample stomach. "I agreed to this in a weak moment," he rumbled as he saw us approaching. "I don't need none o' your jokes, Doc."

"Doc's not tellin' jokes today," Chadwick said. "He wants us to dig up the time capsule 'cause Max McNear's disappeared again."

"What are you talkin' about?"

I explained quickly, telling Sheriff Lens exactly what had happened. When I'd finished he snorted and climbed down off the sulky. "I think you got a screw loose, Doc, but to tell the truth I'd welcome any excuse not to have to drive this fool thing. Come on, let's dig."

Gus Antwerp put down his shovel as we approached and listened to our request. "We just got it buried and you want us to dig it up again?"

"That's right," I said.

"And when we get it dug up?"

"We want to open it and take a look inside."

"You're crazy! You're all crazy!"

I held out the bloodstained book. "This is crazy too, but it's a fact. There's blood in McNear's truck and blood on this book from the time capsule. I want it opened."

"But he *couldn't* be in there!" Antwerp insisted.

"I want to look all the same."

The balding man shrugged and handed me his shovel. "You got ten years on me, Doc. Go ahead and dig."

I started digging and the others joined in. When Antwerp saw we were serious he helped uncover the upper part of the capsule and got the ropes back around it. "The earth is still loose," he said. "We can probably pull it out with the block an' tackle."

A few of us got at the end of the rope but the capsule wouldn't budge. "Get a team of them draft horses," Sheriff Lens suggested. "They'll have it out in jigtime."

Someone went to get a team while the rest of us dug a little more. Up in the stands a low hum of conversation had grown into shouts of inquiry. They wanted to know what was going on and when the races would start. None of us answered them.

When the team was hooked up they pulled the metal cylinder free of the earth in less than a minute. We lowered it to the ground on its side and Gus Antwerp went to work with a chisel, knocking off the spot welds he'd made. Watchin' him work, I began to feel a little foolish.

Gert Friar and April had come out to watch as the time capsule was reopened. I tried to keep Gert back but she insisted on looking. And I heard her scream even before I could see inside myself.

Then April was holdin' her and I was pushin' past the whitefaced Sheriff Lens to peer in at the impossible. There, among the scattered books and tools consigned to the 21st Century, was the body of Max McNear.

W e tried to look at it logically.

Someone had built an underground tunnel to the capsule and gotten the body in that way.

Except that we dug all the loose earth out of the hole and found no tunnel. Found nothing but dirt.

Or maybe Gus Antwerp had the body hidden inside the capsule all the time. Except that Gus didn't even know McNear, and I'd looked into the capsule myself and saw there was no body inside.

Or maybe the capsule had been dug up between noon and the time I found the bloodstained book.

Except that Antwerp and a couple of others were there filling in the hole. "I left for maybe ten minutes to get a hotdog," Gus said, "but there were people in the grandstand all the time, eatin' their lunches and watchin' us. That capsule never budged from the ground once it was buried."

We looked at it logically.

And logically it couldn't have happened.

"What killed him, Doc?" Sheriff Lens asked when we'd pulled the body out of the metal cylinder and I'd had a chance to examine it.

"Blow to the head with some sort of blunt instrument."

"He been dead long?"

"Hard to say in this hot weather, but he's been dead a good many hours. All bleeding's stopped and rigor mortis pretty far advanced. I'd say he was already dead when Emma saw his truck this morning."

"Which means?"

"Which means he wasn't drivin' it. Maybe he was dead on the front seat and the killer was driving."

Sheriff Lens just grunted at that. "But look, Doc, if the bleedin' had stopped, how'd the blood get all over the arithmetic book you found? That looked like pretty fresh blood to me."

"I don't know," I admitted.

"Do dead bodies bleed?"

"Not as a rule. But the blood drains to the lowest point and if there's a large wound at that point the blood could still be oozing out some time after death." I saw April coming and went to meet her. "How's Gert taking it?"

"Not very good, I'm afraid. You might have to give her a sleepin' powder. It's a terrible shock having him come back after a year only to get killed."

"A shock and a damned shame. Who'd hold a grudge that long?"

April led me to the needlework tent where Gert was resting on a cot. Old Emma Thane hovered over her, pressing a damp cloth to her forehead, and Gus Antwerp was holdin' her hand. "I keep tellin' her it'll be all right," he said. "But she's just not comin' around."

"It's been a shock," I said. "She'll be all right after a good rest. Why don't you all go away now?"

When Gert was alone with April and me, she opened her eyes and said, "I saw the top of his head when that door opened, Sam. His hair was all bloody."

She shuddered at her own words.

"Gert, I have to ask you some questions. It's either Sheriff Lens or me, and I thought you'd rather talk to me."

"What is it, Doc?"

"Who knew about that phone call from Cleveland? Who knew he was coming back today?"

"No one."

"Think harder, Gert. You told me when you saw me today. Maybe you told someone else too. Did your boss know?"

She shook her head. "Gus never knew Max, so there was no reason for me to tell him. Oh, he'd probably heard me mention Max, but he never met him."

"How about Emma Thane?"

"Why would I tell her?"

"I don't know. She just didn't seem too surprised when she saw his truck this morning."

She sat up with a little jerk. "There was one person I told. He saw me yesterday and asked if I'd be at the ceremony for burying the time capsule. I said yes, and then I mentioned that Max would be back for it too."

"Who was it you told?"

"Mayor Chadwick."

I found the mayor out by the grandstand, staring at the time capsule that still lay on its side by the dirt piles. He glanced at me with a bleak expression and said, "Damned clever way to get rid of a body, I do say that! Can you imagine their faces a hundred years from now if they opened it up an' found a skeleton?"

"About like our faces this afternoon," I suggested. The sun was low beyond the yellow fence. It was almost evening.

"Yeah," he agreed. "But who killed him, Doc?"

"It had to be someone who knew he was coming back. You knew, didn't you, Felix?"

"What's that?"

"Gert told you he was coming back today."

"She may have mentioned it. I didn't pay much attention."

"Whatever happened to that son of yours? The one Max beat up so bad."

"Joe's away at college," he answered stiffly.

"In the summer?"

He was silent for a moment. Then he said, "I might as well tell you. My wife would, if you asked her. Joe's never been right in the head since that beating. He's away at a hospital. He had to drop out of college."

I stared at where the sun had been, above the yellow fence.

"Enough to drive a father to murder?"

He took a plug of chewing tobacco from his pocket. "Hell, I'd of just killed him and let him lay! This business of hidin' the body in a time capsule is beyond my imagination."

I tried to remember he was only a chicken farmer posing as a mayor. Maybe a murder scheme like this was beyond him.

"All right," I said at last. "I'll see you later, Felix."

"Findin' that body sure shot the hell out of our fair," he complained, more to himself than to me. "Had to cancel the harness racing, and a lot of the side-show attractions people are packin' up. They don't want no truck with the police."

"It was a fine fair while it lasted," I told him.

I went off, anxious to reach the sideshow attractions before they'd all vanished. I found the barker at the girlie show and motioned him aside. "I need some information," I said.

He scowled. "Not from me, you don't."

"I'm not with the police. I'm a doctor."

"We didn't see a thing. Me an' the girls are clean."

"Sure you are. Look, sometimes sideshows do the stunt of burying some-one alive—right?"

"Yeah," he said with a shrug. "I know a guy does it. Stays buried for the whole run of the fair. Folks pay a quarter to look down a tube an' see him resting in his coffin."

"How's it done?" I asked.

"Huh?"

"What's the trick?" I took a bill from my wallet and held it suggestively.

He grabbed at the bill. "Don't say I told you."

"I won't."

"The body in the coffin is a wax dummy. As soon as he's buried he crawls out through a tunnel. Indian fakirs been doin' it for centuries."

"A tunnel . . ."

"Sure, what'd you think?"

I thanked him and went away. He hadn't helped me at all. There was no tunnel to the time capsule, and even if there had been, how could the body have passed through the solid metal sides of the cylinder itself?

I went back to the grandstand, deciding to have a final look at the capsule. Mayor Chadwick was gone and dusk had settled over the field. A few kids playing on the mounds of dirt scattered as I approached.

For a long time I just stood and stared.

Suppose there were *two* capsules, and we'd dug up the second one. No, the books and papers and tools had all been there. Even my school medical log was there with the body. It was the same capsule.

But with a body inside.

I tapped my knuckles against the metal cylinder, as I'd done earlier.

Then I tapped again.

There wasn't the same ringing sound I'd heard this afternoon. Now the sound was different, more solid.

Then I remembered something else. I remembered the screeching of metal . . . .

"So you know how it was done?" a voice behind me asked.

I turned and saw Emma Thane standing there in the dusk, her knobby walking stick held firmly in one hand.

For an instant I almost leaped at her, thinkin' to disarm her. But then she coughed gently and repeated her question and I relaxed. I even smiled. "I think I do, Miss Thane. I think it's just come to me."

"He should never have come back. He wasn't wanted here. The past simply caught up with him."

"Oddly enough, I think it was the future that caught up with him."

"How's that?"

I tapped her walking stick with my finger. "You should be careful of this thing, Miss Thane. Someone might mistake it for a blunt instrument."

I walked away, leaving her standing by the time capsule that was part of her dream.

A pril was standing with Sheriff Lens by the needlework displays when I returned. "Where's Gert?" I asked.

"Her boss is drivin' her home," April replied.

I was done takin' chances with people's lives. "Come on, we've got to stop them! There could be another murder!" Already I was running toward my car.

April came after me. "You can't mean you think Gert killed Max!"

"Of course not."

The sheriff and April piled into the two-passenger front seat with me. "But Gus never even *knew* the dead man," Sheriff Lens argued.

"That's why he killed him," I replied, sounding like one of those paradoxes in G. K. Chesterton's stories. "Didn't you notice Gus holdin' Gert's hand earlier? It's not so strange for a middle-aged man like Gus Antwerp to imagine himself in love with his pretty twenty-year-old secretary. He never knew Max McNear, but he'd heard plenty about him from Gert and others. He imagined

Gert would be swept off her feet by the return of her lover, before he could do anything about it. It wasn't Max's past but Gus Antwerp's future that supplied the motive."

Up ahead we could see the lights of Antwerp's truck. I beeped the horn and made as if I intended to pass him. Then I cut in front of the truck, forcing it to stop. Gus tried to yank Gert from the seat but when he saw Sheriff Lens he let go and ran off toward the nearby woods. The sheriff took off after him.

"Are you all right?" I asked Gert.

She was rubbing her bruised wrist. "I—I guess so. He's gone crazy, Sam. He wanted me to run off with him tonight!"

"I was afraid he'd decide to run and take you with him. Once we found the body he knew it was only a matter of time before we figured it all out."

Sheriff Lens reappeared, alone. "Antwerp went into the river," he said. "I don't think he made it across."

We drove back to town, with the sheriff following at the wheel of Gus Antwerp's truck. He notified the state police to watch for Gus, just in case he'd survived the river. Then, back in the sheriff's office, it was my turn to talk some more.

"It was an odd, impossible crime—but once I figured how the body got into that time capsule, Gus was the only possible killer. You see, the body wasn't put in before the capsule was sealed, or after it was opened. So it passed through those sheet metal walls somehow while the capsule was buried."

"You're makin' it sound even more impossible," the sheriff complained.

"Not really. When I tapped my knuckles on the capsule this evening it sounded different than before. More solid. And I remembered that screeching of metal as it was bein' lowered into the ground. If you examine it closely you'll see there are now *two* thicknesses of metal instead of one. Gus Antwerp put Max's body in a second cylinder, maybe an inch narrower than the one we saw. It was already in the ground, directly beneath the upright time capsule.

"After our mementos were in place, Gus pulled out the metal support —which was also the bottom of the time capsule. Everything fell through to the lower cylinder, which was open at the top, and where Max McNear's body was already hidden. Then Gus guided the larger top cylinder down so it fitted completely over the smaller bottom one beneath the ground. I suppose he greased the sides, but there was still that screeching of metal as they slid together. It was such a tight fit that when the capsule was dug up it looked like a single metal cylinder."

"How'd he do all that without being seen?" Sheriff Lens asked.

"It would have been easy last night, with no one around the fairgrounds. If anyone did see him unloading the second cylinder from his truck he could have said it was a spare. And once the narrower cylinder, containing the body, was beneath the ground there was no danger of its being seen. You'll remember the dirt was piled around the rim of the hole, and the top cylinder was partly in already, actually resting over the bottom one."

"But how'd Antwerp know Max was comin' back?" April asked. "Gert says she never told him."

"We can make a good guess at that. Max was due back today, but he must have come a day early in order for Gus to have killed him and planted the body last night. It's logical to believe Max tried to phone Gert again about his change in plans. She was out and her boss took the call. Instead of givin' Gert the message, Gus Antwerp's love-crazed brain devised this scheme. He told me himself he made the capsule in less than one night. It was a simple job for him to make a second, slightly narrower, cylinder that would slide inside the first one.

"Gus waited for Max's arrival last night and probably killed him with a blow to the head in the front seat of Max's truck, leaving those bloodstains. Then he took the body and the cylinders to the fairground in his own truck. This morning he drove Max's truck to the fairground, nearly hittin' Emma Thane, so it would look as if Max arrived today on schedule and then disappeared again."

Sheriff Lens grunted. "I've heard'a killers burying the bodies in some pretty clever places, but this is the first one I know who tried to bury a body in the next century!"

D r. Sam Hawthorne took a sip of his drink as he concluded the story. "They found Antwerp's body in the river the next morning, and that was the end of it. Another small—ah—libation before you go? What's that? You're not satisfied? I didn't explain about the bloodstained arithmetic book?

"Well, April settled that the next day. One of the boys in line at the time capsule had a sudden nosebleed all over his book. He couldn't put it in the capsule like that, so he just dropped it on the ground, behind some dirt. It had nothing to do with the killing, except that it got me to dig up the capsule and find the body. I like to leave that part out of the story, 'cause it makes me look sort of foolish. I wish you hadn't asked.

"Next time? Well, 1927 was the year of the first talking movie. Northmont was a long way from Hollywood, but when a film company came there to shoot an early talking picture it had unexpected and deadly results. But that's for next time. Come now, let me refill your glass."

THE PROBLEM OF
THE OLD OAK TREE

D r. Sam Hawthorne poured a little brandy from the decanter and settled back in his chair. "September of '27 is a time I 'specially remember, because that's when the folks came to make a talking picture in Northmont. And that's also when a man was apparently strangled to death by an oak tree. But I'm getting ahead of my story. First I should tell you something about the movies in those days, and 'specially about talking pictures."

W e didn't get to see many movies around Northmont in those days (Dr. Sam continued) because there weren't any theaters. Viewing the popular silent films of the day meant a drive into Springfield or Hartford, or even all the way to Boston. A few people had made the trip the year before to see John Barrymore in *Don Juan,* the first film with synchronized sound effects, and people were already talking about *The Jazz Singer* with Al Jolson. Its New York opening was only a few weeks away that September, and the advance publicity promised Vitaphoned songs and some stretches of dialogue in sound for the first time.

So it wasn't surprising that movie-makers around the country were jumping on the talkie bandwagon. Nor was it surprising that some of them wanted to make movies about aviators. The silent film *Wings* had opened in August to critical and popular acclaim, and would go on to capture the first Academy Award for best picture of the year. And Lindbergh's triumph was still very much in the news.

That was why Granger Newmark came to Northmont—to make the first talking picture about fliers. Not the World War I aces of *Wings,* but the barnstorming pilots who turned up at county fairs and rural weekends to risk their lives for a few dollars' pay. Granger Newmark was very much a product of Hollywood, where motion-picture studios were beginning to congregate after their early years in New Jersey. He arrived in my office that first afternoon wearing riding britches and leather boots, with a zipper jacket topped by a white silk scarf around his throat. And I'll admit I didn't know quite what to make of him at first.

"What seems to be the trouble?" I asked, showing him to my office chair. "Sore throat?"

"Hardly! I've come here because they tell me you're the only doctor in this burg."

"That's correct."

"I'm producing and directing the barnstorming film being shot near here. You probably recognized my name."

I'd heard of the film but that was about all. "I've been too busy this week to read the papers, Mr. Newmark. You'll have to forgive me."

"I see." He sighed and took out a slim black cigar. "Well, I can see I'll have to educate you. I'm filming the first sound motion picture about barnstorming pilots. We needed a country setting for some of the outdoor scenes and we chose Northmont."

"Why's that?" I asked, genuinely curious.

"I drove through here last year and liked the area. That big open field north of town is ideal for a small landing strip, and I obtained permission from the owner to use it."

"What field would that be?"

"Gates House Farm. Fellow named Hi Gates leased me the use of the land. It's a perfect setting for *Wings of Glory*."

I nodded. Hi Gates was the shiftless son of a moderately successful farmer who'd died a few years back. Hi, with a broken marriage and a drinking problem behind him, was on the lookout for any money-making scheme which would be labor-free on his part. The idea of filming a movie in one of his idle fields would appeal to him.

"What do you need me for?" I asked.

"Some of the stunt work in the picture's going to be dangerous. A parachute jump and a plane nosing over on takeoff. I want a doctor standing by and we didn't bring one with us."

"Look here, I've got my own patients to tend to. I can't neglect them to watch you making a movie."

"I'd only need you for a few days, during the stunt shooting, and I'd pay you well. They could come get you if there was an emergency."

I had to admit that the past week's business had quieted down to the birth of two babies to farm wives. There was no real reason why I couldn't accept his offer, especially since I knew my nurse April could hold down the office and notify me if I was needed. "All right," I decided finally. "But I couldn't spare more than three days."

"Good! I'll need you Wednesday morning, out at the Gates House Farm. Nine o'clock sharp!"

Granger Newmark was gone before I realized that he hadn't mentioned how much he'd be paying me. But by that time I knew I was hooked.

O n Wednesday morning I left April in charge of the office, with instructions for reaching me, and drove my six-year-old Pierce-Arrow Runabout over the rutted roads to Hi Gates's farm. Even before nine o'clock the place was alive with activity. And sure enough—there was a flying machine at one end of the long field.

Newmark greeted me with enthusiasm and explained that the aircraft was a D. H. 60 Moth, a biplane with two open cockpits and a single engine. Though it looked just like the planes I remembered from the Great War, he told me it had been developed only two years earlier by Captain Geoffrey de Havilland, a British officer.

"It's perfect for the picture," he said enthusiastically. "Looks like those wartime crates all the barnstormers fly, but it's safer and it has a new sixty-horsepower Cirrus engine inside. Best of all, we can tow it along the road with its wings folded, so it's easy to move from place to place during shooting."

Gazing down the grassy runway toward the distant woods I was reminded of one landscape feature worth noting. "The haunted oak," I said aloud.

"What?"

"That old oak tree—the one that's partly dead. Some folks around here say it's haunted. Supposed to have been planted over the grave of a Revolutionary War traitor back a hundred and fifty years ago. I doubt if it's really that old, though."

Granger Newmark studied the distant tree, which stood alone some distance from the woods. "Ugly-looking thing," he agreed. "Can't think of a way we could work it into the script, though. Has it ever killed anyone?"

Though the question was asked in jest, I had a serious reply. "Boy fell from it a few years back and broke his neck. For folks around here that was enough to revive all the old superstitions."

A tall handsome man in a pilot's costume joined us then. I recognized him even before the introductions as a silent-screen favorite, Robert Raines. Newmark performed the introductions and Raines shook my hand firmly. "I hope I won't be needing your services, Doc."

"Hear that voice?" the director asked, aglow with pleasure. "When the women of America hear it, we're going to have ourselves a big *big* star! Half the silent actors will be out of work once the public hears their squeaky little voices!"

Raines grinned boyishly at the compliment. "It's just the voice that God gave me. I do the best I can with it."

"Are you going to be jumping?" I asked, noticing the parachute strapped to his back.

"We're using a double for the actual jump," Newmark explained. "Can't risk our big star on anything like that."

"Don't know as you should risk anyone," I said. "There's not much treatment I can give if his chute doesn't open."

"Don't be silly!" Newmark sputtered. "People were parachuting before there were airplanes! It's perfectly safe."

His statement seemed like such a downright impossibility that I admit I laughed at it. Later when I looked it up I found out he was right—there had been parachute jumps from hot-air balloons before the year 1800. I learned quickly that Granger Newmark rarely made mistakes.

About then we were joined by a young man dressed exactly like the star. "This is our double," Newmark said. "Charlie Bone."

Bone's rough, angular face bore little resemblance to the star's handsome features, but I could see they shared a similar height and build. The camera's eye on a distant falling figure would see them as one. "How are you?" Bone asked me, not expecting an answer. His interest was already elsewhere. "See those clouds rollin' in? Could be trouble."

"My cameras are ready to roll," the director said. "We'll need a shot of you two climbing into the plane, and then the takeoff. You jump out as soon as you can, Charlie, and Raines will bring the plane in."

"You can fly this thing?" I asked the star.

"Oh, sure. I'm a lot more comfortable flying it than being a passenger. We've got some stunt footage we'll stick in later, though. I don't do stunts."

I watched the two men go off, side by side, as Granger Newmark explained the scene. "In the film Bone plays the pilot and Raines is his barnstorming partner. Raines is going up for a parachute jump even though a doctor has warned him the thin air could cause him to black out." He smiled apologetically. "Sorry we've shot the doctor scene already or we could have used you, Doc."

"Acting's a bit out of my line." The fliers had reached the biplane now and been joined by a dark-haired young woman in a long flowered dress. "Who's the girl?"

"Angela Rhodes. Our leading lady. This is her first picture, actually, but I think she's going to be a big star."

I watched her adjust the star's scarf, just as a princess might have done before her knight rode off to joust. Then both men were into the plane with a wave and the director shouted, "Camera! Action! Take one!" Raines waved from the front cockpit.

The cameraman followed the plane as it taxied into position and then took off. For the first time I noticed that Hi Gates had been watching too, standing just a bit behind me. "Hello, Doc," he said when I turned to him. "Never thought they'd be shootin' a movin' picture on my farm."

"I hope you're getting a good price for it, Hi," I told him. "These movie companies got piles of money."

"Don't you worry, Doc." He spat some tobacco juice at the ground. "They don't out-fox ol' Hi. My daddy taught me a thing or two 'bout business afore he passed on."

I doubted if anybody had ever taught Hi Gates much of anything, but I didn't disagree with him. "How you been making out here by yourself, Hi?" I asked. Overhead, the plane was circling back after its takeoff.

"Good as can be expected. I keep hopin' Dorie'll come back, but I guess there's not much hope of that." Dorie was the wife who'd left him when he started to drink heavily. The last anyone had heard she was living up in Maine with her sister.

"Maybe she'll read about them shootin' this film at your farm," I said.

"Yeah. Maybe."

Nearby, Granger Newmark was standing at the cameraman's side. "Keep focused on the plane! Don't miss a thing! He'll jump now when they come over the field again."

The biplane with its two open cockpits had become a mere speck in the sky as it climbed high enough for the parachute jump. As I watched from the ground, glad that I wasn't up there, Angela Rhodes came over to join our group. "Isn't it dangerous?" she asked Newmark.

"No more dangerous than falling out of bed."

I saw a tiny speck detach itself from the plane and start to fall. Then a cloud of white billowed up behind it as the parachute was released. The falling figure was caught beneath a gently falling mushroom and began drifting slowly toward us. "Perfect!" Newmark shouted. "He should land right on the field in front of the camera!"

But the clouds that had gathered on the horizon were moving in now, and the wind was picking up. As the parachute neared the ground we could see it was drifting further off course, toward the old oak tree at the edge of the field.

"Why doesn't he steer himself?" Angela asked. "He's going to hit that tree!"

"Charlie!" the director shouted, but his voice must have been lost in the gathering wind. The parachute came down in the upper branches of the tree, snagged by some of the dead limbs that stretched toward heaven. And beneath it, hanging from his harness some ten feet from the ground, was the limp body of the stunt man, Charlie Bone.

"Let's get him out of there!" I shouted, leading the others toward the tree. Just then I didn't care if I was ruining the scene. There was something about that limp body, swaying at the end of the parachute harness, that had galvanized me into action. "Somebody get a ladder," I called to them, reaching the tree before the others.

Hi Gates ran off toward the barn as I tried to boost myself onto a lower limb of the tree. Already I could see the blue of Bone's face, and the tongue half out of his mouth. I managed to climb high enough to feel for a pulse, but there was none.

"What is it?" Granger Newmark called from the ground. "What's wrong?"

I climbed a bit higher in the tree, reaching out toward the white scarf around his neck. But then I felt something else, and drew my hand away. I came down from the tree just as Hi Gates returned carrying a ladder. "Cut him down carefully," I instructed. "And then leave him here on the ground. I have to call Sheriff Lens."

"My God, do you mean he's dead?"

"Yes, Mr. Newmark, he's dead. And there's a piece of wire knotted around his scarf. He's been murdered."

I phoned Sheriff Lens from the Gates farmhouse and then walked back to the body. The cast and crew were gathered around in a circle, watching while Newmark worked to unknot the wire from Charlie Bone's neck. "You'd better leave that for the sheriff to see," I advised. "It won't do Bone any good now."

"But—but how could it have happened?"

I stared up at the old oak tree. "Damned if I know."

The biplane was circling the field and finally Newmark waved it in for a landing. I think we were all wondering what Robert Raines would say when he saw the body. Because we knew we had witnessed a murder with only one possible explanation. Charlie Bone had been strangled in the plane before he jumped—there was no other way. And Robert Raines was the only person up there with him.

We watched as Raines came running over to the circle, pushing his way through to stare at the body. "What happened to him?" he asked.

"He's dead," I said. "Strangled by a wire around his neck."

"Strangled! Here on the ground?"

"Before he reached the ground. His chute snagged in the tree and when I climbed up to free him he was already dead."

He stared at me with unbelieving eyes. "But he was alive when he jumped! He had to be, to pull the rip cord!"

"That's right," Granger Newmark agreed. "I hadn't thought of that."

I saw Sheriff Lens arriving in his car, and I decided I could wind this thing up quickly. "You could have strangled him with the wire and dumped him out of the plane—and used a second wire or a string to pull open the rip cord when the body was free of the plane."

Raines strode up to me, hands on hips. Close up like that, he was intimidating. "You think so, Doc? I was in the front cockpit, remember? You tell me how I could have strangled someone sitting in the *rear* cockpit, several feet behind me, while the plane was in the air, then attached a string to his rip cord and dumped the body out of the plane. Go ahead, tell me!"

I'd forgotten about the cockpits, but now I remembered that he spoke the truth. I remembered him waving from that front cockpit as the plane took off. He was right—he couldn't have strangled Charlie Bone.

But no one else could have, either.

It was an impossible crime.

Sheriff Lens was not to be put off so easily. "You're telling me the damn tree killed him, Doc?"

"No, I'm not telling you the tree killed him. Trees don't strangle people with pieces of wire—not even haunted trees."

"All right, then—who did? He sure didn't commit suicide."

"No," I agreed. "People can shoot or stab or poison themselves, but it's impossible to strangle oneself to death. You'd pass out before you finished the job."

"Unless you hanged yourself. How about this, Doc—the wire was attached to the chute and when it opened the wire was pulled tight and choked him to death."

"A nice theory, except that the wire's not attached to the chute now. Besides, I've just examined the neck under that scarf and there's no evidence that the pressure came from above. Something like you suggest would have almost torn the head from his body. There'd be evidence of it."

"So how was it done, Doc? You're the expert on these impossible crimes."

"But I've never seen one quite as impossible as this."

There was something gnawing at my memory, though, and I went in search of Granger Newmark. Sheriff Lens could content himself with prowling around the oak tree till I returned. I found the director with his star, Angela, and I suppose you could say he was comforting her. He took his hand off her shoulder as I approached and frowned at me. "What is it now, Dr. Hawthorne? A bill for your services?"

"My services aren't finished yet. I was wondering about that plane Raines and Bone were in."

Newmark gazed out at the field where the Moth biplane stood. "What about it? We won't be reshooting the scene, if that's what you're wondering."

"I'm wondering if the plane has one of those automatic pilot gadgets I been reading about."

This brought a smile to the director's face. "So my star could have set it and climbed back along the fuselage to strangle Bone? Not a chance! There's no autopilot on it, and Raines would be scared to death to try a trick like that anyway."

I learned later that although the automatic pilot had been invented in 1910, it was not widely used on planes till after 1930. Newmark was telling the truth —there was no autopilot on the Moth. It was another good idea gone awry.

"Why are you so interested in who killed him?" Angela Rhodes asked me. "It's no business of yours."

"I was hired to minister to the ill and injured. I failed in that, quite badly."

Newmark smiled. "We won't hold it against you."

"What about the film you shot? Can you get it developed? It might give us a clue."

"The film has to go down to New York for processing. It'll be days before we see anything. You think we carry a darkroom along with us?"

I could see they had turned against me, as if somehow the impossible death of Charles Bone was my fault. And maybe it was—I did seem to attract murder with increasing frequency in those years.

Sheriff Lens was busy questioning Hi Gates, digging into a possible motive for the crime, and I decided that was the smart thing to do. Worrying about the how of it would get me nowhere. Maybe the why would prove more profitable.

"He was stayin' here at your farmhouse, wasn't he?" Sheriff Lens asked. They were in the tool shed near the barn.

Hi Gates nodded. I could smell his breath and I realized he'd been drinking again. For all I knew, maybe he never stopped. "Sure, I got three bedrooms upstairs just goin' to waste. I wait for Dorie to come home an' that'll be never, so I rented them out to some o' the cast and crew. Bone and that cameraman, Zeedler. And one of the extras."

"Any trouble between him an' the others?" the sheriff asked.

"No trouble I could see."

"No fights, drinking?"

"Hell, they'd only just got here this week." Gates looked sly, though, as if he wasn't telling us everything.

"Let's go up to the house," I suggested, "and take a look at Bone's room."

With the sheriff walking a little bit ahead of us, Hi Gates lowered his voice. "I got somethin' you'd want to see. Don't want Sheriff Lens to spot it, though."

When we entered the house I told the sheriff to go over Bone's things while I lingered behind. What Hi Gates produced was a tattered scrapbook full of clippings and credits which had obviously belonged to the dead man. "See this? I got it from his room."

"You stole it?"

His face fell a bit. "I found it when I was cleanin' up this mornin'. But I knew old Lens would say I stole it. Look at it!"

Charlie Bone had worked in silent films during most of the twenties, according to the clippings, appearing frequently in popular two-reel comedies and thrillers. He'd played the part of the old man in Poe's *The Tell-Tale Heart,* and of Edward Stapleton in *The Premature Burial.* There were clippings of his work as a stunt man and double too, and a gravure photograph of him standing with Robert Raines. They were wearing identical pirate costumes for a scene in *Captain Blood,* the 1925 swashbuckler.

"Interesting, but I don't see—"

Hi Gates reached over my shoulder and pulled something loose from under the *Captain Blood* photo. It was a fuzzy picture of a man and woman, naked, on a bed. "Dirty pictures," he announced triumphantly. "Look at the other side."

There were words written on the back that had been crossed out hurriedly. *"Remember this? If you don't want me to—"*

Hi Gates was pulling more pictures free from their hiding places in the album. They were much the same, or at least they seemed to show the same couple in various poses. All were too fuzzy and underexposed for clear identification, and none of these had writing on the back.

Charlie Bone had been blackmailing someone. But who?

The man in the picture could have been Robert Raines.

Or it could have been his double.

The girl just might have been Angela Rhodes, but her face did not show clearly in any of the scenes.

"You comin' up, Doc?" Sheriff Lens called down the stairs.

"Be right there!" I pocketed some of the pictures and told Gates to put the album away in a safe place. Then I went up to join the sheriff.

Charlie Bone's room was bare except for a bed and dresser and chair. He seemed to have unpacked little, and most of his clothes still rested in an open suitcase on the chair. "Nothin' much here," Sheriff Lens said. "Have a look." I glanced hastily through the suitcase and the dresser drawers, but found nothing of interest. Hi Gates had no doubt been through it already, and thinking about that I wondered when he'd had the time. While we were waiting for the sheriff's arrival?

Or had he known of Bone's death even before that? Had he somehow tampered with his clothing, looped the wire around his scarf?

But for what motive? Charlie Bone certainly wasn't blackmailing Hi Gates.

I was on my way downstairs when I encountered the cameraman, Zeedler, on his way up to the room next to the dead man's. I suppose he was a suspect too, but I had to trust someone. "Got a minute? Let me show you something." We went into his bedroom and I brought out the photographs Hi Gates had discovered.

Zeedler grunted and scratched his balding head. "Fuzzy. They look like frame blowups from movie film. There's a lot of this blue stuff around—stag movies. They rent 'em to men's clubs and bachelor parties."

"Recognize the stars?"

He squinted at the blurred figures. "No, can't say I do."

"The man could be Robert Raines."

"Raines? Hell, no! He's too big a star for this sort of thing."

"He wasn't always a star."

"Doesn't look like him to me," Zeedler said, returning the photos. "Where'd you get these?"

"Found them," I answered vaguely. "Thanks for your help."

"Figured out how Bone was killed yet?"

"I'm working on it."

I went back outside and headed over toward the old oak tree. The body was gone and most of the others had drifted off. Zeedler's movie camera sat on its tripod pointed at the sky. A couple of kids from a neighboring farm were playing by the plane and nobody was chasing them away. The cast and crew had simply abandoned their stage and gone off somewhere to ponder the strange passing of Charlie Bone.

I saw something on the ground beneath the oak tree and I stooped to pick it up. It was a hard rubber ball and I wondered if it belonged to one of the children near the plane. I started to toss it in their direction, then changed my mind and dropped it into my pocket. I could see Angela Rhodes heading in my direction.

"Hello, Dr. Hawthorne," she said. "We haven't had a chance to get properly acquainted."

"And I'm afraid we won't have. If Granger Newmark continues with the picture he'll certainly want another doctor on the set now."

"Why? You didn't cause Charlie's death, did you?"

"I certainly didn't save his life. Tell me something—how long did you know Charlie Bone?"

"I just met him last month, when Granger was casting for the movie. But Robert's known him for years. Charlie doubled for him in the *Captain Blood* stunts."

"Who do you think killed him?"

She didn't answer right away. She stared up at the tree, and then off at the plane where the neighbor kids were climbing on a wing. "It had to be someone up there, before he jumped."

"Raines was the only one up there."

"I know."

But was he?

I had a sudden thought and ran off toward the plane, leaving Angela Rhodes standing there alone. "Come on, boys—off the aircraft," I shouted, chasing them away. Then I climbed up to the rear cockpit where Bone had been seated when the plane took off. Was it possible that someone small could have been concealed in the cockpit with him—someone who strangled him and pitched his body over the side? The idea was far-fetched to begin with, and as soon as I seated myself in the cockpit I saw that it was physically impossible as well. Not even a midget could have shared the cockpit with Bone. My legs were cramped and he was a bigger man than me.

But as I lifted myself out of the plane I saw Angela again, off in the distance, touching a finger to her smooth throat. I remembered the gesture from before. She'd touched someone else, adjusted a scarf just before the plane took off. Remembering now, it seemed it had been Raines's scarf. But it could have been Bone's.

Memories, memories. They play such damned tricks on you!

"Dr. Sam!"

I turned and saw April, my nurse, hurrying across the field toward me. "What is it, April—one of my patients?"

"No, Dr. Sam. But they've got the body in town and they need you to sign the death certificate. They couldn't get through on the phone."

"All right. I'll come along. Nothing much to do here, anyway." I told Newmark I'd be leaving and he waved me away. There was no point in asking for my pay. I certainly hadn't earned it.

They'd taken the body to the local funeral parlor, where Jud Miller was waiting to do what passed in those days for an autopsy. "Can't cut into him till you sign the paper, Doc."

I glanced at the corpse on the embalming table and turned away. "What about next of kin?"

"They say he didn't have any. Going to bury him here, I suppose."

"There's no doubt he was strangled?"

"Oh, I'll check his insides, all right. But it looks like a strangling to me. No other marks on him except a bruise on his temple. Probably got that when they were taking him down from the tree."

"Yeah," I agreed. I walked over and looked at it. "Except that dead men don't bruise like this. He was still alive when this happened."

"Maybe when he landed in the tree."

I started talking, to Jud Miller but mostly to myself. "He had to be strangled either before he jumped or while he was coming down or after he landed. Those are the only possibilities. Before he jumped Raines couldn't have reached him, and no one could have hidden in the cockpit. While he was coming down no one could have done it, and a device attached to the parachute wouldn't have worked in this way if it worked at all. That leaves only one possibility: he was strangled after he landed in the old oak tree."

Jud Miller chuckled as he got out his embalming equipment. " 'Tweren't no haunted tree strangled him. More likely the first person to reach him did it before the others arrived. I read a story like that once."

"Only trouble with that is, it was me who reached him first."

"Oh."

I signed the death certificate and went back to my office, feeling depressed. I felt right on the verge of figuring it out, but somehow it wouldn't quite come together in my mind. The only thing I knew for sure was that no oak tree had strangled Charlie Bone. The killer was quite human, and so was the motive.

April hadn't yet returned and I was alone in the office. I sat down at my desk and reached into my pocket to have another look at those pictures. My fingers encountered the hard rubber ball I'd picked up earlier.

Could that be the answer?

Had I made the one mistake no doctor should ever make?

I got to my feet just as the outer door opened and Granger Newmark came in. "I've been looking for you, Doc."

"Glad you're here. I just earned my money. I know how Charlie Bone was killed."

"You do?"

"I did a terrible thing this morning, Mr. Newmark."

"And what was that?"

"I pronounced a man dead when he was still alive."

Granger Newmark smiled slightly and slipped a small revolver from his pocket. "You're a smarter man than I thought. Now give me the pictures you took from Hi Gates."

I raised my hands slightly but made no effort to hand him the pictures. As soon as he had those I knew I'd be a dead man. "Can't we talk about this? The pictures are in a safe enough place."

"I don't have time for games, Doc. This whole thing is coming apart." He motioned with the gun.

"Because of Hi Gates? I suppose you didn't figure on his going through the dead man's belongings and finding those pictures before you got to them. Charlie Bone was blackmailing you, wasn't he? Reminding you of the stag films you produced before you became a big Hollywood name. That sort of publicity could ruin you right now, on the brink of your success in the talkies. And Charlie knew all about it because he'd been your male star in those stag films. So you killed him, in a most ingenious manner. But when you went after the frame blowups he'd made from the stag movie, you found that Hi Gates had discovered them first."

"And even given some to you," Newmark said.

"Did you kill Gates?"

"Not yet. He gave me the rest of the pictures without knowing quite what was going on. But you're a different story, Doc. You know too much."

"You needed a dumb country doctor to work your scheme. That's why you didn't bring one along from the city. Charlie Bone was alive when he landed in that tree. He was simply playing the role of a dead man, as he had before , in two-reelers like *The Premature Burial* and *The Tell-Tale Heart.* I suppose it was a specialty of his. He gave his face a bluish tinge with a bit of makeup before he jumped, and tied that wire around his neck. The scarf kept it from doing any real damage.

"He used a hard rubber ball pressed into his armpit to cut off his pulse. Maybe he had one in each armpit for all I know. Then he let his tongue protrude a bit and acted like a man who'd been strangled to death.

"It was a break for you that the parachute went into the oak tree, because I had to examine him while balanced on a tree limb. Then when I ran in to phone the sheriff, you helped take him down from the tree. A quick blow to the temple knocked him out, and then you strangled him in full view of us all while seeming to unfasten the wire from his neck. Everyone thought Bone was already dead, of course, so even if they noticed you accidentally knock his temple they thought nothing of it."

"That's very good," Newmark said. "Now give me the pictures."

I ignored his request for the moment. "My only question is how you persuaded Bone to act as an accessory to his own murder. I suppose you told him it was a publicity stunt for the movie. Stunt man pronounced dead revives ten minutes later. That sort of thing would get a few headlines, or so you could have convinced Bone. With the cast and crew around he thought he was safe."

"Right again!" He raised the revolver. "But we've had enough talk."

"Once I put the rubber ball together with Bone's movie roles as dead men, I knew how it was done. Maybe his role in *The Premature Burial* even gave you the whole idea. And knowing how it was done, I knew you had to be the killer. Only the producer-director of the film could persuade Bone to pull that stunt. And then I remembered you bent over his body, tugging at the wire around his neck—"

The door behind Newmark opened and April entered with a cheery "Hello there!" It was what I'd been stalling for. Newmark half turned toward her and instantly I threw myself at him, knocking his gun hand to one side.

It was as simple as that.

"Well," Dr. Sam Hawthorne concluded, "that was my one fling at movie-making. Newmark pleaded guilty and served a long term in prison. And *Wings of Glory* was never made. The old oak tree? It was struck by lightning the following year and just toppled over.

"If you'll come again soon, I'll tell you about what happened when a child evangelist came to Northmont and started curing my patients at an old-fashioned revival meeting in a tent. And about how I became the prime suspect in what happened next. Another—ah—libation before you go? One for the road?"

DR. SAM HAWTHORNE:
A CHRONOLOGY OF HIS CASES
[Updated, April 2000]

by Marvin Lachman

The publication of "The Problem of the Country Mailbox" in the Mid-December 1994 issue of *Ellery Queen's Mystery Magazine* marked the fiftieth Dr. Sam Hawthorne story published there by Edward D. Hoch. (His first, "The Problem of the Covered Bridge," had been published exactly twenty years before, in EQMM for December 1974.) At a time when historical mysteries are popular, most writers in that sub-genre have gone back into the distant past, with series set in Egypt and Rome and the London of Shakespeare, to cite just three examples. Hoch's stories are not often recognized as historical mysteries. They are better known as impossible crime stories by the modern master of the classic puzzle. Yet, they fit the basic definition of historical crime stories: mysteries written in the present and deliberately set in the past.

The first Hawthorne story takes place in 1922. In the twenty-six years of his EQMM literary life, eighteen and one-half years pass in the history of Northmont, the small New England town where Hawthorne is a physician in general practice. With three exceptions, the stories are in chronological order, i.e., the past years advance exactly as the series progresses in EQMM. "The Problem of the Sealed Bottle" (EQMM, September 1986) is about events of December 1933; "The Problem of the Invisible Acrobat" (EQMM, Mid-December 1986) is set in July 1933. "The Problem of the Miraculous Jar" (EQMM August 1996) is set in November 1939. It is followed by "The Problem of the Enchanted Terrace" (EQMM April 1997) which is set in the prior month, October 1939. "The Problem of the Unfound Door" (EQMM June 1998) is set in Midsummer 1940, while the next story, "The Second Problem of the Covered Bridge" (EQMM December 1998), is set earlier in the year, in January 1940.

The alert reader, probing between Hoch's lines, will find, in addition to excellent mysteries, many examples of a living history of the United States during the 1920s and 1930s. This made me decide it might be useful to list the chronology of each story in the Hawthorne series.

When the series begins, the United States is in the midst of one of its great social experiments: Prohibition. Bootlegging is background for several of the stories. (Ironically, one of the features of the early tales was a present-day Hawthorne offering "a small libation" to the anonymous listener to whom he will narrate one of the "problems" he solved in the past.) A later story, "The Problem of the Protected Farmhouse" (EQMM, May 1990), about an athlete trying out for the 1936 U.S. Olympic team, has references to Naziism.

Still, what this series does best is to present a picture of small-town life in the United States during that period. We learn of the lives of the people who live in or near Northmont, as well as of outsiders who visit, usually for economic reasons. (They include gypsies, barnstorming pilots and salesmen.) Against the background of the New England countryside and history, we attempt to reach the solutions (before Dr. Sam) to crimes committed in various rural locations, including a covered bridge, a school, in church, in a barn, in hotels, in meeting houses, at the movies, and even in a voting booth. Taken as a whole, they give a splendid picture of rural America. Especially good, because of Hawthorne's profession, are changes in the way medicine is practiced. Then there are many references to transportation, especially the various cars Dr. Sam drove, including his beloved Pierce-Arrow.

As I write this in January 1995, World War II is on the horizon for the series. Hawthorne solves his fiftieth puzzle just after the Munich pact has raised hopes of "peace in our time" that are due to be dashed. Those of us who are old enough remember that World War II on the home front was one of the most interesting periods in recent U.S. history. I can hardly wait to relive it with Ed Hoch and Dr. Sam.

All of Dr. Sam Hawthorne's reminiscences were first published in *Ellery Queen's Mystery Magazine* [EQMM]. Dates when the events took place are recorded below in brackets.

"The Problem of the Covered Bridge" [March 1922]. EQMM, December 1974.
"The Problem of the Old Gristmill" [July 1923]. EQMM, March 1975.
"The Problem of the Lobster Shack" [June 1924]. EQMM, September 1975.
"The Problem of the Haunted Bandstand" [July 1924]. EQMM, January 1976.
"The Problem of the Locked Caboose" [Spring 1925]. EQMM, May 1976.
"The Problem of the Little Red Schoolhouse" [Fall 1925]. EQMM, September 1976.

"The Problem of the Christmas Steeple" [December 25, 1925]. EQMM, January 1977.

"The Problem of Cell 16" [Spring 1926]. EQMM, March 1977.

"The Problem of the Country Inn" [Summer 1926]. EQMM, September 1977.

"The Problem of the Voting Booth" [November 1926]. EQMM, December 1977.

"The Problem of the County Fair" [Summer 1927]. EQMM, February 1978.

"The Problem of the Old Oak Tree" [September 1927]. EQMM, July 1978.

"The Problem of the Revival Tent" [Fall 1927]. EQMM, November 1978.

"The Problem of the Whispering House" [February 1928]. EQMM, April 1979.

"The Problem of the Boston Common" [Spring 1928]. EQMM, August 1979.

"The Problem of the General Store" [Summer 1928]. EQMM, November 1979.

"The Problem of the Courthouse Gargoyle" [September 1928]. EQMM, June 30, 1980.

"The Problem of the Pilgrims Windmill" [March 1929]. EQMM, September 10, 1980.

"The Problem of the Gingerbread Houseboat" [Summer 1929]. EQMM, January 28, 1981.

"The Problem of the Pink Post Office" [October 1929]. EQMM, June 17, 1981.

"The Problem of the Octagon Room" [December 1929]. EQMM, October 7, 1981.

"The Problem of the Gypsy Camp" [January 1930). EQMM, January 1, 1982.

"The Problem of the Bootleggers Car" [May 1930]. EQMM, July 1982.

"The Problem of the Tin Goose" [July 1930]. EQMM, December 1982.

"The Problem of the Hunting Lodge" [Fall 1930]. EQMM, May 1983.

"The Problem of the Body in the Haystack" [July 1931]. EQMM, August 1983.

"The Problem of Santa's Lighthouse" [December 1931]. EQMM, December 1983.

"The Problem of the Graveyard Picnic" [Spring 1932]. EQMM, June 1984.

"The Problem of the Crying Room" [June 1932]. EQMM, November 1984.

"The Problem of the Fatal Fireworks" [July 4, 1932]. EQMM, May 1985.

"The Problem of the Unfinished Painting" [Fall 1932]. EQMM, February 1986.

"The Problem of the Sealed Bottle" [December 5, 1933]. EQMM, September 1986.

"The Problem of the Invisible Acrobat" [July 1933]. EQMM, Mid-December 1986.

"The Problem of the Curing Barn" [September 1934]. EQMM, August 1987.

"The Problem of the Snowbound Cabin" [January 1935]. EQMM, December 1987.

"The Problem of the Thunder Room" [March 1935]. EQMM, April 1988.

"The Problem of the Black Roadster" [April 1935]. EQMM, November 1988.

"The Problem of the Two Birthmarks" [May 1935]. EQMM, May 1989.

"The Problem of the Dying Patient" [June 1935]. EQMM, December 1989.

"The Problem of the Protected Farmhouse" [August or September 1935]. EQMM, May 1990.

"The Problem of the Haunted Tepee" [September 1935]. EQMM, December 1990.

"The Problem of the Blue Bicycle" [September 1936]. EQMM, April 1991.

"The Problem of the Country Church" [November 1936]. EQMM, August 1991.

"The Problem of the Grange Hall" [March 1937]. EQMM, Mid-December 1991.

"The Problem of the Vanishing Salesman" [May 1937]. EQMM, August 1992.

"The Problem of the Leather Man" [August 1937]. EQMM, December 1992.

"The Problem of the Phantom Parlor" [August 1937]. EQMM, June 1993.

"The Problem of the Poisoned Pool" [September 1937]. EQMM, December 1993.

"The Problem of the Missing Roadhouse" [August 1938]. EQMM, June 1994.

"The Problem of the Country Mailbox" [Fall 1938]. EQMM, Mid-December 1994.

"The Problem of the Crowded Cemetery" [Spring 1939]. EQMM, May 1995.

"The Problem of the Enormous Owl" [August-September 1939]. EQMM, January 1996.

"The Problem of the Miraculous Jar" [November 1939]. EQMM, August 1996.

"The Problem of the Enchanted Terrace" [October 1939]. EQMM, April 1997.

"The Problem of the Unfound Door" [Midsummer 1940]. EQMM, June 1998.

"The Second Problem of the Covered Bridge" [January 1940]. EQMM, December 1998.

"The Problem of the Scarecrow Congress" [late July 1940]. EQMM, June 1999.

"The Problem of Annabel's Ark" [September 1940]. EQMM, March 2000.

"The Problem of the Potting Shed" [October 1940]. EQMM, July 2000.